SPANISH
GOLD

Mel Stevens

SPANISH GOLD

TATE PUBLISHING
AND ENTERPRISES, LLC

Published by Tate Publishing & Enterprises, LLC
127 E. Trade Center Terrace | Mustang, Oklahoma 73064 USA
1.888.361.9473 | www.tatepublishing.com

Tate Publishing is committed to excellence in the publishing industry. The company reflects the philosophy established by the founders, based on Psalm 68:11,
"The Lord gave the word and great was the company of those who published it."

Book design copyright © 2013 by Tate Publishing, LLC. All rights reserved.
Cover design by Lauro Talibong
Interior design by Jake Muelle

Published in the United States of America

ISBN: 978-1-62295-542-8
1. Fiction / Christian / Western
2. Fiction / Christian / Romance
12.12.21

PROLOGUE

The cavern, full of warmth and joy but moments earlier, was now a dark and fearsome place. Reuben was hardly out of the opening before I pushed my head outside, trying desperately to move slowly as he had told me, stopping when my eyes barely cleared the edge. He was snaking away through the brush, making not a sound. The brush, while it was thick enough to make such soundless movement impossible, appeared to provide meager cover. Still, he disappeared from my searching eyes within a few yards.

When he moved out of sight, I spent long minutes in prayer. Later, I pushed farther out of the opening and searched every shred of cover that could hide an enemy. Reuben wanted me to stay in the cave, but that would not keep me from being involved if there was a way to help. No one would sneak up on him if I could prevent it.

I had hunted with him and tried to remember everything he had taught me. Never moving my head more than an inch at a time and lowering myself when possible, I made a complete inspection of the hillside, valley, and the ridges that rose on two sides above the creek. I was watching across the stream when Reuben dashed into the timber on that side. He was in a crouching run and dived out of sight behind a rock. The next time I saw him, he was fifty feet into the scant cover. It must have taken him ten minutes to move that far, and he stood absolutely still for so long I was sure he had seen something. When he finally moved, it was to take three steps and stop again. He was in sight for a distance of not more than ten feet and spent what seemed like ages to travel that far. What boundless patience he had. But was there enough day left for him to accomplish his task if he continued at that pace? Keeping up my vigil, I tracked his snail-like progress up the hill toward the old campsite. It gave me an abundance of time to reflect on this man of mine.

It is true that three years ago I had not so much as heard of him, but the day we met became the point from which everything is measured—B.R. and A.R., before and after Reuben. He has said many times that he is homely as a mud fence, and some might agree. The saying, "beauty is as beauty does", could apply in his case. The Rio Grande River in flood stage is not beautiful, with its muddy torrents overwhelming everything it encounters, but it is magnificent, and so is he.

My mind went back to that day. I sat watching my grandfather as he lay near death, the house quiet but for muffled sounds from the kitchen and the labored breathing from the bed. Without a sound, this tall, rawboned man appeared in the doorway. His glance took in the whole room before settling on that frail body. His eyes were full of concern, and the gentleness in his expression overshadowed the rough exterior. In that moment I knew him for a special man, and my heart swelled. I truly believe it got bigger to make room for him.

When I stood, his eyes swept over me, returned to my face with not a trace of boldness in the glance. I was accustomed to seeing more response from a man. In spite of what he has said, I did everything I could to make sure he knew he was following a woman when I walked ahead of him down the hall. I sensed strength like none I had ever known. Half of me was challenged by it, the rest almost frightened.

He was hesitant, even bashful, in telling about himself. It took the whole afternoon to learn just a little, and that served only to whet my appetite. His rich, bass voice sent shivers up my young spine.

When I talked to my grandfather about him, he said, "He is a fine man, but there is no way he will consider marrying you."

"Who said anything about marriage?" I protested.

But it was only minutes later that I was asking, "Why? Why won't he marry me?"

"There is no way you can keep him from learning that you are wealthy. He obviously is not, and it will never occur to him that you are interested in a man with less than you have."

It was from that conversation that two things developed. First, Grandfather gave him the map to the mine, and then I suggested the partnership. It was at that stage of our relationship that I made the terrible blunder of saying that I had chosen the man I would marry. I never dreamed he would assume it was someone else. His reaction almost broke my heart. I would have given anything to recall the hasty words but could only wait and pray that he would see that he was the only one for me. When he finally started courting me, I could hardly contain myself. I will never let him forget that he is the one who makes my life worth living.

I have seen his face when it was unfeeling as a storm cloud, but with Gard and me, none could be more expressive.

That day, his eyes, green as emeralds, flashed as I told about the murder of my father, and again as I related the threats made by the *bandito* who was even now trying to murder him and come after me.

The glimpses I had of him going through the timber reminded me that our friend Ignacio said that he always walks like he is sneaking up on someone. The fluid movement of his body, unexpected in a man so large, propels him with hardly a sound. Even in the most private moments he is the same.

At last I saw him briefly, close to the campsite, watched as he changed course and made a circuitous trek above, then to the southwest of the camp. Trying to interpret his actions, I looked ever closer at the hillside ahead of him. After what seemed like hours, I spotted a man seated at the base of a spruce, concealed in waist-high brush. Had he been there all the time? The thought struck fear in my heart. I would be of little help if someone could sit in plain sight without my seeing him. How I longed for the field glasses.

Vowing to not let anything else escape detection, I made another complete survey of the landscape before turning back to watch my husband. His actions never varied, or so it seemed to me. He moved a tiny distance then paused for what seemed like ten times as long, moving only his eyes. After every third pause, he would turn completely around, moving so imperceptibly that I could only track his progress by the fact that he was facing a different direction. I had seen him stalk an elk in a patch of down timber, but he had never been so deliberate as now.

From a quarter mile away, I could see the well-loved hands. Scarred and granite-hard, with a strength that never ceases to amaze me, they are gentle as a baby's breath when he touches me. They hold our son with a beautiful tenderness. I have seen the same hands control a raging bull and have watched them wrestle a mad cow to her knees. Yet in ministering to a baby calf or taming a frightened colt, the touch is soft and caring.

When he was within fifty feet of his target, I forced my gaze away to look for danger from any other quarter. It was torture to look elsewhere, but I made a complete—and this time, thorough—search. My goal was to move as slowly as Reuben when making my turn. I know he does it better than anyone else ever could, but he was my pattern, and it seemed that I would never complete the turn. I came to a greater appreciation of what it cost him to move so slowly, and it gave me more reason to admire this one I love so dearly.

CHAPTER ONE

S anta Fe couldn't be more than a half-day's ride to the south. A man could might nigh taste the frijoles, tortillas, and fresh beefsteak. My ears imagined the sound of guitars, castanets, singing, and laughter. The señoritas prancing in my head were downright pretty, but I was after being with some I could touch instead of those I pictured in my mind. That brown horse felt it, too. He was stretching his legs for fair and had settled into a ground-eating stride that would cover the miles in jig time.

Then we heard it.

It sounded like a shot, and that'll put a stop to your daydreams, if you're partial to keeping your hair. I pulled up, knowing we were all but invisible in the fringe of trees where we were. My animals were a bay pack mule and two geldings for the saddle, one a *grullo*, or mouse-colored animal, and the brown I was riding. Nothing about my rig would sparkle—no buckles or *conchas*—and the saddle horn was wrapped with leather.

The sound came again, and it was sure enough gunfire. A batch of ear-stabbing pistol shots were followed by two booming reports from a rifle. Then silence again. More shots followed a couple of minutes later. I figured them to be a mile off.

"It's none of our affair, Brownie," I said to the horse. "We ought to circle wide and get on down to Santa Fe. But... that old boy looked to be the right sort, and the other bunch sure don't stack up. Look at the mess they left where they camped. What with whiskey bottles and grub leavings, they were worse'n a den of wolves. Reckon we'll mosey down and have a look-see. If it's that bunch, I'll bet they're after his horses or that gold. More'n likely both."

The gelding moved out in a long-reaching walk that would get us there in short order without raising a ruckus. That brown horse had the nose of a hound dog and eyes like an antelope. I trusted him to warn me when we got near the fracas. Being in strange country with no friends around kept me in cover off to the side of the trail, when doing that wouldn't slow us too much. When the trail dropped into a draw, I veered left along the flank of a ridge. Slowing, I rode close to the backbone of the ridge and spotted a cluster of cottonwoods, which meant water was close by. The brown threw up his head and flared his nostrils.

"Easy, boy, no nickering. We want to catch those boys off guard. Let's drop down and cat-foot a little farther. Then I best leave you boys and slip up afoot. This's a likely spot. You fellows graze a bit, but don't mosey off." My voice was never loud enough to be heard ten feet away.

Shucking my rifle, I tried to sneak up like I'd been taught by Kit Carson. I moved up through cedars and brush to a ground-hugging sage at the top of the ridge, crawled the last few feet, and lay hidden in a spot where I had a clear view of the draw and opposite slope.

That horse had pinpointed the spot, and the scene was about what I expected. A rock slide tumbled down to the rim of the wash. The man under attack was holed up in a jumble of boulders big as freight wagons at the base of a cliff, with the slide strung out along the slope on either side of his fort. His camp was at a spring surrounded by a patch of grass, some willows, and the cottonwoods I'd seen earlier. Cooking gear was on a fire with plunder stacked nearby.

Two bandits were in the rocks to the right of his position, another to his left. A fourth hunkered in the wash, his rifle resting on the bank. I knew what was in the packs by the fire and had few doubts that the men were after them. I put my rifle sights on the man in the wash and settled down to see what developed.

The fellow under my sights yelled, "Move in and finish him off. We've got to get this over with and get out of here."

"You come up here and show us how," one of the others hollered back. "He came close to getting me with that last shot. There's no cover from here on in, and I'm not getting out where he's got a clear shot at me."

"It's easy for you to stay down in that gulch and order us around. How about showing him your head to shoot at," added another.

"You guys are so yellow bellied a baby could scare you out of getting a fortune. Why do I bother with you? I guess I'll have to come do—"

That cantankerous, pea-brained mule of mine picked that moment to let out a bray, loud as any train whistle. Everybody jumped—me included—which made me jerk off a shot. The guy in the draw jumped, or I'd have killed him for sure. As it was, the bullet slammed into the bank just in front of him, dirt exploded into his eyes, and the ricochet sent his rifle skittering. He whooped, fell backwards, clawed at his eyes, and yelled for his buddies to come help. I stayed right still. Much as I wanted to go shoot that mule, I'd rather stay alive, and it's hard to spot a man if he doesn't wiggle around.

The man closest to the draw sneaked down to his companion and tried to get the dirt out of his eyes, while the other two tried to figure out where the shot had come from. Seemed to expect another one. Chief Dirty Eyes was carrying on something fierce, hollering for help. It didn't take long to get him on his horse, which they had to lead, him being blind as a bat. He did raise a fuss. I almost hoped they knew of a waterhole close by. There was no way he could've seen me, but I reckon he'd have given his favorite horse for a chance at me. Well, I didn't tell him to go poking around shooting at folks.

I waited a bit after they were gone then got my outfit and rode to the spring, hollering so the other fellow'd know I was friendly. Got no answer, so I shouted again and started up through the slide rock, hoping he understood I was there to help.

When I eased into the pocket, it was easy to see why he hadn't answered. He was in a natural fort some ten feet across, rocks head-high on all sides. There were openings so he could shoot without much danger. He'd have been all right if he'd been there when they opened the ball, but a trail of blood said he was hit before he got there. He'd spilled a mess of blood and looked to be pretty bad off.

CHAPTER TWO

I let my mind wander back over the past couple of weeks, thinking about how I'd come to be here with a gun-shot stranger. It was 1872. I'd struck pay dirt on a creek so remote and unlikely nobody'd bothered to put a name to it. It was fed by a spring that put out water pure as a newborn babe, cold enough to crack your teeth, and so clear you wouldn't know it was there except the rocks were wet. The stream scrambled a hundred feet downslope then loafed across a park before joining up with a creek that flowed into the Lake Fork of the Gunnison. I had my own name for it—the Clear Fork of No Name Creek.

The mine was just an outcrop that petered out, but not before I filled a poke. I was ready to pull out anyway, having got there in March, with winter's chill making every morning a battle with ice, frost, and oftentimes snow. I figured it to be September now and had no hankering to let winter close in on me. The spring months of April and May'd given me a belly full of that. Summer must've come that July afternoon when I was inside shaving, and it didn't last long enough for me to get back outside.

I'd seen several Indian parties, seemingly after game. None of them had come near. Then one moonless night I was yanked awake by horses pounding across the park. Guns sort of came into my hands of their own accord. In a moment my eyes adjusted to the faint glow from the stars. I recognized the hoof-beats of my two horses and the mule.

There was at least one more animal.

A guttural voice called from across the way, and the strange hoof-beats receded, slowed, stopped. Three voices jabbered some

Indian lingo. My animals continued toward me at a slower pace and stopped fifty feet away. I slipped into moccasins and britches before moving to them. They crowded close, muzzles reaching as I touched each of them in turn.

"It's okay, boys." I breathed. "Stay here while I mosey out and see what they do next."

They say a man's home is his castle. I reckon it's so, but mine was nothing but a dugout with a roof of brush and dirt that had to be fixed up after every storm. Its only good feature was being two steps from the mine. The tiny clearing I needed to work the claim was hedged in by brush so thick it looked like a body couldn't move without raising a lot of clamor. A rambling path, carefully cleared of all growth and litter, allowed me to slip through the trees and brush with nary a sound. I knew every inch of it and could ghost anywhere within a half-hour's hike.

The lack of usual night sounds said that the visitors were still close. Everything was quiet. I moved to my right, careful to stay on the path. I took two slow steps, stopped, and slowly counted to ten. This was repeated over and again as I circled the clearing. It was during one of the pauses that I spotted one of them pussyfooting along a hundred feet away. Freezing, I kept him in the edge of my vision and watched for movement in any other direction. I'd moved into a slight breeze that drifted across the grassy opening, knowing that some folks who live in the wilds are quick as any deer to smell a man.

It was movement that betrayed his spot, and I knew it would be all but impossible for him to see me, long as I stayed still. I never looked directly at him. Wild things will sometimes sense you're about if you stare at them, and some folks are every bit as touchy as any animal. Besides, I wanted to keep my sight fanned out so none of the others could slip up on me.

He was good, sneaking through the trees with no more sound than a breath of air. His travel would bring him within a dozen feet of me. I waited till he moved behind a spruce then holstered my pistol and exchanged it for the knife. It was razor sharp, weighed a full pound, and was perfectly balanced for throwing. I'd taken it off an *hombre* who tried to slit my throat one stormy night, and it was my favorite weapon for close-up fighting.

Impatience has cost more scalps than anything except carelessness, and I'd developed a knack for waiting. But after so long, patience is no virtue, and it's time to do something. He should've been out of the trees by now. Where was he? It was as though he'd gone up in smoke. I almost wondered if I'd seen a ghost.

It was definitely a time to pray, and I did exactly that, silently asking for wisdom and the protection of the LORD. I needed more than my own ability to out-guess that fellow, and the LORD was the only one who could give me what I needed. It's no fun when the other guy's that good. Waiting for deer is one thing, but it smells different when you're the one being hunted. An owl hooted across the park with a muffled answer from straight ahead of me. They were almost good enough to fool me. The one I'd seen didn't answer.

I'll go to my grave convinced that it was the Holy Spirit who warned me. Maybe I'm half-wild my own self. Whatever it was, it saved my bacon. I dropped to the ground and rolled into some brush just as an arrow thudded into the tree where I'd been.

Coming to my knees, I detected a whisper of leather on dirt. The brave leaped into view, tomahawk raised. He paused, eyes scanning the brush. A flick of my wrist sent the knife on its way. It took him in the ribs, slammed into his body clear to the hilt. Breath burst from his mouth, and he sagged to the ground. Blood flowed freely, foaming as his breath came in gurgles. He tried to fling the tomahawk, but it dropped from his grip.

I moved quickly to retrieve the knife and pick up his weapons then retreated to a nest of brush where I could watch the body. Owl hoots came again, one much closer than before, and soon another man slipped into view. He was barely moving, eyes probing every mite of cover. He passed an arm's length from his fallen *compadre* and continued another twenty feet toward me.

Suddenly his head jerked around, and his nose lifted. Reversing direction, he went directly to the body. He was wild as a cougar, but there was understanding rather than instinct directing his actions. He peered carefully around, and his attention quickly focused on my haven. Nodding, he lifted the body to his shoulder and walked boldly across the park, calling as he went. Within minutes I heard them leave.

I figured they'd accepted defeat and gone their way. A white man will carry a grudge and try to get even, but Indians are likely to judge that the death of a companion means the spirits are against them and will generally leave it at that.

I knelt there in the brush and thanked God for his protection and wisdom. Without his warning, I could've been the one who was dead. I hope I never reach the point that I think I can get along with just what I can bring to a situation. I'll always need the extra that the LORD brings, too.

I went back to bed and slept, trusting my animals and the brush to warn of intruders. A half-hour before sunup, I slipped to a point where the park and all around it were easily viewed. I'd started doing that soon after locating the mine and did it every morning. An hour there each day had kept me out of several tight spots with Indians, claim jumpers, and outlaws who seemed bent on stealing my critters. It was also the time I'd chosen to talk to Jesus every day. I'd been taught to pray as a youngster and had found it made a difference when I did it. When I failed to pray, things tended to get messed up, so I'd made it a part of every day. I'd learned that the good LORD didn't care if I talked to him with my eyes open, and that enabled me to do my praying any time and anywhere. He seemed to like it when I prayed out loud, but we could talk silently, too, if that was better for me. I talked silently that morning and became sure that it was time to hightail it out of there and to be quick about it.

I saw a trio of mama deer, each with twin fawns, porcupines, at least a dozen rabbits, a family of blue grouse, and a pack of coyotes. A sow grizzly bear with two cubs frolicked on the ridge a half-mile south, and jays rioted overhead on their daily search for food and mischief. The horses and mule grazed, never once indicating anything amiss. The only thing lacking was an eagle that had soared overhead every day for the past three months. Search as I might, he never showed up. Satisfied, I whistled to the animals, went down, and stopped at the dugout to pick up halters and gear. They met me, the brown nickering softly.

"You boys did right well. Without you, I'd have never known those guys were about. Guess they wouldn't have come, though, if they hadn't wanted you. They'd likely be having you for breakfast about now, Mule. Never could figure why they favor mule meat so, but most of them do. Time or two, I been ready to try it, when you got stubborn. You know, this's the fourth time we've been troubled in the past ten days. Reckon it's time to clear out. The mine's petered out, anyway, and I got a hankering for company better than the likes of you. Let's get out of here."

We were gone before the sun was halfway to the middle of its swing. Rode over Slumgullian Pass, with its everlasting mudslides, then down to the Rio Grande. I'd followed up along that river the prior spring and could've tracked it back through the San Luis Valley, down to Taos and into Santa Fe. But I'd heard tales of the country around the Rio Grande Pyramid and the Window, eye-catching landmarks in the high-up San Juans. The Rio Piedra heads up to the south of them, the Rio Grande to the north. Both rivers end up running generally south, but start in opposite directions, with the Pyramid and Window betwixt them. They were off to my right, beckoning, and it would take only a couple of days to go up and see them. I asked the Lord if it would be all right to go take a look-see, and he didn't raise any fuss. So we veered off and went upstream instead of down, then on up Ute Creek.

What's a mountain for if not to peek over its highest ridge to see what's on the other side? Reckon I figured to someday find a special spot across one of those high slopes, and there's just no way to sniff it out if you don't go. I've learned never to pass up the chance to take a look see at new country. It wasn't just new country; it was some of the prettiest I ever did see. Snow could come any time, but with grass growing tall, bees buzzing on millions of flowers, silvery trout leaping in beaver ponds, rancid black elk wallows, berry patches full of bear sign, deer more curious than scared, an occasional wolf, and scads of coyotes, the world seemed a right nice place. And that eagle, or what I took to be the same one, showed up, coasting in the air currents above us. Trees and brush were decked out in their fall duds, bold and pretty as the señoritas in Santa Fe. I was riding the *grullo* and brown on alternate days, with a pack on that long-legged mule who could walk the legs off any other critter I ever saw. They seemed as eager as I was to look at new country.

It was Ute territory, and they're like most Indians—notional. You may get along fine for months, then one day they could see another white man, decide it's getting crowded, and come after your scalp. So, while I talked some to the horses, pointing out things they might miss, you couldn't have heard me from twenty feet off. I talked some to the LORD, too, thanking him for making all that great stuff and letting me have a look at it. Mostly, I just rode careful, not getting in the open without stopping to look things over mighty well, trying to see what was there before moving out where it, or they, could see me. Can't ever be sure of doing it, though.

I been on my own since age thirteen, mostly in what could be called dangerous situations, and I've seen lots of men die when they got excited and forgot to look before moving. We moseyed along and enjoyed the smell of spruce, the sound of squirrels and jays, and watched that eagle soar and dive.

Like I said, that's some kind of pretty country. It pleasures me to see what's been put here for us to enjoy. Not just the grandness of mountains and beauty of flowers, but the wisdom of animals like the beaver engineering his dams and putting aside his winter food, sticking it in the muddy bottom of his pond where he can get to it when an icy cap seals him in. I spent an afternoon watching a colony of conies, which are wee hares that live in rocks. They gathered grass like a bunch of farmers and stowed it in stony barns. I remember reading in the Bible that they are "exceeding wise," and surely do believe it. Many's the time I've watched a pack of coyotes work together to bring down a buck too strong for any one of them, and it makes me realize that the good Lord gave us some pretty special critters.

Musing about things like that and letting my senses soak up the sights, I rode up Ute Creek and followed its east fork to the saddle west of the Pyramid and Window. Saw nary a soul. I feel sorry for anyone who's not been there—up where there's nobody but me and that eagle, and it was so good I didn't hold it against him that he can fly and I can't. It was worth the trip, for sure. It was also a great place to get a feel for the good Lord and his power and majesty.

We were about to top out and start down to the Rio Piedra when I spotted a fellow, busy as a beaver. Easing back into the timber, I took my field glasses and sashayed out to where I could watch without being seen.

He had what looked like a slender chain like would be on a woman's necklace. Whatever was on the end of it was swinging back and forth, and he stopped frequently, watching it intently. He wandered around for quite a spell, seemingly without any mind about where he was headed, then walked straight for a ways, made a sharp turn to his right, and marched slowly for about thirty paces, did another sudden right turn and covered about the same distance, turned again and walked back almost to his original line of travel. He retraced the first route for about half the original distance and walked the sides of a smaller square. He did it again several times, each time shortening the sides of the box until he was almost circling, then very slowly moved over the remaining ground. He finally stopped, put away his chain, and poked at the ground with a stick. After a few jabs, the stick went in about half its length. He tossed it aside, dropped to his knees and started digging. He excavated for a few minutes then hustled back the way he'd come.

He was gone quite a while, so I eased around and took a good look to see where we were in relation to the Pyramid and Window. We were almost directly west of them, and I laid out a triangle so I could come back to the spot if I ever wanted to. When I went back to the lookout, he was returning on a horse and leading three others. And those weren't any scrub horses. Every one of them was shiny as a new peso, and they were an invitation to any horse thief.

I hadn't been able to tell too much about him before, but his rig left no doubt that he was Spanish. The outfit on that horse beat anything I'd ever seen, what with silver *conchas*, bells dangling all over it, and the bridle glittering like the inside of a lamp factory. I could hear the bells from a quarter mile off. He couldn't have hid in the thickest brush on that mountain. What a get-up to have in Indian country!

He spurred his mount to the hole, jumped off, dropped to his knees, and tugged some sacks out of the hole, which seemed to take all the strength he could muster. When he had six sacks laid out on the ground, he led the horses to them and managed to heave two bags onto each of the animals he'd been leading. He finished by kicking loose stuff into the hole, then mounted and rode back the way he'd come. I decided to wait around and check things out before going to town. I followed a ways to see if he was sure enough leaving, then went to that hole.

I cleaned out the clutter and found some chunks of ore way down in the bottom. Well, sir, I've done a sight of mining and know a bit about ore, and reckoned that to be the richest stuff I'd ever laid eyes on. If that fellow had three horses loaded with the likes of what was spilled in that hole, he could live in luxury a long time. I scouted around for several hours and was convinced there was no mine close by. It was coming on to dark, so I camped at one of the springs that head up Ute Creek and settled down to some serious thinking. Bull elk filled the night with whistles and grunts, the likes of which you'll hear nowhere but in the high up Rockies. Echoes of the challenges bounced from peak to peak as I tried to recall everything I'd heard about those parts.

The first white men to come into that area were a detachment of soldiers from Coronado's expedition. They were dispatched from his camp on the Rio Grande in 1540 and penetrated the region as far as the La Plata Mountains. The next record is of another bunch of soldiers under Captain Juan Maria de Riviera, or some such fancy handle. They were sent out by the governor of New Mexico in 1758, because of oft-heard rumors that gold was being brought out by miners who were ignoring the fact that the king of Spain claimed that all mines were his.

The party visited workings on the San Juan and Piedra rivers but returned home without finding any major operations. Private records show that there was at least one rich mine in the vicinity of the Pyramid and Window that was working a large crew of men all the time Riviera was in the area.

I decided the man I'd seen probably had information about an old Spanish mine but hadn't located it. Next morning I went back to the hole and scouted the area again. I ended up spending the day and found a lot of strange things like rocks arranged in an arc, a sentinel tree with blazes on each side, a passel of small blazes on trees, and a maze of signs that were just plain confusing, although parts of it seemed to make some sense. Of course, I knew where some of it led. I finally decided to get on down to Santa Fe and cash in my ore. This was even higher than the country I'd left, up where winter's never far off. I'd made do with my own cooking for half a year and hankered to sleep in a bed and belly up to a table. I favor far off country, but once in a while the urge comes on me to palaver with folks, and when it does, I'd just as well go to town and scratch my itch.

I headed off that mountain, tagging along after that lucky fellow. He'd used what looked to be an ancient trail that followed the Piedra until the river plunged into a rugged gorge. At that point the trail headed southeast through a park that was a good two-hour ride from one end to the other. The grass rubbed my stirrups as it swayed and rippled in the breeze. It was the prettiest stuff my horses had ever laid eyes on, and I let them enjoy a mess of it as we meandered down through there. A dream formed right then of setting up to raise horses in that park. I reckoned maybe I'd found that special spot over the mountain that had haunted my dreams for years. It seemed like a time to see if the LORD felt the same way, so we talked about it for a couple of hours, and he seemed to think it made sense, too.

Now, this was no city park that a body has to tend all the time. I guess some folks would call it a meadow, but we call it a park, and there isn't anything nicer for raising cattle or horses, maybe even sheep if you're made up so you can stand them. It was about seven thousand feet up, judging by the brush and trees, with some of it going to eight thousand.

We'd come down from the high country some fast, and now we eased our way through that grass, ever watchful for Utes. I reckoned we'd sure see some, since they'd not been up higher, and the second day I came onto one of their camps. I was riding the brown, and he threw up his head and flared his nostrils, so I eased into some brush and tested the wind. After a bit I could smell wood smoke and meat roasting. The camp was empty except for women, kids, and old men, and they all high-tailed for the brush when I rode into sight. With no reason to pester them, I just kept on going.

About a quarter-mile beyond the camp, I spotted a dandy buck mule deer with an oversized spread of antlers and shot him. The Indians knew I was around, and it would take only a few minutes to do what was on my mind. I figured most of the braves were hunting quite a ways from camp, but I used a bow and arrow so they wouldn't come rushing back at the sound of a rifle shot. Taking care so nobody would slip up on me, I gutted that deer then roped his antlers and drug him back to the camp, shook my rope loose, and made tracks out of there. I kept the liver, though. It comes close to being the best part of a buck if you can put some onions with it and fry it soon after the kill.

The trail we followed looked to be old as the hills themselves. Since all the main trails ended up in Santa Fe, I let the ponies stretch their legs, and it took no time at all to get well down toward town. We left the park, dropped down to the San Juan River, and crossed to a steaming hot spring. I stopped long enough to take a bath, scrape off some whiskers, and scrub my clothes, then headed south again. A chain of parks stretched for at least fifty miles, and it was a sight for sore eyes. Maybe only a rancher can fully appreciate something like that, but I reckon one of those fellows who like to paint pictures would thrive on it, and the guys who write rhymes could spin fancy yarns about the way it looks. The parks finally petered out, giving over to valleys and pine-covered ridges. We were slowed considerable by the rougher terrain. When the pinyon and cedars started, I knew we were within striking distance of Santa Fe. It was the tenth day after we left the mine that we came up to the old fellow in his misfortune.

So there we were, and he needed help. He was older than I'd reckoned from his actions in the mountains. The years had weathered his face like a boulder. He lay lifeless except for shallow breathing. I cut away his jacket and shirt and saw that the wound was nasty, but maybe not as bad as I had guessed. I went to the spring, built up the fire, and started heating water and boiling some of his coffee, something I'd done without for too long. His horses were gone, but his gear was still intact. Needing something for a bandage, I rummaged through his stuff and found a fancy sash—the kind Spanish dandies wear. Taking that and the hot water, I set about cleaning him up. The bleeding had pretty much stopped, and I was careful not to get it started again. I folded a piece of the sash, used it to cover the wound, and tied it in place with the rest of the cloth. It made a passable bandage.

I don't make out to be a doctor and sure wasn't set up to care for anyone hurt as bad as he was. I just hoped to get him so he would live till we got to town. It figured to be a half-day's ride, but we should make it by shortly after dark.

I hauled him down and laid him in some shade then cut down two young cottonwoods and toted them to the mule. Removing his pack, I fashioned a travois to carry the patient. I wrapped the tarp around the poles, fastened so his weight would keep it in place, and put my bedroll on top. I put the rest of the pack back on the mule, fastened the poles, one on each side, extending back so they would drag on the ground, put the old man in my bedroll, and tied him in place so he couldn't spill out.

With his horses gone I couldn't bring all of his stuff, so I chose a brush-choked cranny up in the rocks where no one was apt to look and started carting it up. It was no time at all before I came to the sacks he'd brought from the mountains. I opened one of them, and it was full of ore at least as rich as the little chunks I'd found in the hole. That gave me something to ponder. If I put that ore up in the rocks and somebody found it, they were certain sure to take it, and it would look like I'd done it. The upshot of it was that all the gear, his and mine, went up in the rocks, and the ore was loaded on my animals. I put two of his pack saddles on my horses with my saddle slung on top of one of them, made sure our canteens were full, and headed for town afoot.

The sun was a couple of hours past its high point, and I reckoned six or seven hours would get us to town if there were no delays. I'd been to Santa Fe lots of times and knew the area but had never been on this trail. We were coming into high desert, which stretched to the south as far as the eye could see. As we continued moving downhill, the vegetation changed, with the grass more mature and not as thick and lush as higher up but nice. It was a land for cattle, but few ranchers raised anything but sheep, and all of them would still be on summer range in the Sangre de Cristo Mountains. The part we passed through would be winter graze for the flocks.

My animals were trained to follow without a lead rope, so I put that mule beside me where I could watch the old man, and the horses came along behind. We stopped every hour or so to check him. He was feverish but didn't seem any worse. I managed to get a little water down him a couple of times but generally let him be.

I've seen my share of this world, and all of it has its own beauty, but I'm partial to the Rockies, especially come sunrise or sunset. Clouds were building over in the west, and the setting sun painted them brilliant gold, red, and all shades in between, with the hues changing rapidly as the clouds scudded and the sun lowered. Just moments after the sun was down, the full moon rose in the east, which doubled the impact of the scene. This is a mystery of God's creation. Every month, when the moon reaches full size, it rises and the sun sets at almost exactly the same time. I knew that the moon would go into hiding the next morning just as the sun peeked over the eastern rim. Off to the east was the tag end of the Sangre de Cristo Mountains. Seeing them in the combined lights of the sun and moon made it obvious that the name is appropriate. I took the opportunity to thank the LORD for letting me see it that way.

Although I truly enjoy such a sight, plenty of men have got into trouble by letting something like that take their minds off business. Many a scalp's been lost by paying too much attention to stalking a deer or even creeping up on an enemy while forgetting that someone else might be around. If I'd not been alert during that sunset, I would've missed the movement of the man on the travois. It was very slight, the first of any kind he'd made. I stopped our parade and hurried to him. His eyes were open, and he was trying to get his bearings.

Speaking his language, learned from Mexican hands on trail drives, I said, "Friend, you're pretty bad hurt. We're not far from Santa Fe, and I'll get you to a doctor soon as possible. Can you handle a drink of water?"

"Yes, thanks," he said so weakly I could barely make out the words.

I gave him a pretty good guzzle of water, careful not to choke him. He drank eagerly then said, "My outfit?"

"Your horses are gone. The *banditos*. I hid most of your stuff and brought only the ore."

He lay silently, looking into my eyes.

"I saw you dig it up. Followed along and happened to be nearby when they hit you. What shall I do with it?"

"Hide it. No one must know."

He was getting stirred up, so I said, "Don't worry. I'll see that nobody finds it or even hears about it."

He calmed down some. "Do you know Santa Fe?" he asked.

"Been there."

"Do you know Sanchez, the storekeeper?"

"Yes."

"Take me to his house. He'll know what to do." Then, sort of as an afterthought, "But tell no one of the gold. No one."

He made no effort to sit up, and the strain of talking had obviously sapped his strength. He closed his eyes and left me kneeling there beside him, so I got things moving again. It seemed like a good sign, his waking up, but he was in bad need of a doctor.

His talk added puzzlement to the situation, but there were no clues to help me understand why he would trust me, a complete stranger, and not want anyone else to know about his gold. It was a comfort that he was a friend of Sanchez.

He'd called the man a storekeeper, but he was much more than that. His "store" was The Santa Fe Trading Company, which dealt in all sorts of stuff from most any place you could name. He bought and traded for furs from the northwest, some from as far away as Canada; gold and silver from all over the west; and brought goods in from Mexico, the Gulf Coast, California, and other places. Most of it came from St. Louis by wagon, over the Santa Fe Trail. Santa Fe was the trade center for everything west of the Mississippi, and Sanchez had a God-given talent for figuring out how to meet the needs of people. He was known far and wide as a fair-dealing man. His business was flourishing, making him well to do, if not wealthy.

I'd traded furs and gold for clothing, ammo, grub, pack gear, mining tools, traps, and trade goods. Any friend of his I figured to be a pretty solid citizen. Sanchez was a native of Santa Fe, but most of his competitors were Jews. It was unusual for a Spaniard to be interested in commerce. The fortunes of many a Spanish family were built by men of other nationalities who married Spanish girls.

The request to keep the gold a secret made something of a problem, but I figured the solution would be at the Sanchez layout. He lived on the southeast edge of town, close to where the trail from St. Louis came in, and I thought he would be home by the time we got there.

CHAPTER THREE

I glimpsed the lights of Santa Fe from the edge of a mesa when we were an hour north of town. We swung east then south in order to reach the Sanchez house without going through town. Our outfit might not have caught anyone's eye, but the old man had said to take him to Sanchez, so I did it with as little fuss as possible. The merchant had a big adobe house surrounded by a wall of the same material. There were lots of trees and bushes and a collection of outbuildings, most of them at least two hundred feet from the main house. Following the south wall to a gate, I opened it and went through. The smell of hay and horses indicated that a barn was close. Several buildings had lights inside, likely the homes of workers. I went into some trees, tied the mule, and then went back out through the gate, walked around to a gate on the side next to town, and approached the house.

It was fronted by a covered porch that extended along its entire width. It was one of the finer homes in Santa Fe, close to a hundred feet wide and half that deep. The door was massive, of sanded planks, with a hammer hanging from a brass plate on the right side. When I struck the plate, there was little chance it wouldn't be heard. A plump Mexican woman answered the knock. We spoke to each other in Spanish.

"Good evening, Ma'am" I said. "I am Reuben Dove, and I need to see Señor Sanchez. It's a matter of great importance. Is he home?"

"Yes, sir, but he is with another man. Please wait while I tell him."

"I don't want anyone else to know I'm here, so tell him quiet like."

"I'll try. Wait here, please." She closed the door.

I was sure Sanchez would remember me. It was said that he never forgot the face or name of anyone with whom he'd done business and could recall each detail of a transaction years later. The door opened again sooner than I expected.

"Please come in, Señor Dove," the woman said and took off down a hallway and led me into a room. "Please wait here. The señor will be with you soon."

She padded away, her sandals whacking the earthen floor. Voices came faintly through the wall; then a door opened and they were easily heard.

"Then you won't help me?"

"How can I help, when I have no idea where he went?" I recognized Sanchez's voice. "He said nothing to me about going away."

"Let me know if you hear from him. We've got to know what he's up to. The old fool left with three packhorses and has been gone over two weeks. None of the people at his house will tell me anything. I'm about ready to go take over the place."

"What do you mean, 'take over the place'?" asked Sanchez, his voice softer.

"Oh, well, I just mean until he gets back. I wouldn't want things to run down while he's gone."

"I suggest you wait. There are some good people there who handle things the way he wants. Now, you must excuse me. Another man's waiting on a matter of urgency."

They walked by the door, and I saw Sanchez and a short, skinny man with swarthy complexion.

"Maria, please show Señor Diaz out. Good night," said the merchant.

I suppose he had a first name, but all I ever heard him called was Sanchez, usually preceded by Señor. He stood something less than six feet tall and looked overweight, even soft. But I'd seen him lift a two-hundred-pound load with no noticeable effort. His grip was firm, the hand hard as he clasped mine in greeting.

"Are we alone?" I asked.

"You may speak freely," he said; then he continued in English, "Use your language if you prefer. No one else understands it."

"Thanks, I will. I found an old man half a day north of here. Bandits had him cornered, and he's pretty bad hurt, been unconscious except for a few minutes, when he said to bring him here. I don't know who he is. He's in the trees near your barn and needs a doctor."

"Let's get him," he said, moving as he spoke. "Maria, send Manuel for Doctor Archuleta. Someone's hurt. Get the back bedroom ready."

He did know how to take charge and get things done. He led the way through a back door and hurried toward the barn. As we passed one of the houses, he said quietly, "Jose, please come help us."

A figure separated from the shadows and joined us.

"Where?" he asked as we neared the barn.

I led them to the mule. The old man's breath came in gasps. I would be glad to turn him over to a doctor.

"Get him loose, and we'll carry him to the house," said Sanchez.

Jose went to the back of the travois, Sanchez and I to either side of the mule, and we released the poles. When they were loose, Jose picked the ends from the ground, and we walked away from the mule. I took the pole from Sanchez, and led off toward the house, where Maria was holding the door open. Sanchez led us into a bedroom, stripped the covers down, and directed us to lay the travois at an angle across the bed.

He said, "Thank you, Jose. Don't tell anyone of this. Show Señor Dove where to put his animals and take him to the guesthouse. If he needs anything more, get someone to help him." Turning to me, he said, "When you're settled, please come back."

Jose showed me a building close to the main house then took me to the barn and pointed out three stalls in the back. He put hay and oats in each.

"I'll have one of the boys care for the horses, señor," he said.

Mindful of the load they carried, I said, "No, thanks. They don't like other folks messing with them."

I got the animals then went to the guesthouse and unloaded the ore. After watering the horses, I returned to the barn and unsaddled them, rubbed them down, and left them chomping oats, a real treat for critters used to making do in the high country.

Hurrying back to the main house, I knocked softly on the back door and was admitted by Maria. As I entered the sickroom, a man was removing the sash bandage.

"This is a bad wound. What caused it?" he asked.

"It was probably a pistol bullet," I answered. "Four men attacked and shot him before he made it to cover. It was a while before I got to him; then it took about half a day to get here."

"The bullet's still in him. It's got to come out right away. I'll need plenty of hot water and bandages."

"I will get those," said Maria, bustling out.

"Help me get him off this rig and undressed," the man ordered.

As Sanchez and I lifted the patient, the doctor pulled my bedroll off the bed. He instructed us as we got the old man undressed and positioned.

"Now, I'll do better by myself," he said. "We can talk later."

"Let's eat," said Sanchez. He took me to the kitchen and placed food on the table. He said, "We'll continue to use your language when we're alone. We'll be discussing things that need to be kept private. When the doctor comes out, we'll need to speak Spanish."

"He is Luiz Jimenez, a good friend. I'm glad he was able to tell you to come here. His son was killed a few years back. It was the husband of his son's widow who was here when you arrived. That fellow wouldn't be sorry to see Luiz dead so he could move in and take over his place. There's a granddaughter, Luiz's only blood relative, and she's under the stepfather's control. Since Luiz is wealthy, Pancho Diaz would like to have the estate come to her while he's in control. If you'd taken him anywhere else, Pancho could have heard of it. He cannot touch him as long as he's here. You will do me a favor by staying with us to see that he's not bothered until he's well. Can you do that…for me?"

"Well," I said, eating to gain time, "I'd say he may not live through this, but he's a tough old bird or he'd be dead by now. I reckon I'd best stick here for a while. He sort of obligated me to wait till he can talk to me again."

"This is your home as long as you're in Santa Fe. We'll be most happy to have you."

"I need to go after the rest of our stuff. It's hid where I found him, and I don't want to leave it there very long. There's a storm brewing, so if it's all right, I'll get out of here early in the morning and go after it."

"That will be fine. Do you need horses or equipment?"

"No, I brought my saddle, and my critters can handle the load with the gear I left out there. As soon as the doctor's finished, I'll hit the hay then leave early."

"Please have Maria send me word when you return," he said. "I'll have Jose stay close until you get back. Pancho may get curious about the message Maria brought when you came. He hangs around with some bad men, and they might harm my people. I'll be glad to have you here."

"I hope there's nothing to do but loaf and eat your grub," I said. "But if he's in danger we'll face that, too."

As I sat there eating tortillas, frijoles, and the first beef I'd had in months, it occurred to me that the travois had left a trail any kid could follow. Not wanting to trouble Sanchez, I decided it would be a good idea to stay and make sure the bandits didn't try for the gold again. I wasn't sure they knew about it, but it was likely the reason for the attack. We sat and drank coffee like

I'd dreamed of for months; black as the guts of a mine and hot as Satan's oven. When the doc came out, he looked weary and seemed grateful for the cup Sanchez set before him.

"He's a tough old guy," he said. "The bullet was really smashed up, but I think I got it all. You did all anyone could, short of taking the bullet out, and that's pretty tricky. It's best to do what you did. I expect he'll feel some better in a couple of days, but it's a bad wound, and he's old enough to make it difficult. We need to get Elena over here as soon as he comes around. He dotes on her, and she'll make him want to live. If he doesn't have something to perk him up, he might decide it's not worth the trouble. He's going to hurt like blazes for a while."

Sanchez said, "We don't want Pancho to know Luiz is here, so we'll have to be careful getting word to Elena. Florencia will be home tomorrow, and I'll get her to work something out." He added, for my benefit, "Elena's the granddaughter I told you about."

The moon was riding the top of its run when I got back to the guesthouse. Thankful for the moonlight, I poked around looking for a place to hide the ore and decided to bury it under wood in a box by the kitchen stove.

It was an hour shy of sunup when I headed for the spring to get our stuff. The air was heavy with moisture, and dew hung on every bush as we traveled under a leaden sky. I'd be lucky to get back dry. Sunrise was every bit as pretty as the sunset had been, the moon an overgrown pumpkin perched on the western horizon when the sun showed. The colors ran a shade or two darker than the ones of the evening, some of them like the dark feathers on a goose, shading out to white edges.

Morning, like springtime, gives a freshness and sparkle that fades as the day wears on. I've heard tell of folks who don't know the sun comes up gradually, having never seen it until it's full-blown. If there really are people like that, they sure miss a lot. That early sun colored not only the eastern sky, with clouds stacked like tumbleweeds against a fence, but also the foothills and mountains took on the oranges and reds of the sunrise. It was purely pretty and made me realize why God looked on his creation and saw that it was good. It was enough to set me to singing. The horses cocked their ears, snorted, tossed their heads, and wrung their tails some, but it didn't seem to bother them too much.

I approached the spring quietly, swung wide to the point from which I'd shot, and had the spring in full view. Nobody was around, so I rode down, kindled a fire, and started breakfast. While coffee was making, I hauled the gear down then fried venison, made gravy thick as brick mortar, and settled down to eat. After cleaning up, I switched my saddle to the *grullo*, put Luiz's fancy, silver-studded outfit on the brown, and the packsaddle on the mule. Since I'd used my bedroll in the travois, it was easy to get everything on the two rigs, and we set off again.

I'd followed the trail back to the spring but decided to return a different way because of that fancy saddle. There might be a hundred like it in Santa Fe, but I hadn't seen anything to match it. It sure would be pretty for riding where the señoritas could see you but was a mighty poor pick for Indian country. That was no bother now, but if someone happened to be hunting for Luiz and saw that rig, it could cause problems. There was also a possibility that the bandits would track us to the Sanchez place and could be watching. The thought that, unlike most outlaws I'd known, they might be early risers and could be waiting back along the trail firmed up my decision. I rode across that back country, and the storm kept building. Lightning flashed, thunder cracked and the wind got downright brisk. The smell of rain was strong, even though the wind whipped dust into clouds that sometimes hid the sky. Those ponies felt it and maybe figured they could reach the barn and more of those sweet oats before the storm hit.

The brown was a natural single-footer, a gait in which the horse's body never sways from side to side but goes forward in a straight line, with no jar to the rider. All motion is made by the horse's legs beneath the body. A horse that knows the gait will always go to it when he's in a hurry. I trained the *grullo* to it shortly after I got the brown and learned what a pleasure it is for riding. We didn't use it much if the mule was along because he could never learn it, and when he had to keep up with the horses, he shook things up pretty bad. With that storm brewing, those ponies just naturally went to it, and I figured the pack would have to stand up to a shaking.

We were back at the barn and unpacking when the storm hit. I put the animals in the stalls again, fed them, and put up the gear, placing Luiz's saddle in a room with several other highly decorated outfits. Those Spaniards do beat all for flashy rigs, and it does look nice—in town. I put my outfit with some ordinary-looking tack, took both sets of saddlebags, put on my slicker, and sloshed across to the guesthouse. It'd come up a real gully washer. I tossed the bags on the bed and went to the big house.

Maria was bossing four women in the kitchen.

"May I fix you some breakfast?" she asked. She already knew I understood Spanish. In fact, that was what was spoken except when Sanchez and I discussed things privately.

"Thanks, no. Just a cup of coffee, please. Señor Sanchez said you could send someone to tell him when I got here, though."

"Yes, I've already sent Manuel."

"Good. I'm going to check on the old man."

Two women were in the room with the patient. An old lady dressed in black sat in a corner, eyes closed as she said her beads. A girl sat close beside the bed. The old man was peaceful.

"Has he been awake?" I asked the young one.

She stood up and motioned for me to follow her. Her movement going down the hall was lovely as a dove in flight, and I've got to say, tagging along after her was pleasant. In my twenty-four years of living, I'd never seen anyone who came close to being that beautiful. I'd loned it for half a year, and the urge was on me to be with a woman. Sanchez had put me in a spot where it was going to be another spell before I could get to town and scratch my itch. Now, here's this young thing swinging down the hall in front of me, and it made the postponement less of a strain. She wasn't putting on no show, but you set a shapely woman in motion, and notions do come to a man's head. Any man tells you different, he'll lie about other things, too.

She went into a large room furnished with leather-covered chairs and a whopping big leather couch. Plants were in every cranny, and a window looked out over a beautiful flower garden. Bookshelves along two walls bulged with rich-looking volumes.

Turning, she said, "You must be the gentleman who rescued my grandfather. Maria said you are Señor Dove. I am Elena Jimenez." The voice was throaty and vibrant.

Tall and slender, she was anything but scrawny, and her dress didn't hide her young figure. Obsidian eyes and skin like tanned buckskin indicated that she was of pure Spanish descent. I thought of a rose ready to burst into full bloom. Her jaw line extended a good two inches below her ear then angled sharply out to a strong chin. The ebony eyes , big as the conchas on Luiz's saddle, were jewels set between high cheekbones. A crown of hair thick and rich as sculptured onyx framed the lovely face.

I stared, must've been a full minute. When she started blushing at my look, I stammered, "I'm sorry, ma'am. I just came off a mountain, where I spent six lonely months; then I rode for another half a month to get here through some truly beautiful country. I thought I'd seen beauty, but you put all that in the shade. Thank you for making the trip worthwhile. I'm so overcome my mind must've shut down. I didn't know the good LORD made anyone as beautiful as you are. I didn't hear a thing you said. I hope you can forgive me. Can we maybe start over?"

Now, I'm usually tongue-tied with women, but that just wouldn't stay unsaid. I guess it maybe turned out all right, because she kept on blushing and gave me a smile that almost knocked me over.

About that time Sanchez came, and the moment was just a memory. His wife had returned from visiting a married daughter. We went to the dining room, where I met his son, Renaldo, and two daughters, Carmelita and Juanita. During the meal Sanchez brought his family up to date on the happenings of the previous night. He concluded by saying, "We'll say nothing of this to anyone." Turning to me, he said, "Did anyone follow you this morning?"

"I saw no sign of it but didn't come back on the trail. The tracks are washed out by now. Do you think someone followed me?"

"One of my men saw Pancho and four of his buddies ride in from the west. They stopped a quarter mile from the gate you used last night, spent some time looking at the ground, then rode north. My man went out to where they had stopped. There were tracks going both ways from the gate, and he described the marks of the travois. Pancho and his crew seemed to be headed back the way you came in last night." He asked Elena, "How did you learn that Luiz was here?"

"I had no idea he was. One of the men with my stepfather said he was going to take me with him tonight. I slipped away when they left. You're right in thinking they suspect something. My stepfather is afraid of them. I think he would like to have them gone. I knew that Grandfather was away and took the liberty of coming to you. I'll leave if you think it'll bring trouble."

"We'll have no talk of that, my dear. I was going to send for you. Doctor Archuleta said you're the only one who can make Luiz want to get well. As long as Rube's here, we'll not worry about trouble. He'll take care of whatever Pancho and his cohorts think up."

It looked like he might carry on, and while I didn't mind his saying a few things to make me show up in her eyes, it didn't seem fitting to sit and listen to him lay it on too thick. I switched the talk to her grandpa, and we decided to go check on him. Sanchez walked with us to the sickroom, where we found Luiz awake. He reacted slowly to our presence.

"Ah, my friend, you're with us, are you?" said Sanchez.

The oldster seemed to have trouble focusing his eyes. When he looked at me, there was no sign he remembered me.

"This is Señor Reuben Dove," said Elena. "He drove off the men who shot you and then brought you here. Do you remember?"

He stared at me a long time and finally nodded slightly.

"I did just like you said. Don't worry about anything," I said.

He continued to stare at me, so I said, "It's all right."

He turned his attention to Elena, who knelt at his bedside.

"Have him tell you everything," he said, his voice barely a whisper. Rolling his eyes toward me, he said, "Everything," then drifted off again.

We walked into the hallway, and Sanchez said, "Missus Alvarez will stay with him so the two of you can talk. He wants you to tell her something, and you can do it better out of that room. I must get back to my business."

Elena led me back to the library. I followed, taking the opportunity to assess her again. Her clothes were hardly different from those worn by the servants, but beyond that she was like nobody I'd ever seen. She was in a class by herself.

"Do you know what Grandfather wants you to tell me?"

"Reckon he was talking about the ore he was packing. Never saw the likes of it, richer'n anything I ever come on, and six big sacks full."

"Ahhh. Did the banditos know of it?"

"I couldn't rightly say, but they'd camped so's to watch the trail, seemed like, and waited for him to come, then followed till they could take him by surprise."

"But you saved him and the gold as well. We are much in your debt. He'll reward you."

"Wasn't after no reward. He was minding his own business, bothering no one, and those others didn't stack up, so I bought in. Reckon he'd do the same if'n he had the chance. It seemed like something the LORD would do, so I jumped in."

"Most men would have not said anything about the gold. You could have hidden it and let us think the banditos took it. Didn't you think of that?"

"Only thing that come to mind was, I best keep it where nobody else could get it. Never been one to take what ain't mine. Pa always said there's no way you can buy a good name, but it's sure easy to lose one. I've tried to keep mine, much as possible. I always ask myself what Jesus would do and try to follow along that way."

"You've certainly proven yourself to us, señor, and he will repay you."

She was gazing at me, those eyes like dark pools of still water. I wanted to dive in, knowing full well I'd never come up. I could've told her just sitting there with her was more pay than I'd ever got for anything up to then. But that's no kind of talk to make with someone like her, so I sat and twisted my old, knobby, scarred up hands and stared back at her. She was the prettiest thing I ever did see, and there I sat, with a mug ugly enough to scare a wildcat.

"What happened to your fingers?" she wanted to know.

"These two on the left hand? Fool things got caught in a dally when I hooked up to a Longhorn down Texas way. Snipped 'em off, slick as calf slobbers. I was ridin' one of the smartest horses I ever owned. I'd just started ropin' off him; only done it maybe ten times. That rascal figgered out how long it took me to get ready for him to stop after the rope settled over the cow's horns. He waited that long and stopped without me tellin' him to. I wasn't ready, and those fingers were in the way. Good-bye, fingers. I got ready for him to stop from that time on. Made me a better roper."

"What's a dally?"

"It's where you wrap a rope round the saddle horn, so's to snub up a critter after you've got a loop on him. Some folks tie hard and fast, which is where you leave the end of your lasso fastened to the horn all the time. That's pretty hard on the horse and cow both because you let them run clear to the end, then yank them up. The way I do is to dab the loop then take a couple wraps, and jerk them quick. Lots of fellers running round shy some fingers from doing it that way."

"That sounds awful. It must've hurt terribly."

"It throbbed some, couple of nights, but 'tweren't too bad. Get careless, you pay. Had a friend once, up on the Musselshell, set a deadfall so's to trigger a shotgun. Going to get him a bear. Durned if he didn't forget and trip it his ownself. Found him later, his head all…you ain't interested in that. It was some messy. But it don't pay to get careless."

"Weren't you angry with that horse?"

"Hey, he was doin' better'n any horse I'd ever had. How can you blame him for that? I had to be ready when I rode him, and it made me better, too. I can't be mad about that."

"I don't think many people would think that way about it. I'm afraid I wouldn't."

"I've only had one other horse that caught on as fast as that one did, and it makes me wonder how the LORD can make a horse that smart. It's sure a pleasure when he does, though."

"I think it's amazing that you look at it that way. Most people would blame the horse for losing their fingers and be mad at him the rest of their lives."

"I wasn't gonna spoil a good horse. They don't come along like that every day. I want all of 'em I can get."

"That's *wonderful*! I'm going to try to be more like that."

She asked, "How did you know about Grandfather? Were you there when he was shot?"

"No, ma'am. I was following along behind him, though. I saw him when he found the gold, up in the high country. I was maybe a mile away when I heard shooting and decided to have a look see."

"Then you drove the banditos off?"

"I guess it worked out that way. I left my critters and sneaked up to have a look. It was sort of clear what was happening. There were four fellows shooting at a spot on the hillside. I put my sights on the one who looked to be the leader but hadn't made up my mind whether to shoot him when my crazy mule brayed. It made me jump, and I jerked off a shot. It did nothing but knock some dirt into the man's eyes, but it caused them to skedaddle out of there.

"I found your grandpa and did the best I could to fix things so he'd last till we got here. Sanchez took over as soon as we got here. I brought the gold at that time and went back this morning to get the rest of our stuff."

She said, "Grandfather's told me that the gold is really far up in the mountains. Why were you up there?"

"I had me a bit of a gold mine over the hill from there and decided to ride over the top to get to town. I saw your grandpa walking around, swinging something on the end of a chain, and watched till he located the gold and put it on his horses and left. I looked around up there some, then tagged along the way he came off the mountain. I guess the good LORD just wanted me there when he needed help."

"He was dowsing when you first saw him. He puts a nugget on a gold chain and uses it to find ore. Not many people are able to do it, and some people think it's witchcraft, but he's used it several times. His wife's grandfather, my great-great-grandfather, taught him when he was young. It was used to locate most of the great mines."

"Never heard tell of it. Sounds something like water witching."

"I've never heard of that. Is it done by witches?"

"The fellow I saw didn't look like no witch. He used a forked willow switch. Seemed like he could find water ever time, too."

"Where was that?"

"Back in West Virginy, when I was a young'un."

And then she wanted to know about that, and before long I'd told her all about myself. It's good nobody came bothering that day because she had every dab of my attention. A herd of wild horses could've come through there without troubling me none. I did nothing but peer into those eyes and let my mouth run.

I've had some friends along the way, couldn't have made it without them, but don't reckon anyone had been much interested in me since my folks were killed by Indians when I was thirteen. They were good folks and had given me a love for reading, even though we hadn't much to read but the Good Book. They gave me a decent enough handle on ciphers, too, but the three greatest things they done was to teach me to work for what I got and to believe what's in the Bible. That and give me a desire to make something of myself. My pa was a horseman, and I'd grown up with a love for the critters and how to figure what it takes to make a good riding animal. He also taught me some things about how to breed so as to improve livestock. I guess that's where I got the dream of a horse ranch.

She said, "Tell me about the time when your parents were killed. Who did it, and why did they do it?"

"It was a bunch of drunk Indians who did it. They were probably some that my folks had thought were friendly, and they were most of the time, but when anybody gets drunk, they're apt to turn into a different kind of person. It's a good reason to never drink the stuff."

"Where were you when it happened?"

"It was a Sunday afternoon. We'd spent the morning reading the Bible, and after the noon meal, I went for a ride. Pa'd given me my first full-grown horse, and I took him for about a four-hour ride to see if he was as good as he looked. He was a roan with what's called a glass eye, and some horses like that are pretty mean. I should've known Pa wouldn't guess about something like that, but I needed to find out for myself. I smelled smoke when I was a quarter mile away and found the two of them laid out in the yard, all messed up, with the house burned to the ground."

"How horrible! What did you do?"

"Got a shovel and buried them up on the hill where Ma always liked to go in the evening just after we'd eaten supper. It seemed to be her favorite spot on the whole place. I figured she'd like it there. She was one who liked pretty things a lot, and she had a view of half the state from there. I knew she had a better spot, up with Jesus, but it seemed like she'd like it, anyway, so that's where I put them."

"How old were you?"

"I turned fourteen the next month."

"When did this happen?"

"Ten years ago."

"So you're twenty-four now?"

"Yes'm, I will be in a couple of months."

"What did you do after that? You had no house, so where did you live?"

"The war between the states was a threat, and all the neighbors had their hands full. I couldn't ask any of them to take me in, so I headed west to see what I could find. It was a couple of weeks later that I rode into a place where it was obvious they were raising horses. I spotted a slave who was working with some fancy-looking horses. When I asked him if there was any chance I could get a meal for a day's work, he pointed out the owner. When I asked him, he said, 'You tell Charlie over there that you're to stay with him. I guess you can stay as long as you're willing to work with him."

"Charlie was the man I'd talked with, and he was able to hear the owner. He waved to me, and the two of us combed and brushed the horses, fed them, and put them in a pasture. Charlie was a really nice man. He had no family, so I lived with him for about a year and a half. He taught me how to train racehorses, do blacksmith work, care for sick animals, and added to what Pa had taught me about breeding them. The owner ended up with another slave, but I got an education in how to raise good horses. Charlie really knew how to talk to the LORD, so I learned about that, too. When I figured I'd learned about all I was going to, I scatted out of there."

She said, "It sounds like Charlie was a really special man."

"He was. He'd been gelded, so he had no family. I guess I was sort of the son he wished he could have."

"I don't know what that word means."

"Which one? Oh, you mean *gelded*?"

"Yes. What does that mean?"

"That's what they do to a stallion or a bull so he can't breed."

"That had been done to a man?"

"Seems like it was common with slaves, since way back in Bible times. In men it's called making them eunuchs. I believe that's what happened to Daniel when he was taken to Babylon."

"Oh, my goodness. I didn't know they ever did that to humans! That's a terrible thing to do. I almost get sick thinking about it."

"It's not a happy thought, is it? Well, it'd been done to Charlie, and it did make him a gentle man. I often wonder what happened to him. He was a mighty good friend to me."

"You said he taught you how to talk to the LORD. What was so special about that?"

"He didn't just tell Jesus what he wanted or needed; he almost always began by telling Jesus what a great God he is and how much he loved him. Then he would thank him for special things he'd been given, like a time when a colt had been quick to learn something. He would ask the LORD to forgive him for anything he thought the LORD wouldn't like. He would then ask for what he needed or wanted. He always asked if the LORD wanted to tell him something, then he'd wait a while to see if he was told anything."

"That's *beautiful!* What a great way to handle prayer. Was he told things often?"

"It didn't happen every day, but Charlie convinced me that there were lots of times the LORD helped him figure out how to handle a horse so he would get the critter to do what was wanted."

"Is that how you pray?"

"I'm not as good as Charlie, but it sure has helped a lot of times. I couldn't have handled the deal with your grandpa any other way. It's really important to believe that you already have what you ask for. In the gospel, according to Mark, we're told that we're to believe we have what we ask for, and it'll be given to us. It even sounds like it's more important to believe than anything else. I don't understand all about it, but old Charlie could sure get serious when he wanted something, and he almost always got what he wanted."

"That's amazing. Do you think you could teach someone how to do it?"

"I don't reckon it'd be too tough if the person who's being taught knows Jesus as his savior. I'd want to be sure of that before I tried."

"Are you going to stay here for a while?"

"Sanchez has asked me to stay around until your grandpa's all right, so I guess I will."

"We'll see if I can learn to pray like that, if you'll help me."

"I reckon it'll be fun to try. When you want to start?"

"Do you think I can learn to pray so that Grandfather will get well?"

"Do you believe that Jesus can heal him?"

"Didn't he heal lots of people when he was here?"

"That's surely what the Bible says, isn't it?"

"I think so."

"I've read somewhere in the Bible that he's the same, yesterday, today, and forever. If that's true, he can still heal whenever and whomever he wants to. I believe every word in the Bible is true."

"Then teach me how to pray so it'll happen."

"Do you know Jesus?"

"I think so. I've gone to church all my life and try to do only good things. Is there more to it than that?"

"It won't hurt to spend a few minutes to be sure, if that's all right with you."

"That's fine. Tell me how to be sure."

"The Bible says we've all sinned and come short of being what we should be. Because of what Adam and Eve did with the serpent in the Garden of Eden, we are all born with a sinful nature, and we will sin. If I have a bad thought, it's a sin and has to be paid for. In another place the Bible says that the wages of sin is death, which means eternal separation from God, but it also says that the gift of God is eternal life through the blood of Christ. That blood was shed on the cross at Calvary and was sufficient to save us from that death when we accept Christ as our savior. Have you done that?"

"I've been in church all my life, and have heard about Jesus dying and that he did it so people would be saved. Nobody ever told me I need to accept him as my savior. It was always as though he died for everybody, and that was all that mattered. What do I need to do?"

"All it takes is to tell Jesus you know you've done things he calls sin and believe he's done all that's needed to pay for it. You can then tell him you want him to be your savior, that you believe he's done everything that's needed to pay for your sin, and ask him to save you."

"Does it need to be said a certain way? I don't want to do it wrong."

"One of the greatest things I've learned is that God the Father, Jesus, who is God the Son, and the Holy Spirit are all with us all the time. They love us and want us to be saved. They are willing and able to give you the proper words to say if you ask them to. Do you want to?"

"Yes, I do. Can you give me an idea about how to say it?"

"If you talk to Jesus, which I like to do, I would tell him you know you have sinned, and that you believe that he gave his life so that you could be saved. I would then tell him you want him to save you and make you pure. It's not a difficult thing to do."

"Will you pray with me, and maybe add anything that I miss?"

"Of course. I'll be happy to do that."

"All right. Jesus, I know I've sinned by doing things you don't like. I believe you died to pay for that. I ask you to forgive me and make me pure. Thank you for doing that, and for bringing Reuben here so I could learn about this. LORD, I also thank you for Reuben helping Grandfather. If you'll heal Grandfather, it'll make me happy. I ask you to do that. Amen."

I continued, "LORD, thank you for doing that for Elena. I am happy that she's accepted you as her savior and look forward to watching you work in her life. You're wonderful, and you bless me with so many things that I don't deserve. It's a special blessing to get to know Elena. Please help her to understand how much you love her and want to help her. Thank you, LORD. Amen."

When I looked up, she was getting up from her chair and coming toward me. Her face was almost glowing, and the smile on her lips would've put the sun to shame. There was a sparkle in her eyes that turned my heart upside down. I stood to meet her. She reached for my hands and took them in hers.

"Thank you, Reuben. I can say without any doubt that I now know Jesus. What a wonderful thing you did."

"It was an honor to be here when God was working. Now all the sins you've ever committed and all that you will ever commit in the future are forgiven. We're told that we should ask him to forgive us when we sin, and he's faithful and just to do that. That's not so we can keep our salvation but to keep our relationship with him free of problems. Another thing you should know is that when you accept what Jesus did for you, the Holy Spirit comes into you and lives there from now on. We're also told that we are placed in Jesus, but he also comes to live in us. I don't understand how they do that, but that's what the Bible says happens, and I know it's true."

"I'll need some time to absorb all this. Will you please help me?"

"It'll be a pleasure to help any way I can," I said. "I hope I can answer all your questions."

"Does God use you like this very often?"

"Sometimes God allows me to be a part of what he's doing, and it's always a really special time. I'm glad he had me ask you if you knew him and then help you understand. It was a privilege to be here when you did that. You're now a child of God in Christ Jesus."

"Really? I am his child now?"

"Isn't it wonderful? We are told that everyone who accepts him as our savior is adopted by God."

"Then you're my brother?"

"Yes, but you'll be happy to know that you'll never look any worse for it. I now have the most beautiful woman in the world for a sister."

"You just did something nobody else has ever even tried to do. That makes you truly special," she said. "You look wonderful to me, too."

"Me, look *wonderful?* Maybe God will give you back your sight eventually. I sort of took after Pa. I always wondered why Ma chose him over some man who was better looking. I even asked her once, and she said he looked fine to her."

"Not all beauty is on the outside. I already know that you're a pretty special person. What you did for Grandfather looked really good to me, and now you've done something for me that's better than anything that's ever been done before. You look really good to me, Reuben. Don't worry about your outside. I can see beyond that."

I guess you know I felt some good right then. She was the sweetest thing I'd ever come close to, and it looked like I might get to spend more than a couple of hours with her.

We sat and looked at each other for a while, which was pleasant for me, but should've stretched her some. I finally said, "Let's go check on Grandpa, then I could use a cup of coffee if one's available."

"If you'll check on him, I'll get the coffee for you and some tea for me."

"That'll be fine, unless he's awake. If he is, he'll want to see you."

"I'll be back in a few minutes," she said as she scampered down the hall. I stood and watched as long as I could. She was worth watching, I'll tell the world.

The old man seemed to be resting nicely, so I walked down to meet her. She was just leaving the kitchen when I got there and was carrying a tray filled with drinks and some other goodies. I figured she could handle that better than I could, so I walked alongside her. I've yet to see a person who walked so gracefully. She seemed to glide along like a majestic Canadian goose on smooth water, or that eagle soaring among the clouds. She's worth watching from any angle. We were soon back in the library, munching and sipping.

"Where did you go when you left the horse ranch?" she asked.

"I drifted to Texas, where I met up with a cowman named Reed Anthony. He was driving cattle herds north and needed men to ride along with them. I went to Kansas with four herds that first year. The next year he put me in charge of a herd, and we went to Kansas three times and once on north into Wyoming. When we were coming back from Wyoming, I got a look at the mountains north of here and decided to see if I could find some gold. The first two years I made more money from trapping beaver in the winter than I did finding gold, but I learned a lot. Met up with a fellow named Kit Carson, who sort of took me under his wing and showed me lots of things. We covered lots of country, clear up almost to Canada, and got to be pretty good friends.

"I was here in Santa Fe quite a bit, and it's been where I've wintered the last two years. Last winter I met a fellow who wanted to trade me his gold mine for my traps and other gear. That's how I ended up with a mine up north of here, where I came from the other day."

Even a body unimportant as me can't tell everything about himself in one afternoon, but she about milked me dry. It finally came on me to ask about her.

"I've chewed your ear for hours. Now it's your turn. Tell me about yourself," I said.

"There's really very little of interest. I've not had an exciting life like yours."

"Tell me about it. What happened to your daddy?"

"He was shot by banditos when I was fourteen. That's how old you were when your parents were killed, is it not?"

"It lacked a month. How'd it happen?"

"No one saw it. He was riding alone. When he didn't return, Mother sent someone to look for him. They came back with his body. He'd been shot in the back. His money was gone, and his horse was never seen again, so we assumed that it was done by banditos who were passing through the country.

"It was only a short time before my stepfather started courting my mother, and they were married two years later."

I'd lived for years alone or in the company of men, and she seemed like rain after a five-year dry spell. I'd hoped to sit and talk with a woman but figured it would be in a cantina, some gal who would listen, long as I bought. To be in that quiet house with someone who seemed sure enough interested in me was never in my wildest schemes. Along about sundown Carmelita Sanchez came traipsing down the hall.

"Supper's almost fixed," she said. "Can the two of you stay apart long enough to get ready?" She was grinning like a kid with a new way to tease her sister.

It came to me that it had been several days since I last shaved. Scurrying to the guesthouse, I remedied that and put on something better than the duds I'd worn on the trail that morning.

As I was scraping off whiskers, I said, "Old hoss, you best figure this as a one-time thing. That little gal ain't apt to waste more'n one afternoon on the likes of you. It's been sure enough fun, though."

But the next few days were more of the same sweet medicine. She said, "Tell me about that place where you want to have your ranch."

"It's a three-day ride north of here. The San Juan River runs through there, and a bunch of hot springs are beside the river down off the mesa where I want to build my house. The park's at least twenty miles long and will average five to ten miles wide on the mesa. Similar parks run from the river south for probably thirty to forty miles. It's a place where any animals would do well and is so pretty it makes your eyes happy."

"Do you know where your house will be?"

"I didn't really set down and pick the exact spot, but there's a place that looked like it would be a good place to put it."

"Will you raise anything other than horses?"

"It'll be hard to make much money from horses until you have a reputation, so I would raise cattle for a cash crop. I'll probably go to Texas and buy a herd or two to drive to Kansas, then go back and pick up some cows to bring to the ranch. After a few years, the calves raised on the ranch will be big enough so I won't need to go anywhere else to have cattle to sell. It'll be necessary to bring in some really good stallions to get the kind of horses I think I want. I want a bigger horse than you'll find anywhere around here. I'll probably use Barbs like are on the sheep ranches in this area but will use bigger stallions. All of this will take several years, but I can almost see the kind of horse I'll have in a few years. It's a pretty big dream and may be more than I can ever accomplish," I said.

"Who gave you the dream?"

"Well, I think it was the LORD, but when I talk about it, it seems like something I would never be able to do."

"Is God able to do something like that?"

"I'm sure he can, if he wants to."

"How important is it to believe?"

"You do learn quick, don't you? Believing's absolutely necessary."

"How do you overcome that?"

"Well, Paul said in his letter to the churches in Galatia that he lived by the faith of the Son of God, who loved him and gave his life for him. That seems to mean that Jesus will give us some of his faith, if we ask for it."

"That sounds like a good thing to do, doesn't it?"

"I have to apologize to God for forgetting. It's something I do pretty often," I said. "Thanks for reminding me."

"What do you do when you want some of his faith?"

"I tell God I don't have enough faith and ask him to give me some of Jesus's faith."

"What happens?"

"He gives it to me. When I depend on him instead of just thinking I can handle it, things go well."

"Do you mind if I ask him to give you the faith you need?"

"I'd like that. I'm sure God will do almost anything for you. He'll probably pull you onto his lap and ask if there's anything more he can do for you."

"I doubt that he's that easily impressed."

"You don't have any idea how much he loves you."

She gave me a smile that turned me to a puddle of soft butter. I managed to keep from melting clear down into my boots, which came close to happening every time I looked at her. It must've been the third day—I was in kind of a daze—when she said, "I want to see your horses."

"They're sorta like me, not used to polite company. You sure?"

"Of course I'm sure. I'll bet they *are* 'sort of like you.' Come on, let's go see them."

She took to that brown right off, and it wasn't more'n a minute before she'd talked the snort right out of him. I guess he's about half smart, after all. She found a sidesaddle, and nothing would do but I had to put it on that old boy and take her for a ride.

"That horse ain't never had a woman atop him. No telling what he'll do, you start flapping your skirts around him," I warned.

"Well, he's your horse, isn't he? You can surely control him. I'm sure you won't let him do anything to hurt me."

I turned to that horse and said, "You heard the lady. Now, behave."

Danged if he wasn't like a baby calf with her. Never did see the beat of it. Usually jumpy as a buck deer, spooking at every booger, and not a misstep with her.

Along about then I started getting back to normal and was mindful of a few things going on. That was the day I spotted someone watching the place. A flash of light on a bluff northeast of the house did it. I made a point of going behind that bluff when we rode the next morning. There were three sets of tracks going in, two coming out.

"Looky here," I said. "Somebody's using that bluff to watch the house."

Lots of men would have told her nothing about the lookout, but I'd seen my ma come up with ideas that unraveled a lot of knots and reckoned a lady had ought to know what she was up against. Especially since the man on the hill might mean danger to her grandpa and maybe to her. We rode on, discussing the situation.

When she headed back to the house I said, "Let's go a different way. When a body's watching, he probably expects to see a pattern to what we do. From now on we'll not give him any help. We'll ride at different times and go different ways. I'll talk to Sanchez about this, too."

On the way to the house, I picked up my field glasses. The bluff could be seen from the library as well as from Luiz's room. Staying well back from the window, I searched the area and soon spotted the lookout.

Handing the glasses to Elena, I said, "Look just to the right of that big, dead cedar on the point that comes out the farthest. He's at the foot of the tree behind that one." It took awhile, but she found him.

"That's one of the men with my stepfather."

"How many are there?"

"Four."

"He's one of the men who shot your grandpa. The horses are those ridden by three of them."

"How can you tell?"

"I saw their tracks."

"Do you mean you can tell the tracks of one horse from those of another?"

"Most any kid who's spent time in the wilds can do that," I replied.

"I've heard of Indians who can but never anyone else."

"I followed those horses for two days and could tell their tracks anywhere. The thing we don't know is if they're onto the gold, or if they want to kill him for his place."

"I'll go home and see if I can learn anything," she said.

"I reckon not. You're not going back where they can get their hands on you again."

Luiz made rare progress and was soon demanding more of Elena's attention. I never figured to take to playing nursemaid to an old man, but all it took to make her happy was for me to pay him some mind. You never saw anyone get pampered like he did, and he lapped it up like a cat with a bowl of cream. You can't fault a man for enjoying the attentions of someone as lovely as that gal. Thought some of shooting myself in the foot, but she'd have seen through the trick, likely. He still slept a lot, which kept me from suffering too much.

One day the Sanchez girls met us as we came back from our ride and marched off with Elena. I overheard the conversation as they left.

"You don't have time for us anymore," said Carmelita. "All you do is take care of your grandfather and ride with that gringo. It's no fun having you around."

"It's as though we weren't even here," added Juanita. "Leave those men alone and go to town with us. They can get along without you for one afternoon."

"I'm sorry," said Elena. "I've been so involved with Grandfather."

"Not just Grandfather," chided Carmelita. "You don't spend as much time with him as with that other one."

"Remember, he's here to protect us from the men who shot Grandfather. I'm indebted to him."

"Surely you've paid your debt by now. Leave him alone for a while."

"I'll have to ask Grandfather. If he agrees, I'll go."

And that's how I came to spend an afternoon alone with Luiz.

CHAPTER FOUR

The girls were hardly out of sight when he sat up in bed, shooed the old lady out, and said, "Thought I'd never get you alone. Seems like you two are sort of taken with each other."

"You've got me pegged right. Anybody don't think she's something special, you better check him out. Reckon she's just being polite, though."

"I've never seen her this *polite* to anyone else," he said. "You better start ducking if you don't want her to dab her loop on you."

Now that's sort of a loose translation of what he said, but you get the drift.

I snorted and said, "That fever's fried your brain. She's not apt to toss her loop at an old bull buffalo like me."

"Don't argue with an old man."

The way he said it and the grin on his face came close to making me wonder if there was something to it, but I ended up guessing that he was just having fun with me.

The grin left his face, and he said, "Where are my saddle bags?"

"Out where I'm stayin'. You want I should get them?"

"Them and a cup of coffee. Bring a pot and something to keep it hot. It's time we talked."

When I got back he was out of bed and headed for the window.

"I'd stay away from there," I said. "The men who shot you keep a lookout on that bluff."

"How long have they been doing that?"

"Ever since we got here."

"You sure it's them?"

"Yep."

"Who knows about them?"

"Elena and Sanchez. Jose and three or four of his men."

"She knows who they are?"

"I reckon. The ones with her stepfather."

"I didn't want her to know. It's a mess. Her mother's torn up about it, but I don't guess she can do anything."

He crawled back in bed and propped up on some pillows. Taking the bags, he pulled out a packet of papers wrapped in oilskin. He carefully unrolled them and spread them on the bed. He motioned for me to sit beside him and began a tale, purely the stuff dreams are made of.

"My wife's grandfather and five other men went into the San Juans, up where you first saw me," he began. "Three of them had mined and knew what good ore looked like, along with the best ways to get it out. One of them was an expert at drawing maps and laying out trails. He knew what all the different types of blazes meant and how to mark rocks to show directions and distances. One was a hunter-trapper who'd spent a lot of time up there and knew some of the Indians. My wife's grandfather was the dowser. Do you know what that is?"

"Elena told me something about it. I figure that's what you were doing when I saw you up there," I answered.

"I'm not very good, but the grandfather was one of the best ever. He seemed to always find gold when no one else could. The whole venture would have failed without him. Every mining party that could manage it had a dowser. When danger showed up, he was the first to receive protection. The only other person taken care of as well was the priest if they took one with them."

"You say you're not very good, but you sure found that batch of ore," I said.

"But I had these maps," he answered.

"The men started about seventeen-fifty-five and worked together for nearly five years, until seventeen-sixty. The Indians let them mine wherever they wanted so long as it didn't interfere with the tribe's hunting or something like that.

"Their first mine was on Wimenuche Creek, northwest of that park at the foot of the mountains. It runs into the Piedra about where it dumps into that canyon. The Utes left them alone for a couple of months, and they took out a good batch of ore before the Indians decided they wanted to pasture horses there.

"They came home for the winter and went back the following spring, exploring to the west. They found some pretty good deposits, which played out quickly, so they moved farther west into Vallecito Creek. The Utes wouldn't let them stay there long, since it was their favorite hunting ground, so they worked south and then back east over the divide from Ute Creek.

"The grandfather had a time of it because there was so much ore in that territory it was hard to locate any major deposit. After several disappointments he announced that he'd found the mother lode, and it was only a few days before the miners agreed with him. You've seen the ore?"

I said, "There was a dab of it in the bottom of the hole where you got the sacks, and I looked again when I brought the stuff here. Yes, I've seen it."

"The mine was full of ore, all as rich as what I got, some lots better. The vein was wider and deeper than they had ever hoped to find. It was in a brushy nook, tucked away at the foot of a steep, overgrown hillside, so it was easy to work with little danger of being spotted.

"They worked without any other help the first year, but the season's so short that they could only bring out a tiny part of what they could have gotten with a gang of miners. There was always the danger that the Utes would drive them off, and the number of adventurers and robbers increased to the point that they decided to take a bunch of men and enough pack animals to bring out a passel of ore.

"They had to be very crafty and watchful in the operation. They named it *La Mina de la Ventana,* the Mine of the Window, because that landmark could be seen from the portal. The opening was covered with fresh branches when the men were working there. All waste was packed off and scattered over rockslides considerable distances from the mine. When they needed timbers, they used parts of trees that had fallen from snow slides or other natural causes and burned the waste so no cut stumps were left to show they'd been there. When all of the deadwood close by was gone, they hauled timbers from several miles away. The mine was sealed by laying fitted logs horizontally into the entrance, covering them with rocks and dirt and transplanting vegetation to leave it looking undisturbed.

"With the big crews and pack trains, they were able to bring out much wealth, but the season was so short that they were still not able to fully exploit the mine. The third year they took an even larger crew and made a cave in the side of a valley much lower down, a day from the mine. It's somewhere in the Rio Piedra drainage, enough lower so it can be reached in the winter. They packed part of the summer's output to the cache, where they could return after the mine was snowed in. This nearly doubled the amount they were able to bring out each year.

"Toward the end, they built a charcoal furnace and melted the richest ore into bricks. That way they didn't have to pack so much rock.

"Like the mine, the cache was skillfully concealed in an area marked by tree blazes, rocks with small holes drilled in them, and other signs that could be followed by a person with the key to the markings.

"The whole scheme of markings is designed to confuse a person who happens to see them but will serve as an unerring guide to anyone who has the key to them. There are three elements, and all of them must be known before the portal can be found. First, there are natural objects such as trees or rocks artificially marked; second, natural objects artificially arranged; and third, a mathematical calculation based on the way those things are arranged. It's possible someone could figure out the first two parts, but the calculations were known only to the members of the party, and it wasn't the same in every case. They had small caches near the mine, where ore was stored until there was enough to justify a trip to the lower cache. It was one of those small hiding places that I located. Some of the owners stayed at each location to boss the mining and melting of the ore," he said.

"In the fall of 1759, the Indians apparently got scared that the miners would bring too many others into their hunting grounds and warned them that they would be killed if they came back again. The drawing power of the gold was too much, and two of the miners went back the next spring. That year the Indians hounded them constantly, so the owners decided to keep all the ore at the mine and in nearby caches until there were two-pack trains of ore ready to be hauled out. At that time, they planned to make a quick trip to take a load to the lower cache and return for the second load, which would be taken directly to Santa Fe as they left for the winter.

"In September, with winter coming on, seven men were left at the mine to get out as much ore as possible while everyone else went with the pack train to the lower cache. At least one man was supposed to stay on lookout at all times because of the Indians. For some reason the lookout left his station and went into the mine. When he returned to the entrance, he was shot by Indians who had chosen that time to attack. The guard cried out, warning the others, who rushed to his side, where another man was killed.

"Realizing that the Indians could seal them in the mine, the men decided to make a rush for it, hoping to escape and get to the pack train. Only one survived. The Utes were apparently expecting to find all the miners inside and had brought only a small party. After they had caved in the entrance, they went for reinforcements, which gave the escaped miner time to catch the party with the gold. Since no one was at the cache, they decided to hustle straight to Santa Fe.

"Inside the mine and the cache, there's a king's ransom in gold. There's close to two hundred mule loads of ore in the mine and at least that in the cache, along with a quantity of gold bars. There are several of the smaller caches around the mine as well.

"The Indians hit the pack train the next day and killed the owners and a large number of the miners. The grandfather and two others of the owners refused to go back that year. One of those was a Frenchman who returned to his homeland. The grandfather and the other miner remained in Santa Fe. When the others were killed, those two used a part of that year's production to care for the families of the miners who were killed. The gold in the mine, as well as a huge amount of ore and gold bricks that was left in the cache, was never removed.

"The two families were wealthy, and none of them ever tried to find the mine or the cache. My wife's father was content to enjoy the life his father's wealth allowed him, and the gold lasted beyond the time of his death. The grandfather had these maps of the locations, along with full instructions for interpreting the signs, but he wasn't an engineer and didn't understand all that was involved in figuring out the bearings that must be taken from the various landmarks. My father-in-law wasn't a daring person, but my wife was more like her grandfather and was always pestering him for stories about his adventures.

"When we married, the grandfather gave me the maps and taught me the secret of dowsing. I've made four trips up there in the last forty years and managed to find a small cache each time. It's been more than enough, so I've never hunted for the mine. Elena is close to the age of marrying, and with my son dead, I want to be sure she'll benefit from the labor of her ancestor.

"These are the maps, and there are instructions that will enable anyone who has them to live like a king and leave his children a fabulous estate."

He lay back, obviously tired from the talking.

I refilled our cups, using the time to ponder what he'd told me.

"A mule load of that ore would buy just about anything a man could ever dream of. I've seen enough gold to know how good that stuff is. You could buy ten or fifteen thousand Longhorns in Texas with what you brought out," I said. "A hundred mule loads would come to more than my mind can figure."

"It's more than anyone could ever need."

"Why are you telling me all this?"

He lay looking at me for several minutes before answering. He finally replied, speaking slowly. "So you'll know what to do with the map I am giving you."

"Why would you give a map to me?"

"I do it partly so you'll be paid for saving my life. That's a debt that must be honored. Now, wait, I know you didn't do it for hire and would turn down any pay, but there it is. I'll give you this as part payment.

"The gold I brought down's for Elena. I think it's enough so she won't have to worry for a long time, but I also feel that if you have this, you'll see that she gets more if she needs it."

"I'd sure do that."

"The map and instructions for finding the mine are yours," he said. "I'll keep the information about the cache. I might make a trip to look for it but will never go back to the high country. Here, look at them."

He spread the maps on the bed so I could see them. They were the best I'd ever seen. It was easy to pick out landmarks and a scan of the instructions showed them to be detailed and should be easy to follow. He rolled up part of the papers, covered them with the oilskin, and returned them to the saddlebags.

Motioning to the others, he said, "Those are yours. You'd better keep my bags until I am well. They'll pass to Elena when I am gone, along with my other property. She's the only one who cares about me."

"Does she know of these?"

"She knows the story, and I think she's guessed that I have the maps. Whatever you do, don't let anyone else know about them. Pancho's friends may suspect that I have them because Elena's mother knows a little bit, and she lets Pancho do whatever he wants."

There didn't seem to be anything more to say, and his eyes soon drooped. He'd not talked that much in all the time I'd known him and was still mighty weak. It must've taken all his strength to tell the tale.

I'd been pretty casual about those saddlebags, but now it was different. I needed a good hiding place for them. For the moment I put them under my bed.

The girls returned from their jaunt, full of nonsense. It was after supper before I had a chance to talk with Elena.

"Your grandpa and I had quite a talk this afternoon," I said. "How about taking a walk so I can tell you about it?"

"Is it something private?"

"I reckon."

"Then let's go for a ride."

"Let's go."

I saddled up, and we rode out far enough to feel free to talk.

"Luiz told me about the mine and cache this afternoon. He also showed me maps of them. Did you know about the maps?"

"I was never sure, but the stories I heard made me think there would be some."

"He gave me the stuff relating to the mine and kept the others. He said it's mine, but I don't figure that's right. Far as I'm concerned, it's yours."

We rode in silence for a quarter mile. She pulled up and said, "I want to walk."

I jumped off and lifted her down. When she was down, she put her hands on my shoulders, face lifted, looking into my eyes for a drawn-out minute. It's a moment I'll not forget. She turned away and paced slowly across the sagebrush-filled park. I led the horses and tagged along behind, praying all the time. She plodded for a half mile, head down. I was on the verge of asking her if she was mad at me when she stopped and looked back. I was quick to go to her.

"You must build your ranch first. The mine's close by, isn't it?"

"It's a two-day ride to where Luiz got the ore. The mine is likely close to that spot."

"The mine hasn't been seen for over a hundred years, and we're just guessing that someone's not found it. He gave the map to you, and it's yours, but you can look for gold any time. He has plenty for all of his needs, and I don't want for anything. Your ranch must come first."

"That suits me," I said. "We've been gone quite a while. I don't want to get in trouble, so maybe we better head back."

"Oh! It is late, isn't it? Yes, let's go."

As I lifted her onto the brown, our bodies came together, which kindled a fire in me. We rode side-by-side, stirrups touching. She wasn't one to lag behind her man, but would ride beside him and bear him sons to match the country. If there were daughters, they would grow to be like her. A lucky man he'd be, the one she chose.

I lay for hours, watching moonlight creep across the floor then up the wall toward the ceiling. Anyone who's chased gold knows it pulls like a magnet and how easily it becomes a passion that replaces reason. I've trailed many a rainbow, even made some strikes. It would be a lie to say I didn't want to take that map and head for the high-up hills. I could picture myself uncovering the mouth of that mine and walking in to find heaps of nuggets and piles of ore ready to be packed out. If there was but a fragment of truth to the tale, a man would be richer than old King Sol.

Maybe there's a man around who can truthfully claim he wouldn't be tempted by that. A couple of things kept me from going. First, I didn't rightly figure the map was mine, and second, Elena said I should build the ranch first.

Thoughts of what Luiz had said about her caring for me kept sneaking into my head, but I was quick to chase them out. I had about as much chance as a rabbit in a pack of wolves. She'd likely end up with some grandee whose family ran back to the throne of Spain. My folks made sure I never got to thinking too much of myself, and this was no time to start.

I never hired on to be pretty, but if stout or stubborn is needed, I'm the man.. Fellow once told me that, next to me, a toad was downright fetching. Another man said I reminded him of Abe Lincoln, and I whacked him alongside the head. Didn't think he'd ought to go insulting our president that way. Well, when he got up, he told me a story about Mr. Lincoln picking up a full sack of seed corn in each hand and hoisting them up arm's length in front of him. When I tried, it took three times to get my left hand to stay up. Then he told about all the times Mr. Abe had gone broke and how he'd got whopped in a bunch of elections but wouldn't quit and finally, he won. Maybe so there was some likeness, long as he wasn't talking about anybody being as ugly as me.

Somewhere along there my thoughts ran back to something my ma said one time when I got to wondering why a woman as pretty as she was would hook up with a man no better looking than my pa. I just asked her, "Ma, how come you didn't look for a handsome man, but married Pa instead? He sure ain't no prize for looks."

"Son, a woman's heart doesn't see the outside of a man so much as it looks at what's inside him. You know, how he treats her and what he says. Even the way he looks at her can make a big difference. A woman gets so she knows pretty much what a man's thinking by the way he looks at her. Your pa's the gentlest man I've ever seen, and he treats me like I am the only woman he ever wanted to be with. You see, I love him, and to me he's as handsome as any man I've ever seen. You watch the way he treats me and the way his eyes are when he looks at me. He would do anything to make me happy. If a woman loves a man, he's handsome to her whether anyone else thinks he is or not."

It didn't help me understand, but it made good remembering. I'd never seen a woman who made it so plain that she cared for her man as Ma did. And Pa was just as open about the way he felt for her. Maybe, after all, there was some hope for me.

Then I thought of all the gold Elena had and how skimpy my poke would look beside it. No, I best forget any ideas about things betwixt her and me. I couldn't help, though, cooking up some dreams of what it would be like to be matched up with her. I said, "Lord, only you could do a thing like that, but it sure would be nice."

CHAPTER FIVE

One morning I woke up, fidgety as a kid headed to his first dance, and rode out before sunup. It bothered me to stay put and let those birds set up on that hill watching the place. Going back of the bluff, I settled in to wait. The sun was well up when a rider showed. He paid no attention to anything but the trail. He was one of three men I had seen on the bluff. They were taking turns up there, and by now it must be mighty dull. I'd yet to see the leader on lookout.

It would have been easy to learn how early they came out by watching from the house, but I was itchy. Luiz was coming along and needed almost no attention. Nothing had happened, and it looked like there was no reason for me to hang around much longer. The ride was an excuse to get off by myself and study. If they were watching for Luiz, we could expect trouble when he left to go home. The urge was on me to bust up their playhouse before they had a chance to start things.

I waited a few minutes after the lookout showed and was thinking of riding back when he came dusting down the trail, his horse jumping brush and leaping gullies. I waited another ten minutes then started back along the north side of the Sanchez place, headed for the gate on the west side. Loud voices came from a clearing up ahead, and one of them was Elena's.

I got down and hurried to where I could see. Sure enough, it was Elena, struggling with a man. I don't get mad easy, but that sight stabbed a white heat of wrath plumb through me. Three men stood watching, their backs to me. I cat-footed out and must've looked like Samson when he went through that bunch of heathens with the jawbone of a donkey; only I used my gun barrel on the heads of those critters. Not daring to shoot at the fellow who had Elena, I whipped out my knife as I ran toward him.

"Turn her loose, mister," I shouted.

He swung around, and she made a lunge to get loose. He clouted her on the jaw and grabbed for his gun as she slumped to the ground. Just as his gun was clearing leather, I took a cut at his hand. He jerked back, but the blade was quicker. He dropped his pistol, grabbed his hand, and stared at his thumb where it lay on the ground.

Elena was rousing, and I saw that she was mussed up but things hadn't gone far. Her face was bruised, the top of her dress was torn, and she was one irate young lady. She pulled her dress together as I rushed to her, picked up her shawl, and put it around her.

"This is the one who led the attack on Luiz," I said.

"Yes. He's the one I told you about, who was going to make me go with him. That's my stepfather over there." She pointed to a fifth man, lying near the trees.

"What happened to him?"

"He tried to help me, and the others knocked him down."

"You go back to the house while I clean things up here," I said and led the brown to her.

"What are you going to do?"

"String them up."

"You mean hang them?"

"What else?"

"You can't do that, with no witnesses or anything."

"They've been after your grandpa, and look what he was trying just now. Start letting buzzards like this off, might as well all plan to live some place back east. Nobody'll be safe here."

"This is a civilized place. I won't be party to a lynching. There are officials to handle such things."

"Got anybody in mind?"

"We'll find someone. Take them to town. Señor Sanchez will know what to do."

"I reckon. Been there when he done it, time or two."

"You mean—"

"Yep, for horse stealing, which is nothing like messing with a gal. He's got no time for skunks like these."

"When was that?"

"Last time was two, three years back."

"Things have changed. We even have a school for girls now."

"Don't reckon Sanchez goes to it."

"No, but his daughters do. Surely he's changed his mind about taking the law into his own hands."

"I don't mind letting him decide. Never did count it fun, hanging a man."

The other three were coming around, so I whistled up the *grullo*.

"Stand up, slow," I said to one of them. As he did, I yanked his gun from its holster and threw it away. "Now, get on your horse, but no shenanigans. One move and I'll drill you."

He was some careful. Seemed he took me at my word, and good that he did. When he was up, I tied his hands to the saddle horn then fastened his reins to my saddle so he couldn't take off. I went through the same routine with the other two then turned back to the leader. He was so involved making a fuss over his thumb that the only trouble was in getting him to pay me some mind.

By the time I got him on his horse, Pancho had come around. "What's your choice?" I asked him. "You with them or us?"

"I want no more of them. Are you all right, Elena?"

"Yes. Thanks for trying to help."

"What do you want me to do?" he asked.

"Go to the Sanchez place and get Jose."

As he rode off, Elena said, "What do you think will happen to them?"

"My guess is they'll hang anyway. Men who bother women, especially someone like you, don't last long. I suppose folks'll like it better if we don't do it. Hanging four men my own self wouldn't look good, even for something like this. It'll take longer, but I reckon it's best."

"I don't want them to get away with it."

Pancho and Jose rode up.

"Pancho, do you know where Luiz's horses are?"

"Yes, sir."

"Can you bring them to the plaza?"

"Yes, if you want."

"Thanks. On your way, take Elena to the house."

"I'll ride with you," she said. "I want to see them in jail."

It seemed to me she'd earned the right. We tied the horses head-to-tail and struck off for town.

"Jose, you ride along behind and see they don't take off, will you?"

"I'll shoot their legs if they try."

"Good idea."

It was mid-morning when we rode into the plaza, and a crowd was on hand to watch us. Most of the trade was carried on there, and there was a continuous hubbub, with a hodgepodge of people that seemed unlikely in such an out-of-the-way spot. Fall was the busiest time, with trappers, Indians from a dozen tribes, Mexicans, Spaniards, Jews, Gentiles, soldiers, miners, freighters, and drifters all stirred up together.

I spotted Sanchez in front of his place and rode to him then called loudly, " Señor Sanchez, if you have a moment, I need your help."

I wanted to get everyone's attention. Those who hadn't already noticed us were quick to do so, and I continued, "Did I bring Señor Luiz Jimenez to your home a few weeks back?"

"Yes, you did."

"What kind of shape was he in?"

"He'd been shot by banditos and was nearly dead."

"How do you know bandits shot him?"

"He told us so."

"I drove off the men who shot him. These are the ones. This morning they set on Senorita Jimenez. That one told her he would make her his woman, and the others were letting him do whatever he pleased. I've sent for Luiz's horses, which they stole when they shot him. When they get here, it'll be more proof of what they done."

"What you figger on doin'?" a freighter called out.

"We'll let the law handle them."

"You said they was botherin' the lady. I vote fer stringin' 'em up. Anythin' less'll let 'em off too light."

Just then Pancho rode up.

"Does anyone recognize these horses?" I asked.

Sanchez said, "They belong to Luiz Jimenez. See his brand? What do you have to say about this?" he asked the bandit leader.

"I don't know anything about them. Are you going to let this man—" An angry outburst from several men cut him off.

A trader named Johnson came forward and said, "We haven't heard from the lady. Is this true, miss?"

"It is. I went to Señor Sanchez's home to get away from this one. It was the day after my grandfather was shot, and I have helped care for him. These men have watched the house every day, and I am sure they were waiting for another chance to attack him."

Johnson turned to me and said, "If it was up to me, we'd handle it, but they're your prisoners. If you want to let the law have 'em, so be it." He spoke to Elena again, "Is that what you want?"

"I just want to be rid of them. They've bothered me long enough. Reuben's the only one who has stood between me and this one. Whatever he decides is all right with me."

We were directly across the plaza from the governor's palace, where several guards were on duty. One of them came over and said, "The only law around here's the Army. If you like, I'll send for an officer."

"Do you have some place to keep them till he gets here?"

"Sure. Corporal, bring two men and take charge of these prisoners," he shouted across.

"Thanks," I said. "Now, I'm going to take the lady home. She's had enough for one day." I reined around and led the way out of the plaza.

"You'd better leave those Jimenez horses here," said the guard. "The Army will probably want them as evidence."

"Okay, they're in your hands," I said.

"What do you want me to do?" asked Pancho. "Can I help you any more?"

"No, go on home. I'll be over to see you."

Elena had never been lovelier in spite of the bruised cheek and torn clothing.

"What will the Army do to them?" she asked.

"Don't know. Never had much to do with that outfit. If we were in Taos, I'd have Kit Carson take care of it. He's in charge of some kind of Indian matters. We go back a ways, and I know what he'd do if he could. Those boys would hang. I have no idea who's in charge here, or what he'll do. You satisfied?"

"Of course. I'm just glad you came along when you did. Now we owe you more than ever."

"Don't owe me nothing. You being safe is all I want."

She flashed a smile bright as the sun in August. Made me feel like a bear cub with honey dripping from his jaws.

At the house I lifted her down then put the horses away. When I went back in the house, Maria offered to fix breakfast, but I grabbed a cup of coffee and went to check on Luiz. He wasn't in his room, so I sniffed around and located him and Elena in the garden. She was pretty as a new pair of boots. The bruise looked like it wouldn't amount to much, and she wasn't hurt otherwise.

"You all right?" I asked her.

She laughed and said, "You kept me from any real harm. I don't want to think about what would have happened if you hadn't come along. I've been telling Grandfather what you did." Turning to him, she said, "You should have seen him. He's a real man."

"She's the one you should've seen. She done herself proud. Never once broke under the strain."

She laughed again, which was something, coming from a mite of a girl who'd been in real danger an hour earlier.

"What were you doing out there alone?" I asked her.

"When you weren't at breakfast, I looked in the barn. Your horse was gone, so I rode out to find you. I know now that it was foolish, but we've been riding so often, and it didn't occur to me that it might be dangerous."

"We'll fix it so you can ride without fretting. I'll get a pistol and teach you to shoot. Then we'll fix a holster on your saddle. But until those fellows are taken care of, don't you go off alone."

"I've learned my lesson. Are you angry with me?" she asked, looking sorry as a kicked pup.

"I reckon not. Just don't be scaring me like that."

"Is it over, then?" asked Luiz.

"Should be. Don't guess we'll be sure till the Army decides what to do, but it seems to me there ain't much to worry about."

"I want to go home."

"Let's wait and talk to Sanchez. If he says it's okay, we'll do it."

"I've had enough excitement," he said. "Take me to my room."

The next day I rode to Pancho's. The house was in town, but set back from the neighbors, so there was a deal of privacy. I saw some outbuildings with several horses in a corral. He met me when I rode up.

"Come in, señor. Thank you for coming."

The house was small and sparsely furnished but spotless. The rich fragrance of spicy food hung in the air. A lady who looked to be an older version of Elena was busy at the stove.

"This is Lupe, Elena's mother, sir," said Pancho. " Señor Dove is the one who saved Luiz."

Her beauty was unfaded, her form still slender, and I could imagine what her daughter would be like twenty years down the road. She put coffee and some sweetbreads on the table and sat with us.

"How is Elena?"

"Fine. Reckon she'll be over soon." Turning to Pancho, I said, "What do you do?"

He seemed embarrassed and took several sips of coffee. At length he said, "I haven't had a job for a while, but I break horses now and then."

"He's very good with them," said his wife. "He can gentle even the meanest ones and never mistreats them."

"Is that what you like to do?"

"Si, señor. I grew up in Texas and have spent lots of time on cattle rancheros. I'm a pretty good cowboy."

"I plan to set up a horse ranch north of here and will need some good hands. I'll want to buy stock and hope to get most of the horses close to Santa Fe. Do you know the people I'll have to deal with?"

"Yes, all of them."

"It'd help to have a man along who knows them. Think you'd be interested in working for me?"

"Maybe. When do you need an answer?"

"There's no rush. May not do anything till spring. Think it over, and we'll talk again."

"Good."

I sat and jawed with them, trying to get a feel for the man. When I started to leave, he said, "May I ride along? I want you to see one of the horses I'm breaking."

"Sure. Welcome the company."

When he went to saddle up, Elena's mother indicated she would like me to stay.

"Is she really all right?" she asked.

"She's perfectly okay. The fellow didn't have a chance to do anything before I got there. She put up a scrap, and he bruised her some, but it's not serious."

"You're most kind to help Pancho. Many men would make him leave, and it would kill me to be away from Elena. Her grandfather would never allow us to take her, and I don't blame him. We've not done much of a job of caring for her. Those men came here soon after we were married and got some kind of hold on Pancho. I don't know what it was, but he couldn't get rid of them. He's glad they are gone, and I'm sure he'll never get tangled up like that again."

"I'd hate for her to lose her family. She's mighty special. I'll do what I can for your man."

When he came with the horse, I thanked her, and we rode toward town. He had a good-looking horse with much cleaner lines than the average mustang.

"What's the breeding of that one?" I asked.

"It's a Barb. Do you know of it?"

"Yes. They came from Egypt originally, didn't they?"

"I don't know that, but the ones around here came from Spain, where it's a favorite of the king's family. I guess folks close to him brought them over."

"If they've been bred properly, it's one of the purest strains of horseflesh. The Arab's the only other breed that's kept its bloodlines as pure. Are there many of the Barbs around?"

"Oh, yes. I know many ranchers who use them."

The horse had nice action, and although it was smaller than the *grullo*, it moved well and had no trouble keeping pace. When I put my mount into the single-foot, Pancho grinned and switched his to the same gait.

"Is that natural to him?" I asked.

"No, but I always train them to it."

By the time we got to town, I was glad of the decision to try to help him. When we were close to the Sanchez place, I pulled up.

"I like the way your horse's trained. I'll see you again next week."

CHAPTER SIX

Luiz was going home. He had a buggy and was giving his thanks to the Sanchez family.

Everybody in the Sanchez crew seemed to think he'd honored them by letting them take care of him, and he sort of agreed with them. Now, I like that old bird a lot, but that was hard to figure. Guess it's just part of the way Spanish folks think. If your kinfolks are related to the king somehow, or have lots of money, everybody else thinks they owe you special treatment. The more I thought about it, the more I saw that it pleasured all of them, so it must be dandy.

"Ride with us," he said to me.

I tied the *grullo* behind, helped Elena in, and got up beside them. A driver handled the matched blacks pulling the rig, and we went to his diggings. It was a show place, but had been built in the style of almost all the homes in Santa Fe. Like the Sanchez layout, it was of unbaked adobe, had only one level, and was surrounded by an adobe wall.

Inside the fence, there was a difference, though. There were broad porches, or *portales*, on three sides, and all of the windows were protected by iron bars. The grounds included several gardens, stately shade trees, three fountains, and a stream that seemed to meander aimlessly, but closer inspection showed that it had been strategically placed to irrigate all the gardens. Even so, you would have to know Santa Fe to think it grand.

Viewed from the mesa to the north, the town looked to be a collection of mud huts, almost all of them single-story affairs, and all of the same exposed adobe, with straw visible in most of the bricks. Virtually all of the buildings, including the governor's palace, had dirt roofs, and anything but a dirt floor was rare.

I could see right quick that this place was much finer than any place I'd ever been in, including the Sanchez home. You didn't have to guess that whoever built it had never gone hungry. The house contained elegant furnishings that would have done justice to any city in the world. It was comfortable and would stay that way. Almost every room had its own fireplace, and it was laid out so the slightest summer breeze would keep it cool.

We went to a large room near the entrance, apparently the principal room in the house. Luiz said, "We'll be dining in a few minutes. Please join us, and later we'll talk."

The meal was first class and lasted longer than any I'd ever sat down to. We ate in a huge dining area, served by girls dressed all alike who hovered over us, making sure we lacked nothing. I've been in some fancy eating places that don't come close to taking care of you like they did. Later, we drifted to another room, where we sat in leather-covered chairs that sort of swallowed us they were so big. Heads of buffalo, bighorn sheep, elk, deer, antelope, and mountain goat covered the walls. Full body mounts of a bear and a mountain lion rounded out the trophy display. Each of the animals was prime. Whoever shot them was some hunter.

"We want this to be your home," Luiz stated. "You have time to move here today, and we'll make plans later. There's much to decide, and I know you've put off your business while you watched over me. When you're ready, I'll send someone to help get your things. There's plenty of room for your horses, and there are so many empty rooms in this house we get lonesome."

I was puzzled, and it must've shown. Elena chimed in, "Please don't say no. We owe you so much, and this is but a tiny thing. You'll be free to come and go as you please. We won't interfere with you in any way. From this day on, you're to make this your home whenever you're in town."

Well, now, that was something. I'd never been inside a place like that, and now they invited me to live there. It was sure a step up from what I'd reckoned on.

"I'll be moving around, looking for stock. It'll be unhandy to have me in and out at all hours."

They gave me so many assurances that it wouldn't trouble them in the least, and finally I agreed to it. Truthfully, I was just haggling about it to be polite. It'd be a fool thing to pass up something like that.

I said, "I'll need some extra animals if I'm gonna make the move in one trip. There's the gold, plus my stuff."

"I'll take care of that," said Elena. "I want to help you move." She was going to be about as much help as a six-year old, but I'd not be the one to discourage her from coming along. She sent a man to get three pack horses. When they came we tied them to the *grullo*, got in the buggy, and were driven back to Sanchez's layout. We put Luiz's gear on his animals, my stuff on the mule, borrowed the sidesaddle she'd been using, then went inside to say our good-byes.

It was a fine day, and we had a nice ride, even with four pack critters tagging along. I tied the horses behind my mule, and he followed wherever we wanted to go. It was like they weren't there.

It was only four weeks since we'd met, but it had got to where we could talk about most anything, or just mosey along not palavering. She was always finding some plant that needed a name, or I'd see a bird or animal she'd missed, and I had a good time just being with her. Seemed like she was interested in whatever I brought up and was the most fascinating person I'd ever come up to.

We loafed along and got back to Casa Jimenez by early evening. I lugged the gold into the house, and we learned that Luiz was asleep. Elena called for someone to care for the animals because I didn't want to leave that gold lying around, even in his house.

After a while Luiz came out and directed me in hauling it to a cellar. A thick plank door opened from his office. It was concealed behind a tapestry hung on a track so it could be slid aside. He used a key in a recessed lock, and the door opened on solid brass hinges with hardly a whisper of sound. A short stairway led to a room that had been excavated from solid rock. The house was set on bedrock, and this cell was placed so it was completely enclosed by that same formation. The doorway was on an inside wall, so there was no possibility of discovery from outside. It was an outright clever way to hide the gold and appeared to be part of the original structure. From what Luiz had told me about his wife's grandfather, the man had been shrewd, and the room was probably designed by him.

The stairs went straight into a room about six feet wide and fifteen or twenty feet long. There were shelves along the sides and at the far end, and I placed the sacks on one of them. Several similar bags were there, so it didn't seem like there'd been a pressing need for more gold at this particular time.

We closed the cellar door, returned the tapestry to its place, and then we were called to supper. Afterward, Elena dismissed all the servants, and we went to the trophy room.

She served coffee and said, "We have a matter to discuss with you. May we do it now?"

"I reckon."

Luiz took the lead. "The gold is Elena's. She's past the age when most girls marry, and I wanted to be sure she had an acceptable dowry. A bride must have substantial property if she's to get a suitable husband. Since we don't know who the groom will be, she wants to invest the gold so it will increase while she waits. You seem to be ambitious, and Señor Sanchez told us you are a capable businessman. We are asking you to advise us and help in the use of the gold, as well as share in the gains. Will you help us?"

"Whoa up. You've put a new horse in the race. I never expected anything like this. It'll take some considering. There's lots of ways to make money if you've got enough money to put together the right proposition, but this isn't something to rush into. Pa always said to set and ponder a spell before you jump. Reckon this's a good time to heed his advisement. I would never go into something like this without a lot of time with the LORD, finding out what he thinks, either."

We sat and drank coffee and looked at each other. I felt like a fool, what with them thinking I could come up with a plan to do what they were after. I'd never had more'n enough to get things together for another trip to the hills, and here they were, asking me how to invest a fortune. From what I'd seen, a man could've bought half the Longhorns in Texas with what they had in those sacks.

And there was an idea, staring me smack-dab in the face.

I said, "Elena, you know of my plan for a ranch."

Looking at Luiz, I went on, "You remember that park country just this side of where you crossed the Piedra, on the mesa west of the hot springs?"

"Yes. It's pretty country."

"That's where I figure to locate. Planned on taking a long time to build a herd big enough to pay. If you're interested in coming in with me, we could make it lots quicker. Understand, I'm not offering a deal, it's just an idea we can chew on till we see if it makes some kind of sense."

"I was hoping you would think of that," said Elena. "It means so much to you, and I want to see the ranch. It sounds like a beautiful place. I want to have a part in it."

We kicked it back and forth for an hour or so before Luiz said, "I'm still weak and need sleep. Good night."

"I'm going take a look at the stock," I said.

"Let me get a shawl and go with you."

Everything was all right, but it was nice out so we strolled around the grounds. The moon had come full again, making it nigh onto noonday bright. I commented on the pretty of the place, she showed me some of her favorite flowers, and we talked. Back inside, she showed me to a room close to Luiz's. She took my hand, looked up with those big eyes, and said, "Good night, my friend."

I don't rightly know where the idea came from, but I raised her hand and brushed it with my lips. It didn't seem out of place right then.

"Are you sure that having a gringo pard won't spoil your chances of catching a decent husband?"

She smiled and said, "Not the one I want."

"Got him picked out, have you?"

"Of course."

"Lucky fellow, him. You sure wouldn't need no dowry to get any man I know. If this guy of yours has got a lick of sense, he'll grab you and run."

I felt downright glum right then. I reckon you can never tell about a woman. I'd had no inkling she already had a guy cut out of the bunch. She'd been nothing but a lady, and we'd just talked a lot and she'd seemed to enjoy our rides and all, but she hadn't acted like you'd expect of a woman who'd picked out a husband.

It set me back some, even though I'd told myself time and time again there was no use hoping Luiz had it right that she cared for me. Anyway, it knocked me plumb off center. I tried to hide it, but it was a long night, with lots to think on. I talked to Jesus half the night but was so glum it seemed to do no good.

Next morning, I said, "Your mother's been worried. Why don't we ride over and let her see that you're okay?"

"That would be nice. I'll be ready in a minute."

It wasn't far, and we could have walked, but we both preferred to just ride. Her mother was glad to see her, and the two of them went off together, so I walked out to the corral where Pancho was working with one of the horses.

"How many top-notch mares could we buy in a fifty-mile circle of here?"

He thought for several minutes, ticking things off on his fingers. "Maybe five hundred. When would you want them?"

"Next spring, if we do anything. They'd need to be in top shape, have foals at their sides, and be bred back to good studs. If we go through with the idea, we'll buy a herd of cattle in Texas and take it to Kansas, where the railroad is, sell them, then get another herd and some horses to take up north of here."

He was full of questions. "What's a railroad?" he wanted to know.

"Well, now, I've never tried to describe one before. Let's see, it's like a bunch of wagons all hooked together, one behind the other, and pulled by a big thing they call an engine. That engine's got a tank of water, which they heat. That causes steam. They use that to make the engine go. The whole thing runs on two hunks of steel set on pieces of wood about a foot square and maybe eight feet long. The steel pieces are nailed to the wood, and the wheels on the wagons and the engine are fixed so they stay on the steel. They build the wagons, which they call cars, so they can haul animals in some and all kinds of stuff in others. They haul everything like lumber and kegs of whiskey, clothing, and just about anything you would ever think of hauling in a wagon. They have special cars for hauling coal and others for grain. I guess they haul gold ore and stuff like that, too. They even have some fixed up for people to ride in. The engine makes a lot of racket, and it's pretty spooky for a horse."

I continued, "Folks are driving cattle up from Texas and selling them where the railroad ends. It's quite a thing to see when they load about fifty cattle in one of the cars built for that. The engine has a whistle in it that's louder than almost anything you'll ever hear. When they blow that, it causes a stir among horses too."

"I guess I'd like to see one, but it might scare me, too," he said.

"If we do what I'm thinking about, you'll get to see one next spring," I told him. "I'll appreciate it if you don't tell anyone about this until we decide whether or not we're going to do it."

"I guess I wouldn't know how to tell them, since I've never seen a railroad. Is it all right if I talk to Lupe?"

"Of course, but not anyone else."

We walked to the house, where the ladies had the noon meal ready for us.

"Mother wants us to eat with them," Elena said. "Is that all right?"

"That'll be nice," I assured her. "We'll be able to get better acquainted."

They'd fixed a full meal of chili con carne and tortillas with butter and honey with plenty of strong coffee. Elena was full of laughter and as pretty as a new peso. We dawdled over our coffee, but she was ready to go as soon as she'd helped clean up after the meal.

I said, "Thank you for the meal. It was very nice."

Lupe said, "Thank you for bringing Elena. Please do it again soon."

"I'll be happy to do that often."

Elena and Lupe hugged each other, and we went to our horses.

"Let's ride and talk about our business deal," Elena said as we rode away.

"Good idea."

We let the horses pick their trail and headed out from town.

"Have you decided yet?" she probed.

"Not for sure, but I've got an idea that could get us a good start in ranching. Pancho tells me we can find plenty of good mares around here. I know we can buy thousands of cattle in Texas, drive them to Kansas, and make a good stake. Then I'd like to get more steers and a herd of cows to take up to the ranch. We'd have the beginning of a breeding herd, and the steers would be kept for a season. They'd be ready to sell the next spring, and by starting from the ranch we'd get a jump on herds that have to come all the way from Texas. We'd have to be careful, because we'd be buying next spring for the following year, and markets can change in a hurry. If we buy right and the market's strong, we stand to make five or six dollars a head on what we take to Kansas. All we'd be out is wages and grub. We should be able to pay for all the breeding animals out of the profit and keep your gold in reserve."

She had a quick mind and asked all sorts of questions. I'd thought it out pretty well, but she came up with things I'd missed. She asked, "Why not just take the gold and buy breeding stock without going to Kansas?"

"Folks back east are using bulls shipped over from England. They call them Herefords or Whitefaces, and they put on meat quicker than Longhorns. While they cost quite a bit, I think it'll pay to bring in some of them to use with part of our cows. I also want to buy a stallion that will give our colts more size and spunk. He and the bulls will have to come by rail, so we'd have to pick them up in Kansas. I don't see any sense in wasting a trip going after them when we can make some money while we're at it.

"I can spend this winter dealing for mares and leave in February to buy cattle and a remuda. It seems like the kind of thing Sanchez might put together, and we could do a lot worse than follow his pattern.

"Then, too, I just want to use your gold short-term. If we do well with the trail herds, we can buy breeding animals with the profits and have the gold as a reserve. I've noticed that prosperous folks always seem to have money to take advantage of a deal when everyone else is broke. That gold is for a special purpose, and I won't risk you needing it and not being able to get hold of it."

"It's a good plan. How do we divide the gain?"

"Better not worry about splitting it till we've got it."

"We'll make money. You've thought it out well, and it will work. What's a fair division?"

"How about two-thirds to you for putting up the cash money, the rest to me for running the show?"

"No."

"Well, then, you tell me."

"Reverse the portions."

"That's too much for me," I said.

"Then let's each take half."

"That's still too big a slice for me."

"I won't do it if you take less."

"Let's see what Luiz says."

"All right." She chuckled. "He'll agree with me."

I had some gold but just a dab compared to hers, so I made no mention of it. Luiz did agree with her, so that's the way we set it up. I'd ramrodded for Reed Anthony, a Texan who eventually took a couple million Longhorns up the trail. He knew more about the cow market than any man around. I wrote him the next day, hoping he could give me an idea what prices would be like, and then Pancho and I started looking for mares.

When we were getting ready to go on our first trip, Elena raised a fuss.

"I'm going with you," she said.

"I reckon not. You can't go traipsing around with two men."

"But one of you is my stepfather, and that will make it all right."

"We'll likely spend most nights lying out on the ground, and I don't reckon you'd be too pleased with that."

"I know almost all of the ranchers, and they'll gladly let us stay with them," she argued.

"That may be, but I don't reckon they're going be too taken with the idea of you running around with a gringo they never met."

It was as close as we'd ever come to a knock down, drag out squabble, and it sure made me feel sour, but she finally gave in.

"After you make this first trip and see how well the ranchers treat you, we'll talk about this some more," she stated, her face as stormy as I ever saw it, even when that fellow had his hands on her.

CHAPTER SEVEN

You could push a herd a thousand miles with nothing a man had put up to stop you. When you did see a fence, it was a few poles stuck up to keep horses close for everyday use. Herds were free to go to the best grass, water, and temperature. The ranches were big, and those around Santa Fe were grants from the king of Spain. Each was a community, with homes for the workers who had families, while those who were single lived in bunkhouses.

Those with families had gardens and were given meat from the herds. Everyone had access to the ranch storehouse for clothing and other necessities. The crews were fiercely loyal. Sheep were raised on most of the grants.

Not a few of the ranchers were men suited to the time, and they built empires. The weak ones watched their domains dwindle and become worthless. Their holdings were often taken over by others who rebuilt them into prime properties. The men whose grants flourished had a high regard for their resources, not just the land and livestock, but especially the people. They admired keenness, and the workers who showed they were interested were trained, given better homes, and put in the top jobs. Foremen sometimes lived about as well as the owners, although I never knew one who had a winter home in town, like most of the ranchers did.

The second day out, I spotted the prettiest filly I had ever laid eyes on. There might have been another one like her in New Mexico, but we never saw it if there was. She had a proud carriage, arched neck, and a swinging stride that kept her head tossing. Her limbs were delicate but muscular, her coat like velvet over iron. I couldn't keep from comparing her to Elena. The first word that came to mind was "ladylike." In a herd of two hundred, she stood out like a rose in a cactus patch and was the perfect mare to use in building our herd.

I cut her out so we could look her over. She was a bay, had a superbly shaped head, and what horse trainers call a "gentle eye." When I got off to look her over from close up, she cocked her ears and extended her nose. A horse uses its muzzle and lips to check things the way we use our fingers. She touched my hand, continued up to my shoulder, then to my hat. She pushed the hat back and checked my hair, then went across and down the other arm. She continued her inspection, and when she seemed to be satisfied, I touched her gently on the shoulder. In a few minutes, she was letting me rub her withers and scratch her chin. A close examination showed not a flaw. The way she was put together was first rate, and she would've taken the ribbon in any contest. All the horses in the herd showed the Barb breeding, and someone understood how to maintain the best of the bloodline. Which was surprising because not many folks know how to do that.

We'd planned to wait until later to buy our stock, wanting to just get an idea how many and what quality was available, and what the price would be. We were laying groundwork. But that filly was so special I knew I'd not rest peaceful until she was mine.

I hate to pay more than absolute bottom dollar for anything, but that filly was such a splendid animal that price wasn't all that important. It looked to me like she wasn't overly special to her owner, although anyone who kept his herd quality that high would know she was no run-of-the-mill animal.

"I want this one," I said to Pancho. "Whose place is this?"

" Señor Ricardo Martinez. I think he doesn't do much of the work, though. We'll probably have to deal with his foreman, Miguel."

"How far to their headquarters?"

"A couple of hours."

"Let's go. I want to see if we can deal for her right away."

"You want to buy her now?"

"I reckon. Would you let something like that wait?"

"Not if there was a chance I could have her. She's as good as I've ever seen. But all of his are good. Miguel does a good job," said Pancho.

"I'd say that's an understatement. He sure enough knows his business."

It was evening before we met Martinez, and he invited us to spend the night. We ate in the cook shack and slept in the bunkhouse. It was neither better nor worse than dozens I'd seen from Texas to Montana. The food on most ranches is beef, biscuits, and beans. The difference here was that mutton took the place of beef, and the beans were full of hot peppers. The crew took to Pancho right off, and when they found out I savvied their lingo, they warmed up to me.

Next morning, Señor Martinez turned us over to Miguel. He was a wiry little guy who wasn't much for looks, but I'd learned that in men, looks don't count for much.

"What is it you want?" he asked.

"We're after brood mares. I want to start raising horses and need a bunch of top mares. We want to make deals the next couple of months and take delivery next spring."

"Good. We have sixty mares for sale. Shall I bring them in?"

"I'd rather see them where they are."

"Yes, it's better."

We rode a half-hour, accompanied by two wranglers. We soon came to a fence. While one of the riders was opening the gate, Miguel said, "I keep each herd of mares in a separate pasture so we can breed them to the right stallions. That way, I always know the bloodlines of the foals."

"Do you keep track of each colt?"

"Oh, yes. I couldn't tell how to pair the mares and stallions, otherwise."

"Who taught you?"

"My uncle, who raised me. He showed me most of what I know, and I try to improve as I see how things work. We never use a mare after her tenth year, because they become less productive. I also keep the best of the young as breeding stock, and it's easy to get inbred foals if we keep mares too long," he said.

"These are Barbs?"

"Yes. We use nothing else."

"Do you know of the Arab breed?"

"No, señor, I've not heard of it."

"The name is that of the people who developed the breed in a land across the ocean. They, too, kept the blood pure but feel that stallions aren't near as important as mares. Fact is if a mare gets with an unwanted stud, they destroy her, reckoning the bloodline's ruined. I hope to develop a new type of horse and want the gentleness and toughness of the Barb but with some extra size. They'll be for handling cattle, and it takes a hefty, fast, smart horse to really do a job on them.

"A cowboy often has to take care of a mean, old bull with no help but his horse, and that horse had better be able to keep him out of trouble. A cow in a bog hole calls for a strong horse. Anything less and she dies where she is. I figure to bring in some big stallions bred for racing to give size and speed. The Barbs will give the colts a good disposition and a desire to please. I hope to develop a horse with natural cow sense, and then we'll have a real working ranch horse."

"Cows can't run fast for very long. These horses can keep up with them."

"You're right, but I want to catch them quick, so we'll try for lots of speed for a short distance. The studs I want to bring in have lots of staying power, so they can carry a big man all day, even working cows. Most of the men I'll be selling to are a couple of sizes bigger than your crews. They'll sometimes have to use a horse several days in a row, and that'll wear out a small horse. I've noticed that Barbs are pretty gentle. I like that, but most cowpokes want a horse full of fight. Some don't think they're horseback if a bronc doesn't buck—at least first thing in the morning."

We rode in silence for a spell, and it was easy to see he was mulling over what I'd said. After several minutes he said, "Will you breed all the mares to the big stallions?"

"Oh, no, I'll keep a few to keep the strain alive. We'll always need them to improve the others."

"Ah, good. Here are the mares."

They all showed the same makeup as the filly we'd seen the previous day, but none was up to her. As we approached, they came toward us. Miguel stopped and ordered the wranglers to stir them up so we could see their action. It took but a minute for me to pick out a mare with the same build and action as the filly. She was smaller and not quite as showy, but I was sure it was the mother. The other mares were almost as good and would stand up to a close look.

"Can we see some of their colts?"

"Yes, but you'll want to be able to tell which mare they came from," he said and started giving me a rundown on each of them. It's always a pleasure to deal with a man who thinks the way I do, and Miguel did just that. When he spoke of a horse, it's the way I thought of them, and we had a good time swapping ideas about what makes a good horse. As I questioned him, he picked right up on what I was after and often answered before I got around to asking. When I had the herd well in mind, he took us to the pasture where we'd seen the filly.

In every case, the mark of the mare was on her foal, and it was clear that we would be getting good, solid brood mares in the culls from this breeding program. The fancy filly was only one example of the quality we had available to us. She was just as friendly as on the previous day and tagged along as we looked over the herd. I got off to pet her and sensed that Miguel watched closely. I spoke then waited until she came to me before reaching out. She nuzzled me and put her head up so I could scratch her throat then pushed against me as I rubbed under her mane and pulled a burr out of it. I gave her a good rubdown with my hands and cleaned some weeds out of her tail. It was hard to get behind her—not because of fear—she just wanted to keep her head toward me. She was about the gentlest thing I'd ever been close to, but it was gentleness clothed in solid strength.

When I lifted her left forefoot with no sign of fight, I said, "She's sort of your pick of the lot, isn't she, Miguel?"

"Yes."

"Don't blame you. Sure would like to make her the cornerstone of our herd."

There was no reply, so I dropped it. You don't push in a case like that. If we got her it would be because he glimpsed what she could do for us and decided he wanted to help. Pressuring him at that time would be the worst thing I could do. I'd wait and see, try persuasion later, if need be. I figured it wouldn't hurt to ask the LORD to help and did that right then and for a long time that night.

We were almost back to the house when he said, "I'd like her to do something grand. Would you build your breed on her?"

"Sure would. You got no worry there."

"And could I come to your ranch and see what you've done?"

"My friend, you come, often as you can. I'd like your help in improving our herd. Not many men have your know-how about breeding horses. It'd be a kindness on your part to tell us how to do it better."

"I'll ask Señor Martinez to sell her to you."

"Thanks a lot. If there's ever a way I can help you, you be sure to call on me."

I meant every word, too. He's a really good man. With his help we dealt with Martinez for the sixty mares, with foals at their sides, to take delivery the following spring. They were to be handled just as if they were still his. Miguel would see to breeding the mares again.

After that was out of the way, I said, "There's one more horse I want to buy, one of your fillies. Your best one, in fact. Miguel agrees that she'll be the perfect mare to start our herd. I'll pay top money for her."

"Which one is it?" he asked his foreman.

"The one I've pointed out to you often. I would never suggest you sell her, but Señor Dove has such a good plan, I ask you to help him. He understands what we are doing and wants to use the same ways to build his herd."

"You run the horse part of this outfit. If you want her to go, I won't argue. What's she worth?"

I paid the amount he stated—ten times what a top hand makes in a year—and reckoned it money well spent. Gave over the cash then and there, out of my own poke.

Miguel said he'd keep her close so I could pick her up before Christmas.

The rancher insisted we move into his house that night. Seems we'd turned into more than just a pair of riders looking to put on the feedbag. We rode back to Santa Fe in high spirits. I stopped at a saddle shop and ordered a rig well suited to the filly—and a certain rider. Had to pay extra to be sure of getting it by Christmas.

During the next few weeks, we dealt for two hundred mares, picking from fifteen ranches. We ended up with half the top mares within a week's ride of Santa Fe. It sure did help, having a saddlebag full of gold. Without that I would have spent at least ten years getting to where we were in a matter of weeks. I planned to pick up some stallions in Texas as well as the one that would come from Kentucky but bought the best two we came across as we dickered for the mares.

Elena made sure I kept the promise to let her go on some of the trips. She knew most of the ranchers, so it was a help to have her along. There was nothing awkward about it since Pancho was her stepfather, and her mother often went, too. We took a buggy, but she preferred to be horseback and was soon an expert horsewoman. Her pick was that brown of mine, but she could ride most anything after a couple of months.

"We must do all of the business in your name," she said.

"Why?"

"None of the ranchers will sell to us if they know I am your partner."

"Is it because of me being a gringo?"

"That might be part of it, but mostly, they'll not do business with a woman."

"That don't make sense."

"It's just the way things are. Do you know of any women who have businesses?"

"Sure. Seen quite a few in some of the bigger towns. It's sort of common for a woman to own a boarding house or eating-place in most any town. Lots of them have stores where they sell ladies clothes. Some even have saloons."

"Not in Santa Fe. My people won't condone it under any circumstances."

"How do we explain your riding with us?"

"I know all of them. We entertain them when they are in town and visit with them often. They are almost all friends of Grandfather. We'll have Mother go with us some of the time, too."

She kept surprising me with her interest in the business. As agreed, I handled all the deals, but we chatted about every one of them in private.

Things were well in hand by late November, so we just had to loaf out the winter. I slipped away one day and picked up the filly from Miguel. He'd broken her to the halter, but I'd asked him to leave the rest of her training to me.

After my parents were killed, I'd drifted to a place in Kentucky where the owner took me in. Looking back, I saw that he got himself another slave, but it was a kindness nonetheless. He turned me over to the slave who was in charge of the stable. He trained horses for the owner's family, and they wanted their riding stock tame. He taught me his methods, which were different from what I later saw on ranches in the west. He got the horses used to a saddle and never rode them until they'd been worked several days and were no longer afraid of a weight on their backs and knew various commands. It was a method that allowed a man to start using a horse, without fighting, soon after the training was under way.

I used his system on the filly, and it took only two days of thirty-minute sessions, morning and afternoon, to have her ready to ride. By that time, I could mount or dismount from either side, and she was never scared by what was happening—concerned a couple of times but never scared. All I had to do was get her to understand what I wanted, and she was for doing it. I'd never handled one so easy to train. We had a sure winner in her. Adding her disposition and quick mind to a bloodline would guarantee success.

Miguel was amazed by the rapid progress we made. When I rode the filly away after only two days with her reining easily, he said, "Please let me know when she drops her first foal. I want to see it as soon as possible."

"You've got my promise, my friend. Come sooner if you can. I want you to see all of the herd and the ranch, too. You'll envy us living there. Merry Christmas."

"May God go with you, my friend."

I rode her the first hour that morning and two more in the afternoon. She was a natural traveler—loved to stretch her legs and look over new country. Most horses have to be taught to cover ground in a hurry, but it was natural to her. She was alert to everything but didn't spook at rocks, trees, and other boogers like a lot of young horses will. If she was disinclined to approach something, I would ease her up to it so she could check it out with her muzzle, which always took the scare out of her. She had an easy gait, and I pushed her into a trot then a gallop, which was as easy to ride as a parlor chair.

I'd taken over the use of some corrals and a pasture that were left unused when the outlaws went to jail. We'd had no word from the Army about them, and I'd been so busy I hadn't checked on them. I decided to go check on them soon. There was a passable barn, and I'd had some hay brought in. I put the filly there and went to the house. I wasn't ready for Elena to see the filly and had somehow forgotten to mention the corrals. I stopped by Pancho's and asked him to keep an eye on her for a couple of days. He'd have to do some of the finish work, since I'd have a problem working with her and still keeping her away from Elena.

CHAPTER EIGHT

Elena was busy with a seamstress. "Do you like this dress?" she asked and whirled across the room. Spanish women go for bright colors and flowing lines and favor flash, being in the spotlight. Most are slender but don't lack for curves to grab your eye, and they do know how to show them off. Many a high-toned actress couldn't hold a candle to a slip of a Spanish girl when it comes to getting your attention.

The gown was of some shiny cloth, bright scarlet down to the waist. A skirt the blue of a high mountain lake hugged her waist and hips then flared out and flowed to the floor. She danced around the room, graceful as that high country eagle, the skirt billowing out to give a glimpse of her legs. The look she gave me was enough to set me on fire.

"Is it pretty enough for you to take me to the ball?" she asked as she glided to me and held out her arms.

There I was, just in from a six-hour ride, the dust of the trail still on me, but it didn't hold me back from the chance to dance with anyone as fair as Elena. I just naturally gathered her in my arms and swung into a waltz, glad for the times Ma had made me prance with her. She'd told me I'd be glad some day, and this was the day. I don't guess I'd ever pass as the greatest dancer in the world, but we waltzed for several minutes, even without music. It weren't no time till it got to be too much of a temptation to grab her closer than would be proper, so I swung her one last time and stopped. She stayed in my arms, gazing up at me.

"I'm going get your pretty dress all dirty. It's sure fetching, and so are you. I'll take you anywhere you want, in that dress or whatever else you want to wear. What's this about a dance?"

"The Senas are having a fiesta, and we are invited."

"You mean you and Luiz."

"Yes, our family. But that includes you," she said.

"What about the man you've picked out to be your husband? Won't he get mad?"

"I'm beginning to think he isn't interested."

"You've picked a blind man and a fool to boot. Any man ain't interested in you can't amount to much. If he's not careful, I'll butt in on him."

She dropped her arms and scampered off while I stood questioning if I'd spoke out of turn. I wandered to my room and sat long, pondering over the matter. Things had changed betwixt us. When we met, I was lured by her beauty, as many a man has been. After we'd spent time together, I came to prize her quick wit and disposition. When she told me she'd chosen her man, I knew the best I could hope for was to be her friend. Our business setup had kept us together, and the friendship grew. Now it had reached the point that the worst thing I could fancy was to have her married off to some other galoot.

No matter that she had her sights on someone else; he could look out for himself. He couldn't stack up, anyway. It was sure he never seemed to pay her no mind. Men came around, and young bucks swarmed like bees anytime she was out and about, but there didn't seem to be a special one. Of course, I'd been gone a lot, but she was with me over half that time. It didn't look to me like the competition was taking very good care of his claim.

The thought of trying to win her was some mind-boggling. I never reckoned myself to be upper crust of any sort, and she was top-of-the-heap and rich to boot. Came close to giving up before I tried. Then I thought back to the day I killed my first whitetail buck.

Pa was away, only Ma and me on the place. One evening, just at dusk, I spotted a buck that, to my eight-year-old eye, was a monstrous big critter. I was close to the house and slipped inside, careful to not upset him.

"Ma," I called softly, afraid he would hear and bolt. "Come see the big buck."

"My, he's a big one," she said. "Why don't you shoot him? We can sure use the meat."

"What if I miss? It'd be awful."

"Are you afraid to try because you might fail?"

"I don't know. I'd purely hate to shoot and not get him."

"Son, there's no shame in failing if you've done your best. Why don't you plan how you can sneak up on him, decide where to rest the gun, and think exactly how the sights will look on the spot behind his shoulder? When you've got everything planned, go do it just like you've thought it out. If you succeed, you'll have a grand tale to tell Pa, and if not, you'll have an adventure anyway. I'll watch and pray, and you can do some of that, too. If Jesus helps you, we'll have some of him for supper."

Well, I done it. Sat down and planned every move, got the rifle, which stood longer than I was tall, checked the primer, and slipped out the back way. There was plenty of cover, and the wind must've been right or I'd have never made it. Checking for wind wasn't part of my training yet. My goal was to get to a rotted stump, which stood a good rifle shot from where I figured he'd be. I crawled up behind that stump, put my hat on top of it, shoved the gun onto the hat, then slipped into position so the gun was at my shoulder. When I looked down those sights, he wasn't more'n ten feet from where I'd guessed, but he was looking me square in the eye.

I didn't breathe for what seemed a couple of hours, him eye-balling me all the time, trying to see what had caused the commotion. I finally remembered that Pa had said animals can spook if you stare at them too long, so I looked away, but try as I might, my eyes crept back to him. It was getting darker by the minute, and there'd soon not be enough light to shoot. He finally decided that whatever had moved wasn't going to bother him and started browsing. It took him two or three years to move enough so I could put the sights on the right spot. I did the best I could to keep from yanking the trigger, like Pa had said. It was one of those old cap and ball rifles. You feel the trigger break, wait half a lifetime while the primer ignites the charge, there's a shove against your shoulder, then a cloud of smoke blots out everything. When the smoke cleared, the buck was tearing for the trees, and my heart sank. He was in the edge of the woods when he faltered, and in a couple more leaps, he piled up like a sack of spuds dropped off the tailgate of a wagon.

I learned something that day that has since hauled me free of many a tangled snag. I guess this was the first time since then that I'd wanted anything as much as I had that buck. By gum, I'd give it a whirl—forget the cards were stacked against me.

First thing, I got a gold nugget I'd taken from the claim up north and went to an Indian who made silver gewgaws. The chunk was sort of like a slice off the side of an egg, an inch and a half long, half that wide, and nearly a quarter inch at the thickest, tapering down to the edges. Like most nuggets, it was all warty-looking on the surface.

The silversmith was a Pueblo Indian with a knack for making pert things. He showed me how he'd like to mount it, in a complicated layout, fixed so it could be pinned to a dress or to a band of cloth and worn around the throat.

While that was in the mill, I spent every possible minute with her, paid her all the mind anyone could hope for, and saw to it she never lacked what she hankered after. We went for a ride every day, sometimes twice, and stepped out to eat two or three times a week, usually at the Union Hotel. It was on the southeast corner of the plaza, across from the governor's palace, and was the tallest building in town. They served up passable fixings, if you liked Mexican grub. She seemed to take to that kind of handling, and it was easy enough to dish up. I poured on the honey and tossed out every kind of bait I could dream up. The most important thing I did was to spend a couple of hours each day talking to Jesus, asking him for advice about how to treat her and what to say to her. I also asked him to see if he could maybe make her like what I was doing. Somewhere along the way he gave me the idea that she wouldn't stampede if I ever got up enough nerve to ask her to marry up with me.

The gold piece was ready a couple of days before the shindig at the Sena's, and I had it when she came out, dolled up in that fancy gown. One look at her was like getting kicked in the wind, but I stood up to it, took her arm, and led her to a looking glass.

"Stand here a minute, please. No, face the glass," I said.

When she was in place, I pulled out the nugget and fixed it on her neck. Her eyes grew a couple of sizes.

"Reuben, it's beautiful! Take it off so I can look at it."

When she'd examined it, she looked up at me and said, "Where did you get it?"

"Up at the claim I told you about. The one I worked this year. Had it put together here."

"Are you sure?"

"Sure? About what?"

"That you want me to wear it?"

"Not just wear it. It's yours," I said and turned her so I could put it on her again.

You wouldn't believe the look she gave me. "Are you very sure? I can't take it unless you're absolutely certain you want me to be the one to have it. It's too precious to be given lightly."

"I reckon. Had it made up just for you." I put it on her.

Her gaze in the mirror was enough to melt me clear down into my boots.

"I feel like a fairy princess wearing the crown jewels. It's like a dream."

She turned and put her hands on my shoulders, and I dived into those eyes. A feller can only drown once. Don't have any idea how long we stood there before Luiz came along and broke it up. But that hunk of gold was decorating her silken throat when we went to the ball. She got a lot of attention, as usual. All the ladies noticed the neck piece, and it seemed like most of them were a bit jealous. It was a simple thing—I'd no intention of gilding the lily—but it sure did look fine on her. She could have passed for a sure-enough princess.

It was a soft, warm night with not a hint of winter. We rode with Luiz in his carriage, which he directed to a home not far from his. He went inside and returned with a handsome lady of middle age. Elena and I got out as they approached.

"This is Señora Margarita Espanoza, a friend from Raton. I want you to meet my granddaughter, Elena, and our friend Reuben Dove," he said.

Luiz had told me he'd not wanted to marry after his wife of forty years died, but it looked to me like his interest was stirred by this lady. She wore an eye-catching dress and proved to be a good talker. What was even more important, she hung onto every word he said. The old man was livelier than I'd ever seen him, and there was no doubt she was the kind of medicine he needed.

I've mentioned the Spanish women's flair for color and clothes. Well, this was the first full-blown shindig of theirs I'd been to, and they sure put on a fuss. My folks took me to a fancy affair when I was twelve, where the ladies were dressed fit to kill.

Pa had said, "Son, you're going to see some women folk wearing togs they didn't get far enough into. Just remember, you look them square in the eye. Don't drop your eyes even a little bit. I catch you looking as low as their chins, we'll wear out a switch when we get home. The good LORD doesn't want you thinking like you will if you do different than I tell you."

That advice had probably kept me out of a bunch of fights, and this was a time to put it to practice. Some of those gals sure took pride in their shoulders and the rest of that neighborhood. I was glad Elena's dress, grand as anything the others had on, forced folks to imagine some things.

Her perfection that night was nigh on impossible to describe. A person could've looked all night and not found a flaw—*not one!* I thought of a long-stemmed rose moving like a magnificent Canadian goose in a pool of still water. As we sat with Luiz and Margarita with folks meandering around, and then as we danced to the fiery music, my heart came nigh to busting with pride over being there with her.

I was watching Luiz when the music started. Margarita gave him an obvious invitation with her eyes, and he lost at least thirty years in the time it takes to breathe once. He almost jumped out of his seat and had her out there prancing in less time than it takes to tell about it. I looked at Elena, and she was smiling as brightly as I had ever seen her. I stood up, offered her my hand, and we joined them. I may have touched the floor a couple of times, but mostly it felt like I was floating; it was so nice to have her in my arms.

I whispered, "Thank you, Jesus. You've given me a glimpse of heaven."

She didn't say anything, but her arm pulled me a little closer.

The Sena family had the only home in town with more than one level. The dance was held upstairs in a special-built room that occupied the entire west part of that level. There were thirty-three rooms in the place with no inside hallways. All the stairways were outside, and the rooms were arranged so every one of them faced the courtyard.

There were two classes of people in Santa Fe: *ricos* and *pobres*—rich and poor. There was a real upper class, with many of the wealthy ladies using servants as footstools. A dozen women at the party had human stools. I suppose the practice came about because virtually all the houses had dirt floors, which are cold in the winter. They thought it better for a servant to lie shivering on the floor than to have a lady's feet cold. The practice was offensive to most folks from outside but didn't seem to bother the servants, so I never made much of it.

The *baile* was for the ricos and most of the white population, which included quite a few Army men. The room was wide enough for one cotillion and long enough for half a dozen. A raised platform accommodated a first-class string band, including a harp and a chair for the Maestra of Ceremonies—a lady. Tables were placed along the wall for about a hundred onlookers.

As dancers, the Spanish can't be beat. Dancing's a lifetime affair with them—something they learn as soon as they can walk. Their cotillions are very complicated, but Elena had coached me so we could do them together. The common waltz is similar to that done in the States and is known as the Valze Redondo. But the national dance—the one that shows the Spanish women to the best advantage—is the Valze de Spachio, which might be translated as "slow waltz." The music is slow, almost mournful, but the movement is tough to put into words. The first figure could be called a "waltzing cotillion," ending with two lines, each lady opposite her partner. She then advances toward him with a passel of graceful gestures—bowing, sinking, rising, extending hands, and again clasping them and retreating, waving scarf or handkerchief, all in perfect time and with nary a misstep. After a while, following the motion of the "head lady," the couples come rapidly together, and as the music breaks into a lively air, are whirled to all parts of the room in quick prance. This again slows, and they waltz back into a sort of hollow square, from which each gal takes a turn and makes the circuit of the set in slow waltz, teasing different cavaliers with feint and retreat. It sounds childish but is fascinating to watch and pretty much fun for the ones taking part. I reckon most of the men thought theirs was the fairest lady, but none came close to Elena. She played the game when it came her turn to make the circle and flirt, but she slighted everybody but me.

I was surprised to see that several soldiers and some of the sons of white merchants brought their Mexican mistresses to the baile, and nobody paid it any mind. The "girls" were especially polite, unlike the same class I'd seen in other places. It has to come from the fact that they see nothing wrong with their kind of life. I never saw one of them drunk, not a single nasty word or motion, nothing different than the rest of the ladies there. The men said that they are the most faithful, kind, and affectionate women of that class in the world. Since then, many of the couples have married.

As I said, it was a balmy night, and after a couple of hours, I said, "Elena, I need some fresh air. Do you want to take a walk outside?"

"It is stuffy in here, isn't it? Yes, I would like that. We can go down into the courtyard, if you would like."

The moon was getting up toward full, and we found a shadowed nook where we likely wouldn't be noticed. She was a sight, those eyes outshining the moon, ebon hair a soft frame for that lovely face, her form hugged by the gown.

I figured to bust wide open if I didn't say what was on my mind, so I waded right in and said, "Elena, honey, I reckon you know I'm head over heels in love with you. Will you marry me?"

The crazy thing is, she never batted an eye; just said, "I reckon."

I come nigh to falling off that wall. Here I'd schemed how to talk her into it, and she didn't balk, not even a little bit.

"You will?"

"Of course I will. Don't you know that I've been waiting for this since the day we met?"

"But you told me you had your husband picked out!"

"I did. I had picked you, and I almost died when you thought I meant it was someone else."

"I've got to have time to think about this. You really mean that I've wasted all this time, mooning around, thinking you had somebody else, and you were waiting for me to finally get so much in love it busted out of me?"

"Yes. And I spent my time trying to make it obvious that you were the one I love," she whispered. "You'll never know how many times I cried myself to sleep because I'd made you think there was someone else. I fell in love with you that first day, there in the library down the hall from Grandfather's room. It may have been before that. When you walked into his room, I knew you were a special person, and it might have been that moment when I lost my heart to you. It was certainly that day."

"That was the day I fell in love with you. You had me before we got to the library. I suppose it happened while we were in the hall. Following you, watching your wonderful walk, would catch any man who's well enough to take a breath. I can still see that in my dreams."

"I was already hoping you would notice me. I may have waited a few minutes, but not more than that, to fall in love. By the time we went to eat lunch, I was sure you were the man I would marry and would do whatever it took to get you. I'm glad you finally figured it out."

"Well, I guess I'll just be thankful you didn't turn me down. I love you and am happy we will be married. Is it all right if I kiss you now?"

Her answer was to come into my arms and take me where my dreams had never reached. I don't want to know how she learned to kiss like that. I didn't spend any time worrying about it, just went along for the ride and enjoyed it more than anything I'd ever done before. When all was said and done, we were set to be married, soon as possible.

"I'll have to get Luiz's okay, and your mother's, too."

"They won't stand in our way."

I whispered, "Thank you, LORD. You just gave me the most precious thing in the world."

She snuggled a little closer, put her lips against my ear and breathed. "Yes, thank you, Jesus. I waited a long time for this."

I suppose it was quite a while, but it seemed like just seconds before she pulled back a mite, and I fell into the pool of her eyes. She set about giving me a kiss to beat all the dreams I ever had. When I'd recovered somewhat I said, "Young lady, I'll give you just two hours to stop doing that. But if you keep at it, there's no question what'll come of it. We better get back inside."

Young she was, only sixteen years old, but that was one full-grown woman hugging me to her. We had to keep our plans hushed up till I'd talked to her folks, but we were some kind of happy. I was sort of glassy-eyed the rest of the night. *What chance does an ugly galoot like me, all bone and rawhide, have of tossing his loop on someone like her?*

When I talked with Luiz and then with Lupe, they gave their blessings without a sideways glance. Never even seemed surprised, either one. We set the date for early January.

The only thing to mar our happiness was that the Army turned those outlaws loose, without so much as a fare-thee-well. When I heard about it, I stormed into the captain's place to raise a ruckus.

"What's this I hear about you turning those bandits loose?" I demanded.

"What bandits?"

"The ones that messed with Elena Jimenez and her grandpa."

"And who are you?"

"I'm Rube Dove, who turned them over to your men."

"Well, Mister Dove, you never filed a formal complaint against them. Without that, we had no authority to hold them."

"So you just let them ride off! What about the horses they stole?"

"We had no evidence that the animals were stolen. Nothing in our files indicated that they belonged to someone else. I assumed they were theirs."

"It never occurred to you to send for me, I guess."

"Regulations don't call for us to do that."

"What're you here for, anyway?"

"Our job is to protect the population from the Indians," he stated.

"Seems to me all you do is strut like a turkey gobbler. We got more trouble with crooks like those you turned loose than the tame Indians around here. Doubt you'd know what to do if anything but a woman showed up to call you out."

He sort of puffed up like a mad toad and said, "If there's no other way I can help you, I'll ask you to leave."

"All I can say is, it's a good thing the government don't run much of this country," I shot back as I took off from there.

CHAPTER NINE

Christmas was another mild day. I was up and about before anybody else and went to get the filly. The sun was still abed when I got her into the barn and cinched up the tailor-made saddle I'd ordered for her. Compared to the average Spanish rig, it was plain as Granny Jones, but I didn't want it to outshine either the horse or its rider. Not that either of them was in danger of being put in the shade, but neither did they need a flashy outfit to show them off. The saddle was carved first class but had nary an ornament. It was a sidesaddle, of course, and the seat was padded with sheepskin with the fleece on. It would be comfortable after a full day's ride. The bridle was also made-to-order of soft, tanned cowhide, with braided reins that were joined three feet from the ends. I tied the filly alongside the *grullo* at the hitch rack in front of the house then went in to get ready for the day.

Gifts were exchanged after breakfast, and we had a fine time. Elena's mother and Pancho were there for the first time ever. I gave Elena a buckskin jacket, and she gave me a set of Spanish duds, sombrero to boots. I was decked out to flash with the best when I put them on.

After the gifts had all been opened, I said to Elena, "Let's go for a walk and see if your jacket is heavy enough for this cold country."

"It's probably too heavy for today. It looks warm as summer outside. But I'd like to walk, anyway."

She didn't spot the filly until we were almost beside the hitch rack.

She stopped short and said, "What a wonderful horse! Whose is she? And what's your horse doing here? What's going on?" All without waiting for an answer.

She turned to me and said, "What do you know about this?"

"Reckon you could learn to like this sorry thing as much as you do that brown? She looks like she might grow out to be a horse of sorts, some day. Could probably be trained, if we can find someone who knows how to bust mean broncs."

"Is she yours?"

"No."

"Whose is she?"

"Yours."

"Mine? Really? Oh, Reuben, may I ride her?"

"Reckon you can try, but she looks a mite mean. You might see if Pancho can work the kinks out first."

By then she was next to the filly, and there wasn't an ounce of scare in the horse. I'd gotten her used to spooks by having her drag a hunk of canvas, and she would stand quietly, even when it was pulled over her head. The sight of a woman with full, flapping skirts must seem like a pack of wildcats to some horses, the way they take on. The filly never flicked an eye when I helped Elena up.

We spent the rest of the morning putting the filly through her paces. By the time we got back, we had the founding of our herd all planned out.

"I wrote to a fellow in Kentucky, the one who took me in when I was orphaned. His horses are bred for running and beat anything I ever did see for speed and staying power. Sent along a draft on the express company and told him to ship the best stud he could turn loose of. He's supposed to put the stallion on the train so's he'll be in Abilene when we get there with the cattle in May," I told her.

"When will we breed this filly?"

"Soon's we get that big stud here this spring. It takes a month shy of a year to have a colt. We should know in a year and a half whether we're on the right track."

"We are. You've done a fine job, and it'll all work just like it should."

"Lots can go wrong. We could lose the longhorns to stampedes, or the market might go plumb to pieces, or there's dozens of things could happen. I've never yet seen a body's plans work out just the way they figured for them to."

"We are going to succeed even more than we are expecting to. I just know it! Nobody's ever devised such a good plan. You've made provision for everything. You'll do it, too. I can hardly wait to see it! And besides that, as you keep reminding me, we have Jesus guiding us and giving you wisdom. I've never known anyone who has as close a relationship with him as you do. He won't let us down."

Well, she come close to making me think it'd be like that. But I never quit watching over my shoulder for trouble and asking the Lord to keep us on the right track.

We were wedded in January as planned. She came up with a dress that had been worn by the last three generations of her family, and she was a sight. They say all brides are beautiful, but she did beat all. It was typical of the weddings for well-to-do Spanish girls, with so much carrying on it'd make your head spin, but it pleasured her. I figured it was the only time, so let her do it exactly like she wanted it. You'd have thought it was the queen herself, the way the town took on.

Most of the celebration was done in the town plaza, and there was plenty of food, dancing, and entertainment to keep the crowd happy. We were able to slip off and change clothes after we'd done all the things like cutting the wedding cake and similar formalities. We had moved most of my stuff into her room, so that's where we went.

As soon as we were there, I said, "Before we do anything else, I want to talk to Jesus."

"That's wonderful. I do, too," she said as she came into my arms.

"LORD, you've given me more than any man should ever expect in this life. I never had a reason to expect that you would give me Elena to be my wife. Please guide me so I can be the husband she deserves. You know that I love her more than anything in the world, and I want her to have everything she needs and even all she ever wants. I'll fail her unless you keep me on course, LORD, so please never let me do anything that will hurt her. I'm so happy that I know you love her even more than I do, which is hard to believe because I don't know how that's possible. LORD, if it's all right with you, we'll have children. Please help us teach them to know you. I ask this in your name, Jesus. Amen."

"Jesus, you've answered my prayers already. All I can do now is thank you. If you let me bear Reuben's children, I'll be the most blessed woman in the world. You've given me all I need in him, and I thank you. Please make me a good wife. Thank you."

Then she took me beyond anything I had ever dreamed. It must have shown on our faces when we went back to the party. I saw quite a few people start smiling when we showed up again.

At the end of a week I asked, "How soon can we get shut of this crowd? I'm sick of sharing you with everybody."

"We can leave whenever you want. It's time to send everyone home."

"I'll say one thing, it's good this is the only time we'll go through this rigmarole."

"Wasn't it fun, though!"

"I'd as soon we'd packed up and run off, just the two of us."

"Oh, think of all the people who would have been disappointed. All my friends have looked forward to this for weeks."

"I know, and so have you. I'm glad we did the whole show."

"Didn't you enjoy it? If I'd known you didn't want it, we could have—"

"Whoa, sweetheart. I got nearly as much kick out of it as you did. I'm only funning you. You'll have to get used to me doing that."

"You can 'fun me' all you want. Where do you want to go?"

"Since we're heading into the heart of Ute country, I'd like to ride up to Taos and see old Kit. Is that all right with you?"

"Kit Carson? I would love to meet him. I was sorry that he was unable to come to the wedding."

"He must be right busy. Wrote that he'd like to come but had to turn us down. He's some sort of commissioner over all the tribes in New Mexico and Colorado. He'll give us good advice about getting on with the Utes. I want every advantage we can get when we go up there."

Most everyone in the territory knew of Kit. He'd made a rep for himself and was getting some rewards for his services to the nation. His relationship with the Indians was such that he could do a good job in representing both sides. There were lots of people over him who felt the Indians were some kind of animal and that cheating them was the thing to do, and that made it all but impossible to help them very much.

We took off the next morning early, packing a sight of camp gear. I wasn't about to give her cause to complain when we were finally off by ourselves. That mule looked like he had half a trainload of paraphernalia on him, but it was mostly light, fluffy trappings to keep her off the ground. We could have made it to Taos in a long day, but why miss a chance to be alone?

We were blessed with unusually mild weather, so we dawdled for several days as we rode toward Taos.

Elena said, "It's so nice to be able to do whatever we want to. The past few days when we had to try to be sure everyone else was happy makes this time really special. Is Kit expecting us at any particular time?"

"He doesn't know we're coming, so we can do whatever we want."

"Good. I'll tell you when I'm ready to leave here, and you can tell me if you want to leave earlier."

"I'll be happy to have you alone for at least a couple of years, sweetheart. Don't expect me to want to leave any time soon."

"I may want to leave if the weather gets bad."

"I guess the LORD may just keep it nice for a while, just to show he's happy we're married. He can be with us and see to it that we're glad to be together like this."

"Is he with us all the time?"

"The Bible tells us that he never leaves us."

"What does he think about those times we—"

"He designed us, sweetheart, so he knows more about that than we do. He's delighted. He says that we are now one flesh. He truly blesses a couple who is together in him. If he didn't like any part of our loving each other, he wouldn't have made it so good. I know he's glad we have each other, and that includes every part of our love for each other. In fact, I talked with him about it the other day, and he said it's fine. He said when you kiss me and make me the happiest man alive, he thinks that's great."

"Did you really do that?"

"I sure did."

"Did he really tell you that, or are you just making it up?"

"It really happened, darling."

"Mmm, he sure made it good, didn't he?"

"He does things really well. I think he made it extra good for me, though. I'm sure he never made anyone like you before."

"I am blessed more than any woman has ever been."

"No man has ever been given a woman like you. I love you more than any man has ever loved a woman, too."

"Show me again how much you love me, darling."

"Come here, sweetheart."

"Oh, yes!"

We rode into Taos, Elena on that filly, in a scarlet shawl, white blouse, and blue, velvet skirt spread over the horse's hips and down the left side. She sat that saddle like it was a throne, her movements perfectly matched to the filly's. It was enough to make your heart hammer. I knew every man in town would want her, soon as he laid eyes on her. Not a few of them would be inclined to try for her, so I was well armed. Twin pistols swung from my belt, a rifle was in a saddle scabbard on the right side, a shotgun on the left. I wore the flashy outfit she gave me for Christmas and came close to matching her when it came to show. Folks sort of took note as we made our way to Kit's home.

It was in the midst of town, east of the plaza, on the north side of the street. There was a pasture next to the house, right there in town. His was one of the nicer places, with a courtyard and trees to give shade. There were two ovens in the yard. Fires were built up inside of them, and when the fire burned down to a bed of coals, it was scraped out, bread was inserted, the door was shut tight, and stored heat baked the loaves up brown.

There were no windows next to the street. The only way in was through the courtyard, which was guarded by a gate that could be locked securely. I got down and rang a bell by the gate. In a few minutes, a bit of a Mexican girl came to ask who we were and what we wanted.

"Is Señor Carson home?" I asked.

"Yes. May I tell him who you are?"

"Reuben Dove."

In a few seconds, I heard him yelling, "Rube, you old he-coon, come in this here house. Haven't seen you since the Glorietta affair."

I've been up the hollow and over the hump with Kit, and he always seems to bring out a different side of me. I knew what an impression Elena would make on him and wanted him to see her as she was right then, dressed to the hilt and on that filly. I figure if you've got something special, you'd just as well let the world know about it. Anyway, I waited for him to come out, which took but a couple of eye blinks. He grabbed me in a bear hug and pounded me on the back like he'd spotted a nest of snakes there. We wrestled around like two ten-year-old boys scrapping over the only stick of candy in town, but it was pure joy instead of mad.

We'd been through some tough scrapes, and a bond had grown betwixt us stronger than most family ties. We'd shared in Indian fights, spent months in the far-off hills, hunted buffalo, trapped, traded, and lived with Indians and other mountain men. He taught me more than any other man about getting on in the wilds, not just the necessities like how to move without stirring up a ruckus, but reading signs from birds and animals as to when others were about. It was from Kit that I learned to track like an Indian. He taught me patience, and many a time it saved my hair. It shouldn't surprise anyone that we were glad to see each other. A couple of minutes was all it took to get it out of our systems, and he noticed my bride.

He swept off his hat and said, "Where in thunder did you find this beauty? Boy, you done yourself proud! Ma'am, if'n you're hooked up with this galoot, you've bought yourself a dandy. I'm Kit Carson, and my home is yours. Get down off that sorry nag and come in. You're way too pretty to be out where every Tom, Dick, and Jose can gawk at you. The likes of you should be kept for special times. Whoo, boy, you are sumpin."

He always did carry on.

I said, "Elena, honey, this is Kit. Kit, this is my bride. She said she'd never had a close-up look-see at a real live gringo gent and heard you could put on a show, so I brought her up for you to amuse."

Elena looked a mix of amazed, amused, and scared, all at the same time. I guess our shenanigans went past what she expected from grown-up men. We just acted like we felt.

We went into the house, where Missus Kit greeted us. It was a nice home with a comfortable kitchen, a parlor, and five bedrooms. The construction and design were almost the same as that found in Santa Fe. The Pueblos had been using it in their buildings for hundreds of years, so it had proven its worth.

"Haven't seen you since you helped put down the Rebs, Rube," he said. "That was quite a fracas. Sure glad you was around."

"We never had a chance to talk much then. Why were you so upset over them being in Santa Fe?"

"Shucks, if we'd let them keep that, they would've had a base to keep them supplied for a sashay into the mines in Colorado, maybe even Californy. If they'd got hold of that gold and silver, it'd sure have been lots tougher to put them down. We could still be fighting them, or they might've even won. Some folks have said we saved the Union by that action."

"I'd left town a few days before they took over. When you put out the word, folks sure spread it in a hurry. Must've been only a day or two before I knew it and got here," I said.

"I sent out the call, an' we hit them three days later. You got here just before we struck out for Glorietta. They folded pretty quick, and we had Santa Fe back the second day of fighting. Not too shabby for a ragtag mess of volunteers led by a used-up critter like me."

We jawed away a couple of hours, with Elena egging him on to tell about our times in the mountains and how he'd sort of taken me to raise. Noontime came and went before we got down to serious talk.

I opened by saying, "Kit, we're taking a bunch of cows and horses into Ute country. Going to set up to ranch. You know those hot springs alongside the San Juan, in that park country three days north of Santa Fe?"

"Sure do. Pretty country, good as any you'll ever set eyes on. Lot like that Jackson Hole, where we used to rendezvous, ain't it? But it's smack dab in the middle of the Utes. Ignacio's chief of the Weminuche Tribe. You may not know it, but there's seven tribes altogether, and they're every one as mean as any Indians around. You've taken cows up the trail from Texas and know how folks dread meeting up with Comanches. Well, Comanches is scared of Utes, because they raid them most every year. They're always losing horses, women, and kids. They trade the kids and some of the women as slaves. You've sure bit off a chunk if you move in on them," was his reply.

"I figured as much. That's why we're here. Thought maybe you could point us out a way to steer clear of trouble, much as possible. We'd like to get along with them. How's this Ignacio to deal with?"

"The whites have pushed him, and he don't like it a-tall. Government got him to sign a treaty giving up a bunch of high country because miners have moved in since gold's been found around Cripple Creek, and those mountains look like they'd be rich. It's some of the Utes' favorite hunting ground, and they got a dirty deal. Trouble is, they're not through getting dealt bad hands, either. Ignacio's figured it out and ain't happy with whites in general. He's pretty friendly with Ouray, who's chief of the Pine River Tribe. That bunch moved up north and have sort of settled down to farming on the Uncompaghre, close to some other hot springs over the hill. Ouray realizes there's no use fighting, because there's too dadgum many whites, and he's talking peace to the other chiefs. If he's been able to convince Ignacio, you've got a chance."

He continued, "You know, well's I do, you got to be strong around Indians. They hate anything weak. But they do appreciate a body being fair and talking with a straight tongue. You've been around enough Indians to handle whatever comes, well as anybody I know. What you expect me to tell you?"

"You've pretty well done it. I needed to know who to look for. Always pays to know who's in charge and what they're apt to be like. I hadn't a glimmer. It's good to know how they've been treated. We'll have to show them we're not just more whites who want to push them off their ground. But we'll stand fast."

He looked at Elena and said, "You got any idea what you've let yourself in for? This crazy galoot'll take you up where there ain't nobody but Indians and maybe a few outlaws or roughshod miners to keep you company. Every blessed man who sees you's going want to pack you off, and plenty of them will take a shot at Rube to get you. You could be left a widow mighty young if you follow this gent. You best stay in Santa Fe a couple of years till he sees how the Indians act when cows show up in their territory."

"Señor Carson, you have known my husband longer than I have, but you must not know him very well. He says he is going to build the best cattle and horse ranch in the country, and that's exactly what he will do. I am not afraid to go with him anywhere. He rescued my grandfather from bandits, brought him to Santa Fe, helped care for him, and then he captured the men who had hurt Grandfather. He's come to you for advice, but I would never consider not going with him. I've given him my heart and will go with him wherever he wants and will rejoice in doing it. We'll prosper, and you need not concern yourself about my safety. Reuben is well able to care for me in any situation."

Kit sat quiet for a long moment. "Well, young lady, you've sure enough put me in my place. And I tend to agree with you. You've got yourself a sort of halfway man, all right. Fact is, don't know anybody I'd rather have siding me in a scrap. You can't really know what kind of crazy thing you're setting out to do, but with your spunk and the kind of faith you got, I reckon you'll come out right side up. I'd go along and help you get set up, if it was so I could."

He turned to me and said, "Set up a meeting with Ignacio, soon as possible. Don't wait for him to come to you. Find out where he's camped and go, right off. Tell him what you're doing and offer to buy or rent the land. You know better'n to give him guns, I reckon, and I know you won't give him liquor. Trade him something useful that ain't a weapon. Sure don't want anyone accusing you of helping Utes in any fracas they have with whites. You've dealt with all kinds up north, and these won't be much different than Bloods and Piegans. Watch your horses, though. Ain't nobody worse'n a Ute for wanting a good horse. You start raising fancy critters like that filly, an' they'll try to take them off your hands. That may be the worst problem you'll have—if they don't decide to wipe you out, soon's you show up."

I said, "You and me have kept a few from doing what they wanted, time to time. Reckon we'll have a go at it again, if they can't be talked into being peaceful. Thanks for the advice."

We talked the sun plumb down, ended up staying the night. Next morning, as I was getting our gear on the horses, Kit came out.

"Rube, you really ought to leave that gal in town. What I said about every man wanting her's the straight stuff. You're just adding extra danger by having her there. Dadgum it! Thought I taught you better. You can't go taking chances and expect to get on out there. If you got to have a woman, get a plain-looking one to take along."

"I reckon not. You've given me lots of advice, first rate, most of it, but this time I'll pay you no mind. First, it'd be no good without her, and anyway, she'd come up on her own, and that would really be dangerous. I'll consider it, though, and do what I can to keep trouble away from her," I said.

"Can't say I blame ya. That's some woman you've got. You're some lucky."

"I reckon. The good LORD surely opened heaven and poured his blessing on me."

Kit and Elena had warmed to each other right off, but if she hadn't done it before, she won his heart when we were leaving.

She said, "Reuben says you've been like a daddy to him, so I'm going to consider you my father-in-law. We want you to visit us whenever you can."

Then she hugged him and kissed his old, whiskery cheek. It's the only time I ever knew of when he wasn't full of gab. Even looked like he might turn blubbery.

CHAPTER TEN

Pancho and I left in February, and it would be weeks—maybe months—before we could get back. I wondered if it was worth it. My pretty bride put on a brave face, but I suspected it was to keep me from feeling any worse than I did. I'd never done anything as hard as it was to ride off and leave her.

Our last conversation went something like this:

"Let me go with you. You know I can ride as well as anyone, and we're married now, so it will be perfectly proper for me to be with you. We camped out a lot on our honeymoon, so that's no problem."

"Sweetheart, don't make it harder for me than it already is. You've never been near a cattle drive and can't imagine what it's like. There aren't many men who can stand up to it. It's just no place for a woman, especially a lady like you, with the kind of men it takes to get along on the trail. I'll be able to control our crews, but there's no telling whom we'll meet up with. Besides, we'll have several herds, and I may be running back and forth between them, which means sometimes riding all night. It's just not something I can do to let you go along."

"You don't know how tough I am. I can do it!"

"Probably could, but you're not going to, not with me. I care too much for you to risk your pretty neck that way."

That didn't end the argument, but nothing changed. She tried to make it easier for me, though. She found someone to paint a picture of her on a piece of leather. It was a beautiful thing that I cherished.

She said, "I don't want you to forget me. Maybe this will remind you so you will come back soon."

"Why'd you have it painted with you crying?"

"I want you to know how much I'll be missing you. You can see me smiling when you get back."

"What can I give you so you'll not forget me?"

"I've got a picture of you on the back of my eyeballs. I'll *never* forget you!"

"Sweetheart, I'll never forget you either, but this picture is wonderful. Thank you for having it done. Can you teach it to hug and kiss me?"

"Put it over there and let it watch me. Maybe it can learn a little bit."

We took four horses and my mule, so as to cover ground in a hurry. We rode down through southern New Mexico and into Texas, sort of mapping out a way to travel when we would bring the herds back north. I made sure Pancho spent a lot of time looking back the way we'd come, so he would be able to know how things looked from that angle. All country looks different when you're going than it does when you're coming. We picked out ways that would give the best grass as well as having water. It took maybe a week longer doing it that way but would make a big difference when the herds came that way. Pancho had never handled moving a herd of longhorns, so I tried to help him get ready for that, too.

I told him, "I plan to get a herd of maybe four or five thousand cows with calves at their sides. You've never handled any kind of cattle drive, so we'll try to give you a crew who know enough to help you. If the crew knows what to do without being told, they can handle most things. You will just need to decide things like how far to travel each day and which way to have the herd travel. Calves won't cover much ground every day, so you'll need to take it easy. I'd plan to select a good man and have him ride ahead of the herd and pick the best route. He'll decide for you on things like where to stop for the night, how to get the best grass and water, where to go to avoid getting mixed up with other herds, and so on. We'll try to pick that man before you leave with the herd. You'll have plenty to do keeping the crew under control while you're learning. We may send you with a herd of young stuff, which won't need quite as much care, but will be easier to control than a herd of cows and calves. You'll still need to take charge, though, and keep the men in line. Cowboys moving a herd are usually not too hard to handle as far as getting work done. The hard part will come if one of them gets mad at somebody else and wants to fight. If that happens, you'll have to handle it in whatever way seems best. It'll be different every time. I can't get you ready for that, except to tell you it might come up, and you'll be the one who has to handle it."

He said, "Are you sure you want to trust me with something like that? I could make some bad mistakes and cost you lots."

"We'll try to find a fellow who's been up the trail several times and knows what goes on with a rowdy crew. If he's willing, we'll get him to sort of give you a leg up. You've been around long enough to handle it. The main thing is to take charge early and not let trouble build. When you see two men who seem to be causing trouble, separate them so they don't work the same part of the herd. If one of them is working the front of the herd, put the other one in the back and on the other side. Don't have them on night herd at the same time. Things like that will help. If it seems like all they'll do is knock each other around some, maybe you'll just let them work it off, but if it looks like a shooting affair, take control and do whatever it takes to keep it from happening. It's a big job, but you'll do fine. I'd be spending some serious time with the LORD, though."

When we got to Fort Worth, I put out word that we were looking for cattle of all sorts. The third day a man came up to where we were leaned back in the chairs on the hotel porch.

He said, "Hear tell you're looking to buy some cow critters."

I let the chair settle down on all fours and said, "That's right. What you got?"

"I ain't got none my own self, but a fellow I know was telling me t'other day there's a whole ranch full of stock for sale a couple of days south. Said a shyster lawyer fellow's handling the sale of a ranch left by some bird that died a year or so back. Said the guy was in some hurry to get shut of it, so a fellow could likely pick them up right cheap like."

"He say how many there'd be?"

"Claimed there'd been nothing sold off the place since the old guy passed on three, four years back, and there should be seven, eight thousand head. Said the tinhorn don't know a cow from sour milk, ain't never been out to look them over, but is in a sure enough stir to get shut of all of them."

"He say the lawyer's name?"

"I don't rightly remember if he did. Shouldn't be no trouble to find him, though. Everybody'll know about the deal. You know how cow towns are."

"I reckon. Say, I sure appreciate this. Join us for supper?"

"Nope, thanks. My woman's wanting to head back to the place. Hope you find what you're looking for."

I ran into Juan Salazar, a trail hand who'd been with me on the drives with Reed Anthony. He knew how to handle cows and men. After we'd jawed a while, I said, "What you doing now?"

"Waiting for someone to get a herd together; then I'll hit him up for a job. It's hard but better than anything around here."

"How many times you been up the trail?"

"I don't know, ten or twelve, I guess."

"How long would it take to round up a crew and seven horses for each of them? I'm looking to buy a couple of herds and will need two good men to ramrod them. If you can get a crew and remuda together, you've got a job."

"I can have the men by morning," he said. "It might take a few days to find the horses. Did you say seven horses apiece? I like that. A man can take all sorts of grief if he's well mounted, but when his horses give out, he's got a real live complaint. You'll need another boss, too?"

"Yes, you got someone?"

"Remember Jose Gallegos? He was a runt of a kid the first time we went up."

"I reckon. We all sort of took him under our wings and kept him out of trouble."

"He's as good as you'll find anywhere. He'll handle anything that comes along. Still sort of runty looking, but you don't have to worry about anybody running over him."

"See if you can find him. We'll talk, and if things look right, he'll be in charge of the second herd. Meet me at the Frontier Hotel for supper come sundown."

Pancho and I drifted around town then went to the hotel as scheduled. Jose and Juan were waiting.

"Hello, Jose," I greeted him. "Meet my father-in-law, Pancho."

We went to the dining room, ordered, and discussed my plans. It didn't take long to see that Juan had been right about Jose. He was soft-spoken but with iron underneath. I hired him and gave him orders to put together a crew of fifteen men and bring them to the ranch we'd been told about.

Pancho and I left early the next morning. Juan was there when we left. "Bring your crew along, soon as you get the horses together," I said.

He said, "I know of a good bunch of horses a couple days east. I'd like to get just enough horses here to take the crew over there then buy that herd. There's enough for both outfits."

"You're in charge. We won't be ready to start a gather for a few days. I don't want the lawyer to think we're anxious."

We rode two days south and visited with every cowman we met. They all confirmed what I'd heard, adding that all the lawyer knew about the herd was what was on the books of account. The general estimate was that there would be more cattle than he thought. I rode to town and looked him up. It seemed like we might get a mixed bunch that would give us the beginnings of a breeding herd, some young stuff to hold over a season, and part of a herd to trail to market right off.

The lawyer was a pinched-up, stoop-shouldered little bird who acted like a banty rooster we had when I was a kid. His office was dingy and cluttered. He looked up as we entered, squinting his watery eyes over glasses that hadn't been cleaned since last spring.

"What do you want?" he demanded in a raspy voice. Got my dander up right off, he did.

"Hear tell you're looking after an estate that has cattle to sell," I said. "If they're top stuff, we might be interested."

"They're good cattle and will bring a good price from the drovers who'll be buying trail herds."

"What you asking for them?"

"Seven dollars, counting everything from two years up," he said.

"They'd sure have to be good to bring that. Where will you deliver them?"

"The best I can do is let you have the ranch crew to help gather them. They're running loose."

"Let's go," I said, turning to leave.

"Wait! Wait!" His voice changed to a whine. "At least ride out and look at them. We might be able to work out a deal."

"How many are there?"

"According to the books, there should be about six thousand, counting everything. We show four thousand two years and over."

"You'll sell nothing but steers and dry cows to drovers. Anything else would be a real mess on the trail. What about bred cows and young stuff?"

"Well, I'll let you have the cows for five and throw in everything under two years old," he said.

"Way too much," I snorted. "I reckon we'll look somewhere else."

"No, no. Why don't you go look them over. I'm a reasonable man. They're supposed to be really good cattle. You see what they're like and come back with an offer. I sort of need to get that estate settled."

We rode to the place and found the crew nearly afoot, and it didn't take long to see that none of them was interested in anything but one more payday. We looked at the cattle for a couple of days and went back to town. It took most of the morning, but we made a deal. He was desperate to get shut of them, and I took advantage of it.

I said, "You're not gonna' get anybody to do your gather for you. Your crew is almost afoot, and don't look like they'd ever get your cattle out of the brush. Tell you what I'll do. We'll gather the cattle for you and give you three dollars for steers over two years old, two dollars for dry cows and two-year-old steers, and a dollar for cows ready to calve. Your crew can hold the stuff after we get it gathered."

"That's way too cheap," he said. "Add two dollars to each price, and we've got a deal."

"They're not worth that in the brush. We'll go get some ready to drive to Kansas."

"No! Make it a dollar and a half more for each of them, and you can have them."

It took another two hours, but we finally made a deal. We settled on four dollars for steers over two years, three dollars for dry cows and two-year-old steers, and two bucks for cows ready to calve. The cattle would have been worth a lot more if they were gathered and ready to put on the trail. We'd have to get them out of the brush, and some of them had never been handled. We were taking on a big job, but the price made it worth the extra effort. It was 1872, and cattle in Texas still weren't worth much until they were close to a railroad. Many a ranch had cattle that had run wild almost all the time the War Between the States was raging.

The ranch crew would hold the gather after we got them out of the brush. The neighbors had all agreed to give us a roundup of the cows wearing the Lazy T, the ranch brand, if any came up in their gathers.

When Juan and Jose got to the ranch, they had two full crews, each with a chuck wagon pulled by big Arkansas mules and as good a remuda as any I'd seen. The crews were a mix of Mexicans and Negros, which suited me fine. We were going to have Mexicans and Indians for neighbors, and it made sense to have a crew that would fit in.

Juan was worth at least three men, and Jose wasn't far behind him. We had thirty-four riders plus two cooks and were well-mounted and ready to comb those cows out of the brush.

I'd done my turn at chowsing Longhorns out of Texas thickets and have the scars to prove it. That brush has more ways to skin you, jab your eyes, and jerk you out of a saddle than four wildcats tearing up a rabbit. And to put a loop over those horns while you're dodging limbs and jumping boulders isn't a thing you do for fun. But it was there to do, and it's what we came for, so we dug in and went after those doggies.

It didn't take long to find out there were more cattle than anyone had thought. We didn't intentionally let any get away, but sometimes the boys didn't try as hard as they might to get every last one. With the ranch crew loafing around, just herding what was brought to them, no one but my men had any idea how many were still in the hills when we got done. And we could only guess at the number. When all the easy ones were in and tallied, we had over ten thousand head, with more than six thousand fit for the

Kansas market. Better than two thousand cows were ready to drop calves, which was going to make it tough to move everything.

The lawyer had come out for the tally and settlement. When we were done, I said, "There's a few still out there. If you've ever chowsed cows, you know there's no way to get them all."

He said, "You're going to have a mess, trying to move those cows with them calving. What'll you give me to leave them here for a couple of months and for everything else you can gather?"

"It wouldn't hurt to be able to keep them here a while, I'll admit. But as for busting any more out of the thickets, I don't know. We're sort of geared up to take everything and get," I said. "But make me an offer. After all, there was nigh onto twice as many critters as you guessed, so you should look pretty good to the people you're working for. There's no market for a herd that's already been picked over."

Well, he didn't want anything to do with trying to sell what was left, it seemed.

He said, "I'll rent you the place until fall and give you all you can gather by the end of September. That should be worth a thousand dollars."

"You just write me up a bill of sale for everything wearin' the Lazy T, and you've got yourself a deal."

It was his offer, and I didn't dicker, just paid over the cash money. It was worth that much to keep from branding all those critters. Anyone who's never been around anything but a calf branding has no idea what a chore it is to burn your mark on the hide of a steer five or six years old who's run wild all his life. Doing it to ten thousand head would be a man-sized job and maybe cripple some men and horses. It's not so bad on a well-run place with good corrals and a chute, but on a rawhide spread like that one with no pens, we'd have a mess. By fighting shy of that, we were able to cut out the stuff fit to head for market then separate the young stuff that would go to Colorado and turn the rest loose. I hired two men from the ranch crew to stay with Pancho and sent Juan and his outfit with the herd headed for Kansas. Jose and I took his crew and set out to find another bunch of cattle.

We started six day's ride away and worked back to the Lazy T, buying as we went. In three weeks we were back with another six thousand head. We branded as we bought, so all we had to do was make the cut and send the herds on their way. Jose put together a crew to take everything under four years old to Colorado, and they took off, with Pancho in charge. Jose took the other herd and headed for Abilene, following the way Juan had gone.

We had twelve thousand steers and dry cows in the two bunches headed to Kansas. The last herd was handpicked, with every head the same size and weight. We'd not have to shave our price because of differences in the makeup of those steers. I had to pay a premium, but it would come back at trail's end.

I took three extra horses and headed up trail after Juan. It was no small order, with him having almost a month head start. It took eight days to catch up to them, and I was glad to have four more horses there for my use. The four I'd ridden were sort of used up and enjoyed loafing along for a while.

The cattle were in good shape. Juan never said anything about trouble, but I learned from the crew that they *had* met up with a wrinkle or two. I had no worries with him in charge. He never looks for trouble but is ready if it comes—and it does if you're dealing with cattle and men. There were usually Indians around to demand that we give them cows for letting us pass through their territory. We gave them weak ones or strays that showed up time to time. At one river crossing, a bunch of them lined up and told us we had to give them ten steers or we couldn't cross.

Juan rode up to the chief and said, "You've got bows and arrows under your blankets."

"No, no we got nothing under them. But if you no give steer, we go get 'um. Then you be sorry, fella."

"I say they're on you, right now. You figure to shoot us, first chance you get."

"We want to smoke peace pipe, but we gotta have meat to feed our families. You give steer, and we go. Ten steer."

"You're a lying scalawag. You figure to shoot us, soon as we start cutting out the steers."

The two of them jawed back and forth like that for ten minutes or so. The chief was a scruffy, wore out old bag of bones, but he had fifty or sixty braves behind him, and some of them looked like they had nothing but mean in them. If they got the jump on us it could go hard.

Juan finally had a belly full of the palaver and jumped his horse into the chief and knocked him off his cayuse. That caused his blanket to fly open, revealing a strung bow and a quiver full of arrows. The chief was humiliated and led his men off, gesturing in a mean way as he did so. We were all well armed, while they had nothing but bows and arrows, so we didn't worry about the four-to-one odds in their favor. They didn't bother us no more.

Once in a while, we would end up with a bunch of strays in our herd from some other bunch that had gotten in trouble. When we did, we had to stop and make a cut, which is a sight to behold. The men select their best cutting horses and ride into the herd to pick out the strays. When one's spotted, the horse senses it and takes over with no guidance until he's clear of the herd. At that point the steer will almost always try to get back in the bunch, and there's a battle between horse and steer. A good cutting horse will put his head down so he's eyeball to eyeball with the steer and seems to read the steer's mind so he can stay one step ahead all the time. There are few things nicer to watch than a top cutting horse in action, and most cowboys, this one included, would rather ride a good cutting horse than most any other chore.

There was one tough stretch that tried the patience and staying power of the men and animals. It was a ninety-mile section with no water. Those of us who'd been up the trail knew what was in store and didn't relish it.

"How you reckon to handle it?" I asked of Juan when we were at the start of the bad stretch.

"We'll stay here close to water tomorrow. The next day, we'll water again about midday then head out. You know we'll have to push them day and night till we're through it. The second night we'll send two men ahead with half the horses. When they hit water and come on back, we'll have fresh riding stock to finish the drive."

"Sounds like what we've done in the past. Should work again," I said.

We watered the herd then drove them back the way we had come. We usually went the other direction but wanted them to be as fully watered as possible when we started the dry drive. There was nothing unusual about the first day. The cattle were used to traveling a full day without food or water, and we went only half a day. By the end of the second day, the doggies were restless and noisy.

Along about noon the third day the whole herd was feeling mean. A steer with horns almost as long as his body hooked the horse Mike, a black cowboy on his first cattle drive, was riding. That horse was ready to come apart at the seams from thirst and started a rodeo through that part of the herd.

Juan and I were riding toward the top of a ridge to see if we could spot the horse herd coming back from the river. I heard the racket and hollered at Juan. We were able to get two of the cowboys to help and rode into the cattle a short distance ahead of the uproar. The four of us cut out about a hundred critters at the very back of the herd and got the bunch where the upset was taking place headed away from the rest of the cattle.

That youngster was every place except in his saddle for about five minutes. There wasn't a strap or string on his saddle that he didn't use, along with the saddle horn, to keep off the ground. I thought he was gone several times, but he was nimble and came out the far side still on that horse. He was some mad at that steer that hooked his horse, though. It took him a couple of minutes to get everything in place; then he started hunting that steer.

The four of us who'd watched him and had kept the stampede from spreading were bunched together, all of us laughing. Mike didn't see anything funny. He came charging back through the bunch we'd cut out. He got almost to the middle and must've thought he saw the steer that had started the whole thing. It wasn't but a few seconds before he was beside that steer. He had his rope loose and used it to wallop that longhorn in the face. The steer didn't take to that at all and made another swipe with his horns. I'm sure his target was that cowboy, but he raked the side of the horse again, and we had another rodeo underway.

A couple of other wranglers had come back by then, and the six of us had our hands full for ten or fifteen minutes before we once again had the small herd cut off from the rest of the cattle, and there was little danger of things getting out of hand.

None of us had paid any attention to Mike during the excitement. When I looked for him, he was nowhere in sight.

"Did any of you see where Mike went?" I asked the other riders.

None of them had, and he wasn't anywhere toward the front of the herd.

"Where's that steer he was fighting?" asked Juan.

He wasn't in sight, either, so we separated to see if we could locate the cowboy, his horse, and the steer. I rode to the top of the ridge Juan and I had been on and saw the steer and the horse. They were having their private shindig on the other side of the ridge, and the horse wasn't doing very well. That steer had hooked his neck several times and was stalking him with the obvious intention of finishing the fight in a hurry.

I rushed down and drove the steer back toward the herd. That horse had been gored at least ten times and was bloody from the saddle to his nose. The steer wasn't bloody except on his horns, but he could barely walk and had a whole side caved in where the horse had kicked him. It took a while to find Mike, and that was a shock. The steer had managed to hook him and get him on the ground. It looked like the whole bunch had run over him, and there wasn't a lot left to bury.

The worst part of that episode was that none of us knew if Mike had ever accepted Jesus as his savior. It sure makes a difference when you don't know where a fellow is going to spend eternity. It was tough to know what to say when we laid him to rest.

At the end of that tough drive, man and beast soaked up water like dry rags, and a full day of rest followed for everybody when they weren't on watch.

With that headache behind us, Juan put one of the crew in charge and back-trailed to check on Jose. From that point on, he traveled between the herds, keeping everything under control. I scooted ahead to Abilene to feel out the market.

Buyers and sellers were just getting prices established. The first thing I did was send wires about the stallion that was to come in from Kentucky and the bulls from Iowa. An answer soon came that the bulls had been shipped so they should arrive any day, but there was no answer concerning the horse. I pestered the telegraph operator day after day and sent a total of seven wires but got no reply.

It took two days to visit all the herds in sight and meet all the buyers in town. It seemed like we should be able to get at least twelve dollars for our steers. I rushed back, slowed the herds, and took them on a roundabout way that allowed them to feed several hours each day. We could see them put on flesh as we moseyed along. The first bids for them were higher than I expected, and we averaged fourteen dollars for each and every animal. We had paid just over five on the average, and our cost for wages and supplies ran about two bits for each critter we delivered. We wouldn't do that well every time, but it was a fine start.

The delivery took a little over three weeks, and I was nervous as a pimply faced kid headed for his first time out with a gal, what with imagining all sorts of things that might have gone wrong with the stallion. The twenty white-faced bulls came in during the second week, and we put them in a corral at the edge of town.

The last steers were to be shipped back east, and delivery was called for at the rail yards. As we were pushing the last of them into the pens, a train pulled in. We were at the end of the tracks, so the train came from the east. I glimpsed a car with three horses inside, and felt a rush of excitement, wondering if one of them was the stud I was waiting for.

I hurried through the final details of delivery, made excuses, and rode off looking for the car with the horses. Since few stock cars from the east carried cargo, it wasn't hard to find one that had been placed at a loading chute. However, the doors were open, and it was empty, as was the pen next to it. I hailed a railroad man and asked if he knew anything about the horses.

"The fellow who came with them asked about a livery stable and hotel. Said something about a man named Dove. Took off toward town," he responded.

I put spurs to my horse and rushed to the livery, where I did a running dismount, hurried inside, and almost collided with Charlie Jimson.

"Charlie, you black son-of-a-gun! What are you doing here?"

"Aw, Rube, boy, I nevah bin so glad ta see anybody in ma whole life! Yoah doan know what a time I'se had." He moaned. "I bin in jail foah times, 'cused o' bein' a run-away nigga hoase thief."

"Come here and let me see you," I said and hugged him like a long-lost brother, which is how I felt. This was the man who'd taught me about training horses back in Kentucky.

After a bit he said, "You gotta see da hoases I brung ya. Dey's rat back hyar, an' you'se goan lak um real good!"

He dragged me to the back of the barn, where we found the three I had spotted in the rail car.

"Charlie, they're nice, but I just sent for one. How'd you get all of these? You didn't bring a bunch of cheap studs, did you? I told Partell we wanted the best. Let's get them out where I can look them over."

"Oh, dey ain't nuthin' wrong wid dese hoases! You got no idee what you can buy crittahs foah since de wah. I got us a 'leben year ole, whut has sired some o' de bess runners roun' de country, dat's de big 'un, an' a foah year ole whut's bin outrunnin' evahthang in sight. De little 'un's jes' a yarlin', but he's gwine be de bess ub de lot, you wait an' see!"

I'd forgotten how excited he could get, but his arm-waving, jumping, and carrying on reminded me quick enough.

"All right, Charlie, settle down. Let's get them outside."

He changed completely when he started handling the animals. He was all gentleness that spoke volumes about his love for them. It was another reminder of the character of this man who had been my only friend during that tough time. I wasn't surprised when he tossed the ropes over their necks and took off, all three following at his heels. Outside, he handed me two of the ropes, grabbed the withers of the biggest one, vaulted to his back, and put him through his paces. The stud had plenty of speed and was easily controlled. Tall and rawboned, he stood at least sixteen hands, probably more. He was in running shape, with not an ounce of fat, which was what I wanted. It would be close to a year before we used him for breeding, but it's a good idea to always keep stock in good condition. Charlie rode the four-year-old next, and he showed up just like he'd said. His body and form was almost identical to the older horse, and speed showed in his every move. He was well mannered, as could be expected from any horse under Charlie's care.

After riding the two older ones, he said, "An' now foah de bess paht. I'se gwine show you a real hoase, an' dat's foah shoah."

He took the yearling and led him at a walk, then a trot, and finally a lope. His appraisal of the youngster was borne out. Young as he was, he showed the best of his breed, standing within a few inches of the older animals' height, with a smoothness of action that promised exceptional speed and agility.

"How did you ever talk anyone out of them?" I asked. "It's hard to imagine things being so bad that a man would sell them."

"You got no notion how bad things is. Dat's one reason I come wid 'em. Ole Massa Partell's got no work fo' me anymoah, an' dese was his lass good hoases. He said yuh was de one man he din't mine sellin' 'em to, an' dat I shud come wid 'em. Said if'n yuh had dat much money to spend on hoases, yuh'd shoah nuff have work fo' me. He done paid paht o' de money to de train man foah shippin' de hoases, an' dey said it was a free ride foah a puhson ridin' wid 'em. So I cum 'long an' cayed foah 'em. Y'all ain't gwine mak me go bak, is yuh?"

"No, don't you worry, we've got a place for you, all right," I said. "You've no idea how glad I am to see you. You did a great job getting them here, and we're going to need your help using them. We'll talk about our plans as we go along. Let's eat, then we'll get things ready to head home."

With the horses back inside, we went to the hotel, and Charlie had his first meal in a white man's dining room.

"Whar am I s'posed to go eat?" he asked.

"Just stay with me."

"I cain't go in der wid ya. Somebody'll pitch me out, quick as scat."

"They better not try it."

"Ya mean I'se gwine eat with *you*?"

"That's it. Don't worry, it's all right."

Seemed he was proud as a kid with his first pony, sitting with me there among all the other folks. When Jose showed up and I introduced them, the Mexican never blinked an eye, and that impressed Charlie even more. He was used to everybody having to cater to white folks. The two of them would have been considered poor company by some, I reckon, but they were valuable to me, and I gladly shared table with them. I'd sent Juan and his crew to the Lazy T in Texas to finish the gather and start that bunch north. When we had all of the steers delivered, I sent Jose and all but three of his hands to help in Texas. It would be no picnic, with over two thousand calves alongside the cows, an extra thousand cows, and the ones we had missed in the first gather. I estimated they would find about five hundred extras and sent money with Juan so he could offer a dollar a head for anything brought in by the neighbors. When the lawyer found out that we got more than four thousand head, counting only those that were two years and up, he threatened to sue, but it had been his deal. I'd made no offers, just paid what he asked, no dickering.

We found a saddle and some guns for Charlie and headed for home with the bulls and stallions. We had a chuck wagon and enough riding stock to let us handle the herd without wearing anything down. The trip was without incident, although driving bulls isn't the greatest way to spend an afternoon. They can be as contrary as anything alive, and ours spent the first week or so fighting, even after traveling halfway across the country together. They finally settled down and sort of drifted along with us.

With the few bulls, so few horses, and one wagon, we hardly raised any dust. That was a real change from the drives with thousands of hooves stirring dust from dawn till dark. I heard no complaints about that. We moved as fast as we could across Kansas, with no mountains to hold us back. Charlie had never seen so much country from one spot, with so few trees to hinder his view. It wasn't long before he was missing the trees that are so thick in Kentucky, and the dry air was a dramatic change from the humidity he was used to. He was amazed at the numbers of game animals. When I suggested that he shoot an antelope,

I thought his eyes would pop out of their sockets. It was worth the whole trip to watch him. I could hardly wait to take him elk hunting.

The trip gave me a chance to give those studs a taste of handling cattle, and they caught on pretty fast. They had no natural cow sense but were quick to learn that when a bull quit the bunch, the idea was to catch up to him and turn him back. It was another story the first time I roped from the four-year-old. He was scared of the rope at first then had no idea what to do when the loop was on the bull. We almost had a storm, but one of the cowboys bailed us out. It would be hard, waiting two years to try the yearling.

We kept a sharp eye peeled for Comanches, with those fancy stallions along. Never saw an Indian who wouldn't rather steal a horse than eat, and the three we had would beat anything those boys had ever had a chance at. We had a few narrow scrapes but were careful to camp where we had a good field of fire and always acted like we were going to be attacked. It made for short nights, what with guards out constantly. I had that brown, and he could smell an Indian half a mile off. Several times we moved in the middle of the night because he got snorty. We cut across country, going southwest out of Abilene, and when we hit the Santa Fe Trail, I took one of the cowhands aside and said, "I'm going to put you in charge here. Charlie and I are going on ahead. All you need to do is stay on this trail till you hit Santa Fe. You up to that?"

"How do you think the other fellows will like that?"

"If you're going to be the boss, you'd best be ready to handle them, whether they like it or not. You up to it?"

"Oh, I can handle them, all right. I was just wondering."

"Okay. I figured you could or I'd not have picked you."

The next morning Charlie and I took the stallions and four other horses and forged ahead. We could cover several times as much ground as the bulls, and I needed to get back. It would take quite awhile to arrange delivery of the mares we'd bought and get the herds from Texas lined out for the ranch.

We kicked up some dust and made the Martinez ranch, where we'd bought the filly, in three days. I was looking forward to a visit with Miguel, but got better than that. Elena came flying out of the house as we rode up. I was off that horse and had her wrapped in my arms quicker'n scat.

"Seeing you is better than a cold drink after a month of dry camps," I said.

"I know! You'll never know how much I've missed you."

"Why are you here? Nothing's wrong, is it?"

"Everything's fine. I couldn't endure sitting around, doing nothing but think of you, so I talked to Señor Sanchez. He said you would almost surely come here first. I took a chance that he was right and came out a month ago. I arranged to have all of the mares brought here."

"You done that all on your own?"

"Yes. Is it all right?" She looked like she'd bust out crying if I even looked like it wasn't.

"I reckon it's sure all right. You saved us a passel of time. We can head for our ranch right quick, now. I'm plumb proud of you."

It was hard, but we managed to be polite until everyone had seen the new horses, business was taken care of, we had eaten, and visited a decent eternity. Then we slipped off and had our private get together.

I said, "That likeness you had painted for me was sure a treasure on the trail. Can't tell you how many times I looked at it. But it don't come close to measuring up to the real thing. Didn't hug back worth shucks. You're the prettiest thing to ever walk on two feet."

"I didn't even have anything look at. All I had was the wonderful memories of our honeymoon."

"Let's make some more memories."

"Oh, yes!"

It only took a couple of days to get to where we could turn loose of each other again.

We headed for town at least a month ahead of schedule. With a foal beside every mare, we had to loaf along, but watching those youngsters cavort made it a pleasure. If there ever comes a time I don't like to watch baby calves and colts, I'll hang up my spurs.

At Santa Fe, we put the mares on pasture, and I decided to head south to locate the herds from Texas.

Elena said, "You're not going anywhere without me."

"There's no way I'll argue about that. Get things together for at least two weeks on the trail. We'll have another honeymoon."

Pancho was to take things slow. I didn't want him coming too early and using the winter range of the ranchers while he waited for me. We met him six days southeast, and he had things under control.

"Looks like you done right well," I said. "Can't see that you've lost many steers."

"A hundred and six, at last count. We had to give about fifty to Indians. Most of the others were lost at river crossings."

"That's downright good for your first drive. I've seen drovers do worse after years of taking herds up the trail."

"I had lots of help. That black fellow Mose sure knows what he's doing. If he hadn't been along, I'd have made a lot more mistakes. He really should have been running the show, instead of me."

"He wouldn't have taken the job. I sent him with you knowing he'd be your top hand. He's been with Juan the last few years, and Juan said he could handle things but didn't want a bossing job."

We drifted with them the next couple of days just to be sure how things were going.

The third morning I said, "It'll take you about a month to reach the ranch. We'll take Lupe along with us, since we'll have wagons for your stuff. Here's a map of the way from Santa Fe to where we'll be. Just keep drifting slow and easy so the critters will stay in good shape. We'll likely have things ready so we can let them scatter when you get there."

We left for the ranch with four wagons, plenty of tents, and other gear to lodge and feed everybody for at least two months. We took along a blacksmith as well as Lupe and three other women who would help Elena cook and take care of the household.

The scenery around Santa Fe isn't very exciting, but by the second day, we were into some better views. That brought a problem, though. We couldn't see as far ahead. I had a hankering for a look at the San Juans. Elena had never been in that area, and she was delighted with the oak brush and berry bushes. When we got into the aspen and pines, she was a joy to watch. The game wasn't much in evidence because of the herd, but I was able to show her a few deer and elk. I kept an eye peeled for the Pyramid, but going up through the hills of northern New Mexico, it's all but impossible to get a look at anything but nearby peaks. One afternoon I got impatient.

Elena was riding beside me, and I said, "Let's ride up and see if we can spot some landmarks."

We rode to a saddle between two pinnacles and there it was.

"Look at that," I said. "That's Rio Grande Pyramid."

"Oh, Reuben, what a magnificent peak! It towers above the whole range."

"Isn't it something? It's easy to see why it got its name, isn't it? Can't see the Window, though. Let's ride on up a ways. Maybe we can spot it, too."

It took most of the morning to find a point from which we could see the second of our landmarks.

"The mine's somewhere in that area," I said. "Guess we'll probably think of that every time we see those two sights."

"Will we be able to see them from our house?"

"No. See that highest mountain off to the right? That's Pagosa Peak, and it's going to pretty much hide the others from where we'll build."

Although summer was more than a month old, shawls of snow still hugged the shoulders of the entire range to remind that winter is never far away from the place we'd chosen for our home.

We left Santa Fe in early July, but I'd arranged for a crew to go ahead to ready things for building our house and barns. We sure didn't want to be in tents when it turned cold. The men had been given detailed instructions of where to go and what kind of logs to cut. They had a stockpile of logs trimmed and squared, as well as rocks for the foundation, so we could start on the house as soon as we picked the spot.

While the crew was unloading the wagons, Elena and I rode to the top of a ridge east of the park.

"Okay, darling," I said, "where do you want to build your house?"

"I can't decide that alone."

"It's going to be your home, so it ought to be where you want it."

"There must be lots of things to consider besides where I would like to have it. What should I look for?"

"Well, there's a spring down below here at the edge of the park. It wouldn't hurt to have water close. It don't have to be right next to the house, though. We can build a cistern and fill it from the spring. You'll probably want to be fairly close to some trees to slow the wind down a mite but not so close you can't see what looks good to you," I suggested.

"Will it be better to build in a low place or up higher?"

"You don't want it so everything runs to the house when it rains or during spring thaws, so clear down in the bottom ain't the best spot."

"Then somewhere not too far below the spring would be all right?"

"I reckon."

"Let's ride down and see where we have the best view of those two peaks. What are they called?"

"That first one's Pagosa Peak. T'other one's Black Mountain."

"I want to be able to see them from our bedroom window."

"Suits me. I reckon these San Juans are as awesome as any range in the world. I've spent time in the Tetons, Bitteroots, and Black Hills in Montana, Idaho, Wyoming, and the Dakotas and gawked at Pikes Peak from far out in the plains. But of all the places I've been, there's no place the equal of these southern Rockies for looking at. Or for grazing livestock. The peaks rearing up out of that park come nigh to being as pretty as you."

She was a joy to behold as she finished choosing the spot to build. Once the site was selected, the carpenters went to work, and in jig time they had the walls up and were started on the roof.

Pancho brought in his herd right on time. We sent one of his riders back to find Juan, Jose, and the other herds and guide them. Since the area was strange to all the animals, the crew herded them that first summer. It was good they did what with grizzlies and wolves. If it hadn't been for those predators, we'd have just let the beef run loose after they knew their way around, but it would take several years to cut the numbers of the beasts down to a point where it was sort of safe to leave the herds alone.

Indians aren't much for eating beef. Their taste runs more to venison or buffalo. But they love to steal horses, and ours were a special drawing card. We all packed shooting irons, and it's good we did. A problem I didn't expect was the growing numbers of miners—plenty of them worse than any Indians. Kit had given us good advice about it being safer for Elena to stay in Santa Fe. With most any other woman, I might have followed his advice, but we didn't regret the decision to make the start together. It was dangerous, but we took things as they came.

When things were well under way, Elena and I rode off looking for Utes. We found a couple of braves and managed to let them know we wanted to see their chief. They didn't savvy English or Spanish, and we didn't talk their lingo, but we got it across with signs. We managed to figure out that Ignacio would be gone for two weeks. Their camp was a half-day's ride to the west of us.

We went home and got some corrals started. When the two weeks were up, I made ready to go see Ignacio.

"I want to go with you," Elena said.

"You think I'm going to let those Utes have a chance at you? Not on your life. Remember what Kit said about them packing off women from the Comanches?"

"They'll know I'm here before long. At least two of them already do. Remember, I was with you when you talked to those braves week before last."

"Yeah, you're right. Shucks, I always get a kick out of showing you off, anyway. Guess if we're going to live among them, they just as well get to know both of us. Reckon it's a fool move, but let's do it."

I wouldn't trade the times we had together for all the gold in those hills. We enjoyed God's creation like few folks ever do. I don't expect to ever get used to the idea that she chose to hook up with me. She's a purely nice person and feels, like me, that there are times to be quiet and soak up the scenery. Seems like most folks have got to be jabbering all the time, but we could ride side by side for hours and not say a word. Which makes a lot of sense in rough country.

I looked over at her on that filly and said, "Being here with you's worth more than all the gold in these hills. I still can't figure out why you chose to hook up with me. I could ride for a lifetime and do nothing but look at you and praise God for letting me do it. I don't know what's waiting in that Ute camp, but it'll be all right because of this. You had a great idea when you decided to come with me. I love you, sweetheart!"

She loved me with those eyes, which came close to knocking me off my horse. "I guess he knew nobody else would bring me out here where I can see all this beauty and have the pleasure of riding this wonderful horse, being loved by the best man in the world. He knew my life would never be complete without that, so he gave me you."

"I'm going to be quiet for a while. If we keep talking, I'll stop and haul you off that filly. I'd better calm down and tend to business. I'm gonna keep looking, though."

"I will try to behave, too. I don't dare look at you very long—it gets dangerous fast."

"I guess we'll just have to settle for a quiet ride."

"I reckon. I love you."

"I love you, and I'm sure glad you're here."

"Hush!"

We rode through columbines and sego lilies, so many you couldn't begin to count them. I never learned the names of all the different flowers, but they're sure pretty and smell good. We kicked out a bunch of elk close to the Piedra and watched them trot through the pines, heads high, testing the breeze for danger. I felt a kinship, since we, too, had to be always on the lookout.

Horse tracks and other sign got thick as we rode on. I pointed it out to Elena and motioned for silence. While we had almost no chance of getting to the camp without being spotted, I'd done just that a couple of times. At the least, I wanted to spot them first. We swung off the trail, rode north half a mile, and took a trail that showed nothing but deer tracks. We were like a couple of wildcats, sneaking through pines, the duff underfoot muffling our horses' hooves. We slowed to a crawl at each crest, easing up to each of them so we could see over before going on. We began our approach at mid-morning, and it was full noon before we peeked over the top of a ridge next to the Los Pinos and saw the Utes' camp.

CHAPTER ELEVEN

It looked like a fixed camp, with many wickiups mingled with the tipis. The wickiups were built of logs and brush, with walls on three sides and were used for cooking and other chores that could be enjoyed more in the shade. They also gave protection from wind and other rough weather. The open side almost always faced east. We saw women, kids, and dogs throughout the camp, and at least fifty braves were puttering around. It looked like what I'd seen among friendly tribes up north.

A tipi bigger than any other stood in the middle of camp. We sat our horses for half an hour watching. During that time, half a dozen men went to the big tipi. They each stopped and talked for a time then left. I pulled out my field glasses and looked the man over. He had a proud carriage, his posture erect and head high whether sitting or standing. His clothes were pretty much like all the others'—buckskin britches and a vest, with moccasins on his feet. The women were dressed in buckskin, too.

Their horses were grazing along the river. Between the camp and the river was a stretch of dirt where no grass showed. Utes love horse races, so I figured that was a racetrack. Carcasses of a half dozen deer hung in a clump of pinyon trees where there was shade. There was a sort of arena in the middle of camp, probably for powwows and dancing.

I searched the area carefully and could find no sentries. Even so, we chose an untraveled way to ride until we were almost to the camp, then we hit the main trail and went in, bold as a full-blown army troop. Nobody took notice until a dog yapped when we were a hundred yards from the first tipi.

I reckon no woman like Elena had ever before ridden into their camp of her own freewill, and she caused some stir. She was a sight, as usual, and I knew it was risky to take her where those Utes could have a look at her. She would come to their attention sooner or later, and this way we got to choose the time and place. It was a tossup whether there were more dogs or kids, and they all jammed around us, raising a ruckus that must've scared every deer off the mountain. The kids made a little less noise than the dogs, but they all trailed along as we rode toward the big tipi.

The women looked us over carefully then went back to their fires. It was noon, and it wouldn't do to keep the men waiting for a meal. The men tried to look unconcerned, but I noted that they all slipped toward the edge of camp, and we ended up surrounded by them.

The tipis were built of sturdy poles and plenty of hides. While I'd found Indians a bit hard to figure, it didn't seem like these were on the prod. It looked like we had guessed right about the chief, since he came to meet us, kicking dogs and grunting at kids. He was the tallest Indian I'd ever seen. He stood a couple of inches over me. Most of the others were chunkier than those up in the Dakotas, as well as the Apaches who roamed the plains west of there. Our confab started off in signs, but I soon picked up on the fact that he knew Spanish pretty well, and things got easier.

"I'm looking for Ignacio, chief of Utes," I said. "You look like the man."

"I am Ignacio. Who you?"

"Name's Dove, Reuben Dove, and this is my woman. Kit Carson told me to come see you."

"You know Carson?"

"We're friends for many, many moons. He's sort of a pa to me. He says you're all right. We want to be friends."

"Get down. We eat."

When we dismounted, a crowd gathered. About half the men spent their time eyeing Elena, while the rest looked over our horses. I'd brought the four-year-old stallion, and he was some horse. Letting them see him was like bringing Elena—they would find out before long, anyway.

"Sit," said the chief, indicating some blankets in front of his home. "How is Carson? He is a good man. You good friend to him?"

"I reckon. If'n it wasn't for him, I'd have been buzzard bait, many a time. Yep, we're friends for many winters."

"He talks with straight tongue. Not like most white eyes. Which way you talk, like Carson, or with snake's tongue?"

"It don't matter much what I tell you, you'll find out before long. I say that I speak like Carson, and you'll see that it's true. Here, this is from him." I handed him a blanket Kit had sent along.

I'd warned Elena that we might end up eating dog, mountain lion, or who knows what. I think we got venison, but you never can be sure. Whatever it was, it never bit back. We were thankful to sit and eat instead of other things that might have come to pass. Three women brought the food to us. When one of them was handing me a bowl, she almost dropped it and started chattering like a kid who'd seen his first elephant. It sure did make me want to learn their lingo so I'd not be in the dark, times like that.

Whatever it was that got her heated up caused a stir. She called to several other women who came and jabbered with her, all of them pointing at me and carrying on. Since nobody seemed to be mad, I just kept on chewing and grinning. We'd brought some trinkets and handed them out after we'd eaten.

Ignacio said, "We talk inside. My wife will take care of your woman."

He brought out a pipe, stuffed it full, lit it, and handed it to me. We'd each take a puff then hand it back. Kept at it till it was nothing but ashes. Took awhile, but he finally settled back.

"Talk now."

"We've brought a bunch of cows and horses into the parks east of here. You know the hot springs? Well we're putting up some houses, barns, and corrals near there. We want to use the grass in that area and in those parks that run off to the south. Don't mean to mess up your hunting or anything. Won't shut you off from going where you want. If the snow gets deep, we'll need to move into lower country, down this way. We'll not bother the deer or elk, except to take a few for meat, like you do, but not near as many.

"We're putting up a few fences, to keep the herds divided, but there'll be plenty of ways for you to go through, and they won't keep the game from moving. We know it's your land and are wanting to pay you for it. If you'll sell it, we'll buy, or we'll pay you for the grass, whichever you want. We want to be friends."

Now I had no such innocent notion as that he didn't already know where we were and what we'd done. You don't move into an Indian's domain without his finding out about it right quick, and we'd been doing a lot of things that would have come to their attention. But it didn't hurt to let them think we expected them to be surprised.

He sat, not a move nor a word out of him, for nigh onto an hour. Never would have guessed a body could sit cross-legged like that for so long. I didn't want to upset him, so I sat, too. Got downright cramped toward the end. To make it worse, I had no idea what was going on with Elena.

Finally, he said, "I ride over soon and see if you tell it straight. I give answer then. We make deal or run you off."

It took me four tries to get off my haunches, but he just stood up like he was ten years old and sauntered out of the tent. I hobbled after him, legs atingle from going to sleep. It was pretty stuffy inside, and the fresh air was sure enough welcome.

My bride was the center of attention, circled by a bunch of women. She was laughing and carrying on with them as though she hadn't a worry in the world. They hushed up in a hurry when Ignacio showed up. Elena came to me, with an escort of women.

"You ready to go?" I asked.

"Whenever you want. How did it go?"

"He's going to ride over for a visit and will give us an answer then. You never know."

"Will he come alone?"

"Reckon not. Generally, a chief'll have a passel of braves with him."

"Ask him to bring his wife. I would love to have her as my guest."

I hesitated only a few seconds then turned to Ignacio. "My woman wants you to bring your wife when you come. She's been made welcome here today and wants to give the same."

He asked me to say it again, then again, before nodding and saying something to his wife. Turning back, he grinned and said, "She come."

I guess we'll never know for sure, but I reckon that Elena being there and giving that invitation made a big difference in how we made out with the Utes down through the years.

He stopped us from leaving, saying, "You stay, eat soon."

We'd no desire to offend, so we stayed, then nothing would do but we had to spend the night. I wasn't much taken with the idea, but Elena was having such a time, learning to cook Ute vittles using native plants and all that I gave in. It was a learning time for sure. I've no doubt we were the first white couple to ever stay there as guests, and the kids never tired of staring at us like we were some kind of critters brought to give them a look-see. Didn't seem like they differed much from any other kids, and we had our share of a good time.

The men wanted to race the stallion, but that would have been a losing proposition. They hadn't a thing that could hold a candle to him, and you don't go into their camp and beat them at their game. Not and stay friendly. One of the men, called Lame Turkey, got pretty pushy about it, but Ignacio put a stop to it.

"That horse would run yours into the ground. Be glad you don't have to be shamed by losing. This man came as a friend. He'd be your enemy if he beat you, and it would be your fault. Wait a while. We'll see that horse run sometime."

They put on a powwow around a big fire with dancing, drum whacking, and howling that would've been downright scary if the chief and his wife hadn't been sitting there showing their teeth every time I looked. We were given a tipi all to ourselves and settled in. If it hadn't been for all the barking dogs and howling coyotes, it would've been peaceful.

When we were snuggled in the blankets and furs they gave us, Elena said, "Do you know what all the commotion was about during the noon meal?"

"I've got no idea. Whatever it was, it sure got some of them stirred up, though."

"Did you kill a deer and give it to some of them last year when you were going to Santa Fe?"

"Yep. Forgot all about it. Ran into their camp an hour above where our house sits and then spotted a buck. Had a fool notion and shot the bugger and drug him back for them."

"Well, Missus Ignacio was there, and she remembered you. It was a nice thing, and I think you're going to be glad for doing it. The women were all saying that they would tell their husbands to give you what you want. I'm glad you're such a nice man. If you weren't, you wouldn't have helped Grandfather, and we might not have met. And I wouldn't have gotten to spend a night with you in an Indian camp."

She stopped and gave me a big hug and as sweet a kiss as anybody could dream up. "My great-great-grandmother was a prisoner of a Ute chief. My great-great-grandfather[1], the dowser I told you about, bought her from him. I mentioned that and some of them had heard about it. I think that may make a difference, too."

---

1   This refers to Molly and Reuben from Santa Fe Riches.

"I reckon we'd better get the LORD involved in this. LORD, it looks like you can handle anything, even a camp full of Utes. That doesn't surprise us, but we want you to know how much we appreciate what you're doing. I thank you for leading us to come, which, as you know, was Elena's scheme. I think it may be what'll make Ignacio decide to be friendly. Thanks for giving me such a great, smart wife. Please keep me from doing or saying anything that'll keep this from working out well for us."

Elena continued, "LORD, you know how wise Reuben is, and it's because he listens to you. Please keep guiding him so we can become friends with these Indians. I love you, LORD."

She rewarded me as only she could, with the treasure of her love. We left next morning first thing and scooted back to get ready for their visit. I wanted the livestock well scattered so the Indians wouldn't think we were going to take too much grass away from the game animals. I also wanted to get the house as far along as possible so they could see we meant to stay.

Ignacio, his wife, and ten braves showed up a couple of weeks later. The walls were up, and the roof was being nailed down when they got there. We tried to give as good as we'd got, and by the time they left, we'd agreed to rent a section of summer grass some fifty miles long and thirty miles wide, along with the lower country for winter range. It cost us four hundred cast-iron Dutch ovens and twice that many double-bitted axes. They'd never used either one, and it was something to watch their faces as they saw those Mexicans shape the timber with the steel implements. The Dutch oven part was worked out between Elena and the chief's wife. I'm sure it changed the way meals were fixed in the Ute camps. We were also to pay them four hundred fat steers and twenty horses every fall, with another two hundred steers added if we had to move into the lower country in the winter. Altogether, it was a fine start.

As they were leaving, I gave each of them a horse. They were all fine animals, but the crews had picked out culls. They just weren't the best cow horses, but Indians weren't going to be working cows, and it didn't shave the value in their eyes. Lame Turkey got the fastest thing my boys would turn loose of. I wanted to keep peace with him if I could. He spent most of his time poking around those studs and that filly. Especially the filly. Part of the deal was for the tribe to leave our stock be.

"That is just for our tribe," said Ignacio. "You'll have to make peace with others, if you can."

"You keep your boys off, and we'll be happy."

I knew very well there were going to be some young fellows looking to shine with pretty little gals who'd end up making a try for our riding stuff. And I wasn't at all sure Lame Turkey would stay in line. We could be in for a fight now and then. Well, it wouldn't be the first time. Altogether, we'd made out real good.

CHAPTER TWELVE

We got word in August that Luiz and Margarita were getting married, so we rode down in September for that. It was a full-blown wingding that ran on a full week. The whole town turned out for it, along with a crowd from her home in Raton. Must have been three hundred folks there. The two of them were like a couple of kids, which made all the rest of us happy, too. We enjoyed the get-together but were glad when we could break loose and head home.

By fall we had houses up for us, as well as for Juan, Jose, and Pancho. We were also well along with building a bunkhouse, cook shack, and a barn that housed a blacksmith shop. They were laid out so each place had some privacy but was in a position to help defend any place that came under attack. We had to handle whatever came along and couldn't look to anyone for help. What with putting up the buildings, fences, and corrals, as well as keeping track of the herds, we had our hands full. Didn't even have time to ride over the whole range that first year.

We'd freighted in furniture and other fixings to make our house comfortable. It was a solid place with four fireplaces for the hard winters I figured we'd face. Our bedroom was off at one end so we'd not be bothered. Elena showed a knack for figuring out what looked good and made the place right livable.

We pulled some men off the building operation and set them to cutting grass. We stacked it then put up fences to keep critters out so it would be ready if the snow got so bad the young stuff couldn't scratch for themselves. The older critters would do okay unless the snow crusted, in which case we'd have to push the herds to the lower range.

Our fall roundup showed a loss of seventy-eight calves and six foals in spite of our constant watch for bears and wolves. It was still a good first summer, and we were almighty thankful.

We kept in touch with the Utes right along, what with them drifting by and us running into them on the range. We set up a time so we could give them the stuff for rent of the land. We met at Chimney Rock, which was as far as we could take wagons. It took four freight rigs to haul the axes and Dutch ovens.

Lame Turkey had spent considerable time sniffing around the ranch all summer. I come up to him three times, lying out in the brush. Always figured he had his eye on Elena. Four other times I saw him sneaking up to the corrals where the stallions and our best mares were kept. It was clear that he'd like to get his hands on the filly or one of the studs. Never gave us a reason to go after him, but he was always close to being on the warpath.

When we made the delivery, he strutted some and made a speech about how he was the greatest hunter in the tribe, which he might've been for all I know. But he ended by saying, "White Eyes Dove is big man when he can shoot deer with boom stick. Let him stay and hunt with bow, like me. Then we see what kind of hunter he is."

Now, I'd spent enough time amongst Indians to know you don't turn your back on a dare like that. Not and keep any kind of league with them. I turned to Ignacio and said, "You got a spare outfit I can borry?"

"We'll find one for you, if you care to join us."

"Can't stay long, but we'll give it a go for a couple days, if you don't care."

"We'll be glad to have you along."

We spent a few hours laying out the places where everybody would hunt, what time, and so on, and then turned in. When we were in bed Elena said, "Can you do it?"

"You mean get a deer with a bow?"

"Yes. The last thing we need is for Lame Turkey to make you look bad."

"I reckon. Always used bows and arrows out in the wilds. They make no racket, and sometimes that's worth your life. Body hear you shoot, they might come looking for trouble. I reckon he'll not show me up too bad."

The toughest part of taking game with any weapon is getting close enough to be sure of your shot. Old Ignacio may have seen to it that I got one of the best spots, and it could be he even had some of the braves sort of push a deer or two my way. It did seem like the animals wanted me to come out on top. About all I had to do was sit quiet and let the critters come to me. By the end of the second day, I'd put down four deer and an elk.

Lame Turkey had three deer and two elk, so we just about came out a draw. That suited me fine but didn't do much for the way he felt. We gave most of the meat to women whose braves had been killed but kept the back straps from the elk. Elena jumped right in and helped the women skin and cut up the carcasses, which made her shine in their eyes.

When we got back to the ranch, I took Juan and Jose, and we went after our own winter meat. I also took Charlie Jimson with us. Wanted him to be in on the hunt and also see what was required of the horses so he could do the best possible job of training them.

I remembered his reaction to shooting an antelope. When I put him on a bull elk with seven points on each side, he started shaking like a leaf. The bull was accommodating and stood till Charlie could get a solid rest for his rifle. I've never seen a man as tickled as he was when that elk went down with his first shot. He was scared silly when I said he had to butcher that big rascal, but I talked him through it, and when it was all done, we had one happy fellow.

We returned after we'd taken five bull elk and three big, four-point bucks. It was early, the sun just peeking over the ridge back of us, but the crew was milling around the corrals like a herd fixing to stampede.

"Something's wrong down there," I said. "Bring the string on in, I'm scooting."

The *grullo* must have jumped twenty feet, I jabbed him so hard, and we made the barn quicker'n it takes to tell.

"What's wrong?" I asked as Elena ran toward me.

"The filly's gone. Somebody stole her last night."

"Pancho, get everybody back here at the barn," I yelled. "Don't let anybody go riding off till I have a look at what tracks there are."

There'd already been too much stirring about, and I had to go clear out in the trees before I could make out much. There was no doubt she'd been stolen. I found where he'd left his horse and gone in afoot. Couldn't tell if he'd ridden her back or not, but it looked like he'd led her to where his pony had been tied, then got on his horse and took off with her following along. He'd not been in a rush about it, because the horses had gone at a walk.

"Put my saddle on that four-year-old stud," I hollered. "I want a fast horse for this."

The stallion was ready by the time I got to the barn. Juan and Jose were there. "Spread the crew out and make a swing to the west. Take it easy and watch for the trail to see if he cuts north or south. I'm going to get on his track, and by gum, whoever it is, he'll not be keeping that filly."

"Got any idea who did it?" asked Juan.

"Looks like Lame Turkey's footprints. Didn't recognize the horse tracks. 'Twas an Indian, though—unshod pony."

"You take care. That booger's got it in for you. He's apt to lay up, like a crippled bear, and wait for you to show. Might even double back on his trail. Want me to come along?" asked Jose. "I'd like to get him in my sights. Never could stand that rascal."

"No, you can do more good keeping the men strung out right. Leave some of them here to watch. I'm surprised he went for the filly instead of Elena. He'd like nothing better than to haul her off. He could be using the horse to draw us away, then creep back for what he's really after."

Elena said, "You're not going after him alone, are you?"

"I don't want anybody to worry about. I do better alone. If there's somebody else along, I'm tempted to depend on them to do things the way I would, and that almost never happens. If I'm alone I know how everything is done, and it's better that way."

"At least pray with me before you leave," she said.

"That's worth doing. LORD, we'll talk more later, but for now I ask that you give me wisdom so I can catch the person who took our filly and bring her back safely. I also ask that you give Elena peace while I'm gone. We trust you to do this and thank you for it. In Jesus's name. Amen."

She said, "LORD, please bring Reuben and that filly back safely." We kissed and I ran for the barn.

That thoroughbred was ready to go, and we made tracks for a while. There'd been no effort to hide the trail, which didn't make sense. I rode hard, the tracks plain enough so I could follow at a lope. Things changed when we hit the Piedra. The trail headed down the rocky slope to the stream and never reached bottom. Took me the better part of an hour to circle far enough to pick it up again, and I'd lost all the ground I'd gained earlier. I was praying full time and am sure it would have been even more difficult otherwise.

Seems he never figured I could pick up his tracks again, and it made him careless. I saw where he'd switched to the filly, and then it was an easy thing to follow, what with the extra weight on her back making her shod hooves dig in deeper than before. She was a joy to ride, and he tried her out some, going into a trot, then a gallop, which tore the trail up so I could go off to the side and still be sure of not losing him.

It was so I could've put the stallion in a run without losing the trail, but it's not my nature to go tearing into a fracas like that. I eased along, knowing he had no mind to eat the horse. Before long, he swung off to the north, headed for the tall timber, and I knew we were in for a long day. Or week, maybe.

He knew the country, and from that point on, he took advantage of that knowledge. If the filly hadn't been shod, it's possible he'd have given me the slip, but the shoes kept leaving scrapes on rocks and cutting into logs and dirt. If he'd stayed on his pony he'd have done better, but he didn't, and it sure never troubled me. His heading off like that was worrisome, though. It showed that he wasn't so sure of not being trailed, after all, and would more than likely try to draw me into a trap.

I slowed down and did as much looking ahead as watching for his tracks. If he set up to shoot me from the brush, I'd ought to be able to pick out where it might happen. Wasted a lot of time circling likely looking spots, then having to locate the trail again when none of them checked out. The sixth guess was a good one, though. I located what looked to be a decent place to lay up and take a body by surprise, then took off up the mountain so as to by-pass it. Rode over a ridge, went far enough west to be sure I'd not run into the ambush, then struck back to find the trail again.

Had to look quite a spell before I saw where he'd sure enough swung off and headed back alongside where he'd just come, off where it wouldn't show to anyone following him. When I was certain sure he'd doubled back, I set off afoot. Now we were getting close to a showdown, and if I didn't want to be the loser, I'd best settle in and be a better sneak than he was. I cat-footed along a ways, sort of ghosting my way, nigh onto being sure where he'd gone but not certain enough to bet my hair on it. I felt the ground for sticks and stuff that would be noisy, never looking down, but making sure when my weight went down there'd be nothing snapping. Hadn't gone more'n a half mile till I spotted the ponies tied and waiting. The spot I figured he'd gone to was another quarter mile along the slope, so I sort of split the distance up and scooted to where I could almost see where I guessed he'd be and still keep the horses located.

I crept into a pocket of rocks where a spring freshet had washed out the dirt and spilled a mess of branches and other trash. It was no easy thing to sneak into the midst of that jumble without raising a racket, but I got it done and had myself as nice a spot to wait as you could ever plan out. There was no way to get to me from the rear, and I could see everything for fifty feet in every other direction. The horses were in plain sight, and he'd have to get where I could see him if he went back to them.

Trouble is, I ain't the only one who can think. That fellow laid out the rest of the day, clear into the dark of night. My belly growled, my throat parched, and my bones ached from setting in that rock pile. I had to figure he'd spotted me and would try for me in the dark, or else had waited to go back to the horses. Either way, we had ourselves a guessing game. If he'd seen me, he could either come after me or just slip back to the horses and try to get away. If he was just waiting around hoping I'd still show on the trail, there was no telling how long before he moved.

Now, setting in a rock pile trying to outsmart a horse thief may sound exciting, but let me say loud and clear, it's not my idea of fun. But then I'd not come out to have a picnic, so why holler. There was lots of time to study on what he might do, and I didn't think he was having much more fun than I was. No telling what kind of a hole he'd set up in, maybe worse'n where I was. It came up cloudy, making things sort of like the inside of a mine. It had been black earlier, with no sign of a moon, but the clouds blotted out the stars, too.

The wind started moaning in the trees off to the north, and before long it was shaking things around me, scattering leaves and whipping branches like it was serious about storming. There were two sides to that, too. It made it so I could think about sneaking down close to the horses, since any stir I made would be pretty much covered by the wind. The flip side was that I couldn't see for shucks, and he might be creeping up to me, easy as not. One thing I did was to move enough to ease the ache in my legs and backside. I've been in lots of places where it was more comfortable to pray but not many where it seemed more important, so I had one of the longest times with the LORD I've ever had. I reckon it was what made it so I could last it out.

The hours sure poked along. There not being any stars, it was hard to tell how much time went by, but I got a belly full of doing nothing and started snaking down to the ponies. The wind did make it hard to tell what was which, far as noise went, but I wasn't running no race. Seemed like an hour, but more likely it was half that, before I made out the horses. I was on my hands and knees, just barely moving, and it was easy to fit my back against a tree trunk, get my rear under me, and there I was, ready for him to make his play. One thing I'd figured for sure was that he'd not go anywhere without that filly, after all the trouble he'd been to.

The rain came, and I sat it out, making sure my rifle stayed dry. Can't let a thing like that chase you to the house. It only lasted half the night, anyway; then things settled down to get cold. I've spent a couple of worse nights, but not more'n that. If I was cold, he must be, too, and there was no use crying over it.

Just about thought he'd fooled me when I spied him, like a piece of cloud flitting through the trees. He was coming from where I'd hid out in the rocks. He must have been disappointed at not finding me there and figured I'd left for good. Leastwise, he wasn't too cautious, even skidded on some wet leaves— something I'd never seen an Indian do. I was surprised to see that he was packing a rifle. That put a whole new shade to the deal. He walked up to his horse, bold as brass, spoke to him, and started untying him. He was off to the side, so I could shoot without hurting either horse. I guess I'm not very bright, but it singes my scruples to shoot even a body like him, unless he's had a warning.

First, I moved that rifle so it was pointing right at his belly button; then I thumbed that old hammer back. When it clicked, you'd have thought a bolt of lightning had hit him dead center. He jumped two feet, seemed like, straight up, and came down facing me, and I was looking down the barrel of his gun. My bullet took him in the throat, and I figured we could change his name to Plucked Turkey.

Took me a while to calm those ponies, especially his. He wouldn't have nothing to do with me for a spell, but I finally got him settled down. Had it to do all over again when I tried to sling that dead body onto his back. Hardly seemed worth the effort, but I did want Ignacio to see what had gone on. When I had the body bundled up so it couldn't slip off, I hopped onto the filly and rode to the stallion.

There was a slicker and enough stuff to make a meal behind the cantle of my saddle, so I set about to have my first meal in a day and a half. A fire helped shove the cold away, and a pot of coffee comforted the inside of me. Bacon and a cold biscuit fixed me up to ride on home. Ignacio wasn't too happy when I dumped the dead brave in his lap, but there wasn't much he could say. I didn't stay around to palaver; just said what happened and rode out. If he wanted to jaw about it, we'd do it after we both had time to cool off.

CHAPTER THIRTEEN

A month later, with a storm moving in, I sent riders to every corner of the range. Wanted to be sure things were shaped up in case it came up a real blizzard. I chose to ride the upper reaches of the park, where some of the best cows had settled in. Took a couple of hours to get there, and not a cow in sight.

The natural thing in a case like that is to look for tracks, and sure enough, those cows had been herded away from there. I'd seen the horse tracks somewhere before but couldn't place them right off. Four riders had pushed the herd off toward the high country, which made no sense at all. Most anybody would know there was no chance of going across the mountains that time of year. Rustlers would have taken them over the ridge to the east, then tried to slip down the other side where we'd not see them.

I sifted along, staying off to the side, and ended up on the slope east of the Piedra. The wind was starting to get serious, but I was curious. It was a half hour before I saw anything. The cows had been shoved a couple of miles up the west side of the Piedra and were drifting back toward the park where they'd been. I got out my glasses and searched the area, and before long spotted three horses in some timber close to a rockslide. The slide ran down almost to the creek, so there was no way to go up or down that side of the valley without passing along between the slide and the river. The riders were laid up in the rocks, watching back the way they'd come.

Looked to me like somebody had set up to bushwhack whoever came after those cows. I don't make out to be a mind reader, but there were a few things about the setup that bothered me. First, where was the fourth man? Four riders had moved the cows from the park, and now there were only three horses and as many men. The other one had to be somewhere. I glassed the whole country and found nary a sign of him.

I wanted to go down and put a bullet in those snakes but held off to mull it over. It was also a great time to pray. Finally decided I'd be better off heading home to make sure the fourth guy wasn't back there raising a ruckus. The more I thought of that likelihood the less I liked it and ended up in a dither. I watch things sort of close when I'm moving about and had seen nobody on my way up, but that meant very little. Many's the time I've watched a man ride by not a hundred feet away from where I stood, with him never knowing he was closer than a mile to anybody.

Well, sir, I headed my cayuse in the general direction of home, looking for a way off that hillside. Rode the rim for maybe five miles before I picked up a trail that led along a bench. It was easy to follow, so I kicked that horse into a lope and made some time. Now and again I spotted some old blazes on trees, but it didn't impress me at the time. The Indians had told me the only trail through there was the one I'd followed down from the high country. At the moment, the only thing I wanted was to get to the house quick as possible. I had a strong hunch that whoever was involved in moving the cows had more in mind than what I'd seen.

The trail eventually cut up over the ridge away from the park, so I left it and worked down through the trees. It was fairly open there, and I soon hit a game trail, and before long was in the park a couple of miles from the house. The storm was moving in fast, packing dark with it, though it was only mid-afternoon. I rammed spurs home, and my horse spurted across the park like his tail was afire.

I'd sent every rider out, so the only ones at the house were the women, the man who cooked for the bunkhouse crew, the blacksmith, and Charlie. The carpenters had left a week earlier.

I was packing a dread that this setup was a threat to Elena. If anything happened to her, all we had would be worthless to me. I got real serious with the LORD about then. I'm certain sure he knows how I feel, but I didn't want to leave any doubt, so I made sure he knew I wanted him watching over her.

The wind had come up a man-sized blow. The noise covered the sound of my approach, even at a dead run. At the barn, I stepped off, which caused the horse to set down on his heels and slide to a stop. Once on the ground, I settled down to sniff out anything that might be out of whack outside the house. Using the cover of the barn and corrals, I slipped to the back of the house and went in through a door that led to quarters for the women who helped Elena. It was quiet—way too quiet. A sixty-foot hall ran through there and opened into the kitchen. It was time to be cooking the evening meal, but I heard nothing. The house was built of ten-inch logs, so no wind noise came inside. The place sounded mighty like nobody was to home. I'd seen smoke from the chimney, so the women had been there recently.

I slipped into the kitchen, scared of what I might find. It stood empty as a dry pond, saying loud and clear that something was mighty wrong. Somebody had probably put the women where they could be kept quiet. Might even be a guard with them. The dining room or parlor would be a likely place, and I didn't want to waste time getting to our part of the house, so I went back outside and around to the office, which was next to our bedroom.

Elena'd spent a lot of time planning our quarters. As a result we ended up with a set of rooms that were joined so we could move about freely without going into a hall, but still made it so we could shut each room off from the others when we wanted to. An outside door led to the office. A double fireplace opened into the office on one side and the bedroom on the other, but the openings were offset so only the most heedful visitor would notice. Alongside the fireplace were doors that connected to the bedroom and a small parlor. The bedroom opened to the parlor and to a setup that had closets and a room with a mirrored wall and a table where Elena did her magic with hairbrush and other gadgets. With all the doors open, we could move about and maintain contact easily, but the office was usually closed unless one of us was working there.

I unlocked the door then waited until the wind died down, hoping to get inside without warning anyone who might be in there. All the doors were closed, but you can't be too careful. Light showed at the bottom of the door to the parlor, and less light came under the door to the bedroom. From that, I was almost sure that if anyone was in the rooms, they were in the parlor, but figured that the door between bedroom and parlor was open. I pulled off my boots and moved into the bedroom; then, watchful as an Indian snaking up to a prize buffalo, I slipped toward the door to the parlor.

I heard Elena's voice and knew immediately that she was mad as a wet hen. Hearing her raised my spirits considerably, though. If she'd been hurt, her tone would have been different, so I could still hope to keep her from harm.

"There's still time for you to leave before my husband gets here. If you do, I promise to keep him from following. But if you're here when he returns, you know as well as I do that you have no chance of living to see another day," she said.

"That skunk won't be coming, and you'd just as well get used to the idea. He's already been shot by my men when he followed some cows we drove off. I made sure he was going after them before I came here. You've got no more husband, and I'm going to take his place."

I couldn't recall ever hearing his voice before.

He continued, "If you treat me nice, you'll not get hurt, and we'll get along just dandy. But it really don't matter to me. Either way, soon as my men show up, we'll take care of the rest of your crew and then you and me're gonna finish what we started that other time. You just come on over here and snuggle up to me while we're waiting. No use putting it off any longer."

"How many men did you leave to kill my husband?"

"Three, the ones who were with me in Santa Fe. And Pancho will come in with us when he sees how things are. He never could stand up to me."

"Do you really think the four of you can handle our crew?"

"We'll take them by surprise, hit them from cover. Don't worry; I've got it all figured out. Now get over here, like I told you to. It'll be lots easier on you than if I have to come after you."

"If you touch me again, you can count on hanging for it. I talked Reuben out of it last time, but he was right, and I won't stand in his way again."

"You're the dumbest woman I ever did meet. Can't you understand? That man of yours is lying up there, already starting to rot. My men'll be here any minute now, and then you'll maybe get the idea."

"You left three men to kill my husband? Why did you run away? Why not stay and help them? Is it your style to fight only women?"

"Go ahead and flap your lips. Ain't gonna do you no good. But I'll take the sass out of you quick enough, once your crew's out of the way. In fact, I think I'll give you a sample here an' now. Get over here, and I mean now."

"You're the one who doesn't understand. Reuben would never ride into a trap. I've watched him too long to think he would be fooled into following cows into an ambush. You need to realize what kind of man you're dealing with. He's the most careful person I've ever seen—always on the lookout. Any trap you set is bound to fail. By now, he's discovered your trap, and he'll be here soon. You had better be gone before he arrives. The other thing you don't understand is that God watches over Reuben and will never allow anyone like you harm him. I enjoy that same protection."

"You do more talking than anybody I ever saw. I said to get over here, and I ain't gonna say it again. Come here, or I'll come over there and use this knife. You won't be so purty with your face carved up, but maybe you'll do less jawing."

I almost couldn't take having to stand and listen to all that without doing anything. I couldn't take a chance on him seeing me until I knew exactly where they were and how easy it would be for him to reach her. Having them talking was the best thing I could hope for. The parlor was laid out so half of the furniture faced the bedroom door, and even with no light in the bedroom, if I moved to where I could see him, there was a good chance he'd spot me, too. Besides, as long as they were talking, his attention was on her. Much as I hated what he was saying, it was better than lots of things that could have been happening. Then, too, their voices helped me locate them, and I was almost sure that they were on opposite sides of the room, with Elena in a chair that faced the bedroom.

"You'll have to do more than talk," she said, and her voice was noticeably closer.

"Don't you try to run away, you little… You go through that door, we'll have our get-acquainted party right now."

"You'll have to catch me first," she said and scooted into the room where I was and on through to the office.

As she went by, I said softly, "Good girl. Stay in there."

With her out of the way, I stepped into the doorway just as he was jumping up from the sofa and turning to go after her. He was maybe fifty pounds heavier than when we'd last met, and it had done nothing for his looks. He stopped short, mouth sagging open.

"How—" he started. Then turned and scrambled toward the hall door.

"Hold it right there," I yelled.

He paid me no heed and made it through the door. I could've shot him, but I didn't want to mess up our place. I turned back to the bedroom just as Elena burst through and into my arms.

"I knew you'd come," she said. "I wouldn't let myself believe otherwise."

"His scheme wasn't a very good one. A kid could've seen through it. We've still got him to take care of, though. Can't let him off this time."

"I tried to warn him, but he wouldn't listen."

"Yeah, I heard some of it."

"How long have you been here?"

"Couple minutes. Was trying to get to where I could see both you and him. Didn't want to bust in there without knowing who was where. Too much chance of his getting hold of you."

"What will you do now?"

"Soon as I get my boots on, I've got to find him and put him away."

"Wait for the crew. They'll be here soon. We've got to get the women, too. He locked them in the storeroom."

"Wondered about that but couldn't waste time looking."

She headed out through the parlor, and I said, "Hold up, honey. That feller may still be in the house. Let me go."

"I'm going with you."

We started through the house with me leading the way, gun in hand. When we were about halfway to the kitchen, a gust of wind came whooshing down the hall.

"He just went outside," I said. "Now he's in trouble. That's a man-sized storm out there. No sense chasing after him tonight. Unless he runs into some of our men, we'll let him go till the storm's past."

"Let's get the others loose, then," she said and led off to the kitchen.

"Hold on, honey," I said, "there's always a chance that booger didn't leave. You stay behind me."

We didn't dawdle but made sure nobody was around as we went from room to room. When we reached the kitchen, she hurried to open the door to the storeroom. The women and two of the men were huddled together.

"Where's Charlie?" I asked.

"Oh, Marse Rube, yuh shudda hollered fore yuh opened de doah," he said and stepped out of the corner beside the door. "I wuz all set ta bash sumbody's haid in." In his hand was a post that had been set in the floor to hold up shelving. A pile of goods and shelving lay in a corner.

"Should've knowed you'd take care of things," I said.

"Whar is dat booger?"

"Outside, seems like, an' I don't envy him none."

None of the crew had seen any of the outlaws. The storm had struck with a vengeance, so we could do nothing but wait and see if they were still around later. It was late when everyone was satisfied there was no longer any danger and settled down for the night.

After we were in bed, I said, "You'll never know how scared I was that something would happen to you before I could get here."

"I guess nothing has ever scared me like it did when he came into the kitchen, pushing Charlie in front of him with his hands in the air. Then when he started talking about your being dead, I just about flew into little pieces."

"I thought being away from you last spring made me realize how much you mean to me, but today did it even better," I said.

"When you went after Lame Turkey, I was worried almost sick, but not like today. I guess Kit was sort of right when he said we would be in danger here."

"He never was one to say that things are worse than they really are. This sure does make me think on it a little more, though.

We've got the start of what I've always dreamed of, but it wouldn't be worth a wore out boot if you weren't here with me."

We went on like that for quite a spell, and she finally said, "We need to have a baby. That way, if something does happen, at least I'll still have part of you."

"I don't know. That would sure cut into our time together. You ever seen how much care a little one takes?"

"I know. I planned to wait a few more years before suggesting it, but this situation's made me think differently. As Kit said, I could be a widow awfully young."

"We'll pray about it, anyway. In fact, let's do it right now. I haven't really taken time to thank the LORD for the way he handled things."

It was almost an hour later when we said the final amen and spent some more quality time together.

The storm raged for four days and nights, and we couldn't get out even to check the stock. When it finally blew itself out, at least four feet of snow lay on the level, with drifts up to twenty feet deep where an obstacle caused it to pile up. The cattle had drifted with the wind and gone into the shelter of timber on the east side of the ranch. We lost a few calves that got caught out in the open, but it was a small loss considering the force of the storm. The herds moseyed back into the park, found open places where the wind had blown the snow clear, and were soon browsing on the cured grass as though nothing had happened. Within a week the sun had melted the snow off half the park, and you would never have guessed we'd gone through a big storm.

As soon as we were sure the cattle were all right, I took most of the crew and went looking for the outlaws. None of us found any sign until we rode over to the Ute camp a week later. It seems that three of them straggled in the second day of the storm, and the other one made it to them that night. The Indians took care of them until the storm broke then headed them for Santa Fe. Juan, Jose, and I trailed them for five hours, and there was no doubt they kept going. Jose was in favor of chasing them as long as it took, but Juan and I had other ideas. As long as they were gone, we could forget about them until spring. Nobody in his right mind would be staying out in the timber during winter.

We spent the next three weeks making sure all the herds were on decent feed and that they were scattered enough to keep from damaging the grass. It was tough work. There were places where we had to either fight through drifts or ride a long way around the deeper snow. We were able to get it all under control, with every animal on good feed.

I came in from the final day of moving cows, tired as I'd ever been. It was full dark, and I may have given my horse less attention than usual before I trudged to the house.

Elena met me in the kitchen. She kissed me then fixed a plate for each of us, placed the meals on a tray, and said, "Let's eat in our rooms."

I finished washing up and followed her, which was the best part of the day. I have no idea how she makes walking such a beautiful event, but it always is. It doesn't matter if she's ahead of me, beside me, or coming toward me; there's nothing any more pleasant.

"Did you have a hard day?" she asked.

"It was just a long one. I think we've got the cattle where we want them now. That was a big snow storm, and we had to move a lot of cows from one place to another. It looks like we'll be all right if we don't get another bad storm, though. We need to be thankful for that."

"We've got something else to be thankful about, darling."

"What's that?"

She put the tray down, turned, and put her arms around me. That's always a great thing to have happen, so I just naturally kissed her. She placed her mouth next to my ear and said, "*We're going to have a baby!*"

I pulled back a ways so I could see her. She had as bright a smile as I'd ever seen. If I'd not been happy before, that did it. I took a deep breath and said, "With a ma like you, he'll be the happiest kid on earth. I reckon God'll have to teach me how to be a pa."

"You'll be the best daddy any child ever had. *You're a natural!* A man who loves calves and colts like you do will have no problem with a baby."

"You're as happy as I've ever seen you, so I reckon it's great. I'll maybe get used to the idea by the time he gets here. I love you, Ma."

"I love you, Pa! Kiss me; then let's eat."

Nothing ever tasted better... The food was good, too.

CHAPTER FOURTEEN

In February we started getting ready to head for Abilene again. The animals had stayed in top condition all winter. It took us a month to gather and sort them, even though we'd loose-herded them all the time. We had almost no problems with Indians. They seemed to be entertained by the amount of work we put into caring for the critters.

We made up two herds of steers and two of cows that looked to be barren. Juan was in charge of the steers, with a top hand to watch over each of the herds when he was away. Jose took the cows in the same manner. The steers went out first, with two days between them to leave room for each herd to run without getting into the other. It's bad enough to have trouble with one bunch without letting it spread.

While Abilene lay to the northeast, the mountains forced us to go south almost to Santa Fe before we could head east. I wanted to stay west of the trail that comes up from Texas, so we cut north over Raton Pass into Colorado, hitting the Purgatoire River where it flows down out of the LaVeta country. That river was named by a Frenchman, and he said it "Puh-ga-twah," which cowboys made into "Picketwire." Most folks ended up calling it the Purgatory, but it's all one and the same. Since it runs northeast into the Arkansas, we sort of followed it until we were close to the big river then cut west, crossing the Purgatoire so as to swim the Arkansas upstream from where the two joined up. Then we struck off northeast again, using feeder streams that ran into the Arkansas for watering the herds. There were no cow outfits in that region, so we spread the herds out so they sort of went alongside each other. Buffalo grass was lush and tall, and the doggies kept putting on flesh as we traveled. We had rains time to time, which freshened things and settled the dust for a few hours. The best part was that the rains kept the streams running so we had few dry camps. Antelope were in sight most every day, buffalo were often close by, and we were trailed by Indians several times. They'd no reason to bother us, with all that game around, so we stayed alert and doubled guard when they were close but left them alone. My big concern was that they would try for the horse herd. We'd be in some kind of trouble if we lost a bunch of riding stock.

One pack of braves shadowed us a couple of weeks and finally made a try for the southern-most remuda. That was one of Juan's herds, and he wasn't much bothered. He had some daredevils, and they seemed to look forward to a brush with Indians. I wasn't there when they made their try, but we lost nary horse nor man, while at least three of them carried lead when they hightailed out of there. From what the boys told me, they hit about a half hour before it was time to bring the cavvy in for the boys to cut out mounts for the day, and the wrangler was already pushing them toward the wagon. Juan had been leery the evening before and had posted a couple of extra guards with the horses. When the raid started, the extra hands were in place to give them a surprise, and it left us in good shape—for the moment.

One thing about most Indians, they don't hold a grudge over a deal like that. They'll beat you if they can, and if not, will back off and wait for a better day. That bunch paid a high price and got nothing, so they rode off and let us alone. A white man might have got all proud and ornery and maybe gone on pestering us.

There was a dry stretch some two hundred miles into Colorado, or maybe even in Kansas for all I know. We went two days without water and came to a streambed that was still damp, so we knew it had been running recently. We stopped the herd about a mile back and cut out maybe five hundred steers. We drove them into the creek bottom then pushed them back and forth, up and down the creek for close to an hour. After their hooves had worked that sandy bottom into a mud hole a half mile long and knee deep to a tall Indian, we drove that bunch on east a ways and let them graze for a couple of hours to let the mud settle then brought the rest of the herd in to drink. It was a trick I learned from Charlie Goodnight and one that saved the day many a time. A herd really gets touchy when they go without water more than a day or two.

Cowboys are rambunctious critters, regardless of the color of skin they wear. Most don't think they are horseback if they don't have to rodeo some every time they saddle up. They call it "working the kinks out," and it's a morning ritual. Our crews sort of smiled up their sleeves when they saw how tame those horses of mine were. I had ten personal mounts divided among the herds in order to do all the traveling it took to keep in touch with the four herds. Each had been hand picked before we started the gather, and there wasn't a one that ever bucked with me. The grins were gone by the time we got back home, because each of my horses had proven he would stay with me all day and do whatever was needed. I never had to worry about them spooking at a booger in a bush or shying from an imaginary danger when I was trying to get some work done. They were ready to go when I stepped on and stayed that way until we off-saddled at night. I'll have a go at staying on a bucking horse if something goes wrong but don't want to get broke up just to prove I can ride. Time or two, I let a rope get under my horse's tail, which leads to all kinds of excitement, but it's been a while since I was that careless. It takes something like that to make one of mine break in two. After they watched my horses, several men were trying to get their mounts so they were more like mine. Several of them had made real progress before we got to Abilene, which was still the end of the tracks.

Boredom and dust were about the worst things we faced on that drive. It may sound like high adventure to take a herd over the trail, but let me say, it gets tiresome. The days are all alike—with breakfast under the stars and supper the same. When dawn comes at four o'clock and sunset near nine at night, it makes for long days in the saddle. There's the roping of the day's horses, saddling, getting the herd lined out, then following them all day long. The men riding drag had the worst of it, and we rotated that duty so nobody had to eat so much dust every day. The best men were assigned to ride point, which was the most comfortable but required the most work keeping the herd headed the right direction. Every herd has a leader who's first out of the chute in the morning, always ready to go. There are also those that always bring up the rear guard and have to be prodded to keep up. The heat from several thousand bodies made those spring days awful hot at times. We always switched mounts at noon.

The wind was worse than anything else. Northern New Mexico seems to have a constant wind, March though May, and the plains of Colorado and Kansas are in a direct path from whatever fan the Almighty uses to stir the air. It calmed down most nights, but there were times we didn't even get that relief. After several weeks of continual wind, man and beast are ready to blow up. It became an enemy of the worst kind, constantly hounding us, and there was no way to fight back. If you were alone, as I often was, it kept a noisy, dusty cloud all about. Around the herd, especially downwind, the dust was an added weapon it used to beat down your spirits. A lot of that plains country is subjected to year-round wind, and it's hard to see why anyone would live there. I guess those who do have never been in the quiet peace of the mountains. When we made camp, we were careful to select the downwind side of any cover.

A bright spot on the trip was the arrival of wild geese on their spring flight to the north. They hit the river by the thousands, and we took advantage of it to vary our diet. I had a Colt revolving shotgun, and it was pure pleasure to get into a flock of the big birds and bring down enough of them to feed the crews on fat, juicy meat—some of the best you'll ever stuff in your mouth.

It was gently rolling country, with no large watersheds to concern us but plenty of small streams. Greed is an awful thing if it's allowed to go unchecked. I've seen places from Texas to Montana that were literally destroyed by men who thought range capable of carrying five thousand cattle would feed many more. The result is always the destruction of the range.

The only real excitement we had was about a hundred and fifty miles from Abilene, where a bunch of crooks tried to cut one of the herds. There were six of them, one wearing a badge, and they rode up as we were eating breakfast. Most of the boys were cross-legged on the ground, having beef, biscuits, and coffee before heading out to the herd. I was on the far side of the chuck wagon when I heard them ride up.

"Who's bossin' this outfit?" a voice called out.

"What you want with him?" Juan asked.

"We bin gettin' complaints 'bout y'all pickin' up cows that ain't yours. Gonna cut the herd."

This sounded sort of familiar, so I reached over and slipped my rifle from its scabbard before stepping around the wagon. I knew him, and he knew me.

"You still running your shorthorn games?" I asked. "I figured you'd have learned by now."

These fellows were running an old game that I'd already encountered, so when I walked around that wagon, the working end of that rifle was pointed in the general direction of the leader. It didn't take but a second for him to remember me. When his gun cleared leather, I shot him and covered the others before they knew what had hit them.

"What's the idea, mister?" said the fellow who was just to the left of the man I'd shot. "You're in real trouble now, shootin' a sheriff. We don't want trouble, but you can't get away with that."

"I reckon you didn't notice, he drew first. Look at him. His gun is out. We'd met before. You know, well's I do, he ain't no sheriff, and if you're anything close to smart you'll take him and leave the country. I see a couple more of you who were there the other time. I see you again, it's going to be open season for killing skunks. Ride out, before we get our dander up."

They turned in a hurry, and I said, "Don't leave his carcass here for us to mess with. Just leave that gun alone and take off the badge. You're through playing games with it."

Two of them got off and flung the body on his horse, and then they all left in a rush.

The boys wanted to hear the story.

"Some of this same outfit hit a herd I was pushing into Dakota Territory some years back. They come up with the same story, and I knew it was a tinhorn trick, because we'd just sold the herd and had run a complete tally on it ten days earlier. Hadn't been near any other cows since. The fellow leading them was a big, mean-looking bird who thought he had an easy thing. When he didn't get his way, he came back at night and tried to catch me coming away from the fire, thinking I couldn't see good, I reckon. Learned early on not to look into fires and could see him as well as he could me. When he went for his gun, I jumped aside and managed to get him. He got me, too, but only through the leg. The rest of the trip was a mite unpleasant, though. Reckon I seemed sorta hair-triggered, shooting like I done just now, but the good LORD says, 'Fellow lives by the sword'll die by the same,' or something like that. Man drags out a gun, he better be ready to have somebody shooting back at him."

Juan said, "You said something about a shorthorn. What'd you mean?"

"You know how most folks in Texas think the only cow worth owning is a longhorn. They assume that anything else has no quality. It's got so lots of folks call anything or anybody a shorthorn if they don't stack up to their standard. I figured it fit those guys as much as anyone I'd ever seen."

"I can't argue with you about that. That was as poor a bunch as I've ever run into."

When I reckoned we were close to Abilene, I told Juan and Jose to loaf along five more days, then get on some good grass, and stick there till I got in touch. I took off to find out who was buying and what the market was like. Only a couple of herds were ahead of us, and they'd been brought up the previous year and wintered in the Indian Nation southwest of Abilene. Buyers were there, though, and anxious to talk then go look at our herds. I did a sashay around and looked over the other herds. Neither of them had cattle as good as ours, and they weren't uniform in size. When I learned that they'd brought twelve dollars a head, I knew we were on green grass. After arranging for three buyers to meet us, I headed back and met our cattle five days from railhead.

We sold for prices ranging from fifteen dollars down to twelve. With a total of almost twenty-seven thousand head, we had us a good year's business. After delivering the herds, the boys had a night in town, and then we headed back.

Abilene was a roaring place, with all the usual ways to part a man and his pay. It seems like whiskey, gambling, and fancy women are never far away when money starts showing. Most of our crew was young and reckless, but we left with everybody, and only a few of them worse for wear. Juan and Jose kept a pretty tight rein on their crews, and I made them leave all their guns at camp.

Other herds showed while we were getting shut of ours, and the prices went down fast. In a few days there were sixty herds reported, and the town turned sure enough wild. The herds were a sight, with close to two hundred thousand cattle in an area not twenty miles square. It takes a special breed of man to handle the tough life of the trail, and when they got to town after weeks of loneliness, pressure had built to the point of busting and often blew up when mixed with rotgut whiskey. Memories of the drunk Indians who killed my family kept me from ever wanting to drink, but most who trailed herds to Kansas had no such qualms. It made for a lively, noisy town.

As soon as the last cows were delivered, we headed for Texas to replace what we'd sold. With nothing but horses to handle, we made about sixty miles a day. We met hundreds of herds headed for the railroad, and I was floored by the size of the market.

We located two brands for sale intact and made deals for both, as well as for a herd of young steers from a rancher who held out for too much from buyers who were there earlier. He lost several thousand dollars by being greedy but was a good sport about it and had a laugh at his own expense. He said, "I'll make it up next year. In the meantime, you're welcome to them."

While most of the crew started gathering cattle on the ranches where we'd bought the entire brands, a skeleton crew set about branding the steers from the other ranch. As soon as we finished the gather, we sorted out the cattle that could travel at a good pace and made up three herds, each one with over four thousand head and started them up the trail. Juan was over them, while Jose handled two bunches of cows and calves. I took three horses and a mule and took off for home.

I would've liked to stay east of Santa Fe and touch in Taos but knew that if anything serious had happened at the ranch, Elena would have gone to Luiz's place if she could. So I veered west and stopped for a quick visit with Luiz and Margarita then made tracks for the ranch and Elena. A man gets truly lonely after he's used to being with a real woman. There were so many things I wanted to know and see that it was impossible to keep from pushing those ponies as hard as they could stand. I changed mounts twice a day, which took the sting out of the fast pace, and none of the animals were hurt by the trip.

I knew home was close when I rode into the first park and saw some of our cattle at a stream. There was an abundance of grass, and the stock was in excellent shape. I met one of our riders and stopped to talk.

"Spread the word. I want everything pushed north and east of headquarters. We're bringing five herds from Texas and don't want any of them mixing with the cows that are here now. These young ones ain't been exposed to Texas fever, and they'll catch it sure if the herds mix before the ones coming up have been through a winter here. Ever see what the fever does to a cow?"

"No, what does it do?"

"Makes them so feverish their skins actually crack open. There's no cure for it. All you can do's stand an' watch them die. It's no fun."

I passed the hot springs just shy of noon and pushed on to the mesa top. When the house came into view, I spurred hard and did a running dismount then jumped to the porch. Elena came dashing out the door and into my arms as soon as I hit the ground. I was very aware of her condition and didn't hug her with my usual vigor.

She said, "Squeeze me! I won't break."

It didn't take much to get me started, and we made up for lost time.

"I may never leave again," I said. "It's too hard, being away from you. I love you, sweetheart. Let me see you. You feeling all right?" All this spaced between kisses, with her talking at the same time. I finally said, "Maybe we best get inside and you can tell me what's been going on."

Later we went to look things over. Pancho and Charlie had been busy, and we had a fine crop of calves and foals. The grass looked even taller than the previous year, and the stock was doing fine. We wouldn't market any of our young stuff for at least two years, and it might be four before most of them were ready, but we were in a good position to wait, with the profits from the current sales to add to our resources.

CHAPTER FIFTEEN

We made some history by bringing in horse-drawn equipment and cutting several hundred acres of that strong grass. It cured into some of the best hay you could want. Ignacio came close to boogering over that deal.

It was just two days after we put the first crews to mowing the hay that he and about twenty of his braves came storming onto the place. I knew right off that we were close to having a first-class shindig, because all of them were armed to the teeth.

"Get down and set," I invited. "Wasn't expecting you, but we'll put on a pot."

"We didn't come to eat. What are you doing to our grass?"

I knew when a Ute don't want to eat or palaver before he gets to the matter at hand, it's a right serious affair.

"We cut hay last year. What's the problem?"

"You never cut this way! That machine go 'snick, snick, snick,' and grass falls like there's a million whistle pigs eating on it," he said. "You'll clean out those parks, and the deer and elk will go hungry all winter. What will we eat then?"

"Hey, amigo, just because we're cutting it fast don't mean we'll take any more than we have before. This is lots easier on the men doing the cutting. We want to get the hay stacked pronto in case a storm blows up. Fact is we'll probably not have to cut as much, if we can get it stacked real soon. We lost a lot last year when it got wet in the fields before we could get it put up. We're after keeping your deer and elk in good shape, just like you are. You think I want you after my cows? Not on your life, I don't."

There was a lot more jawing, but after an hour or so, they rode off. Some of them stayed close by to see to it we left lots of grass standing, but we never heard any more about it.

The hay was really important to us, so we would have fought about it if necessary. We'd fared well our first winter, but if it hadn't warmed up after that big storm, we'd have been in a heap of trouble. Horses can forage even in deep snow, but cows aren't made to dig out grass if the snow gets a crust on it. I hoped we would be able to keep that hay for several years.

We were excited about the approaching birth of our child, and I wanted Elena to go to Santa Fe where she could be under the care of a doctor, but she would have none of it.

She declared, "Our son can be born here at the ranch as easily as the Indian babies in their tipis."

Lupe and the other women sided with her, so I gave in. None of them seemed concerned. As a breeder of livestock, I couldn't help wondering how our bloodlines would match. My pa had been Dutch-German, while Ma was Irish, top to toe. In rancher's lingo, when you cross that mix with pure Castilian you have to wonder what it'll bring. It turned out to be a good match, as it has in everything else. Our son, Gard, named for Pa, was born August 19, and he was a lusty, healthy boy if there ever was one. His green eyes and dark hair showed his Irish blood, while he had the fine bones and facial lines of his mother's heritage.

It was September before I had time to look at the trail I followed the day of the attack on Elena. Some of the cows had ranged up into the timber on that side of the park, and in the process of pushing them back where they belonged, I crossed the trail. The cattle were drifting with no prodding, so I took off up the mountain. It was early, and I was planning to be out until evening, so there should be time to see where it led without being gone beyond the time Elena would expect me back. I was maybe an hour from the house when I hit the trail and let my horse follow it through the timber. It led through some rough country, finally leading all the way along the west slope of Pagosa Peak and then forking. One fork went around the north side of the peak and looked like it would end up on Four-Mile Creek. The other led to the northwest in the general direction of the Pyramid. Choosing that one, I followed along and finally came to the main trail about an hour's ride above the crossing of the Piedra. There was almost no sign that a trail led away from the main track, but after a half hour I located a sort of beacon blaze at least a quarter mile up the hill. Heading for it across the unmarked slope, I was soon on the fork by which I had come down the hillside. I concluded that whoever had blazed the trail had taken special care to not leave the main fork at the same place each time, so there was no evidence of the other trail until you were well away from the main one. I took that to be a sign that this could be the way the Spanish miners had gone to their cache. It seemed like the sort of thing you could expect from men who had been so careful in hiding their treasure.

I followed slowly back the way I'd come, watching for any sign of another trail. I felt sure the cache wouldn't be right along this one, even though it was well concealed. At last my search was rewarded with the discovery of a tiny blaze high up on a tree a hundred yards off the path. Heading toward it, I located another beacon blaze, down toward a bench five hundred feet below the fork I'd been following. The trail, or what might have once been one, led into some really rugged country. I was able to follow for less than a mile before coming to a spot that was definitely not safe for a horse. Heading back, I found a maze of marks and other indications that this was maybe close to the cache. The trail twisted and turned, and if I'd not heard about the complicated markings, I would have figured somebody'd lost his mind and spent his days of being mixed up blazing a trail through that draw. As I was leaving the area, with no idea where the cache might be, I found what was surely an old campsite. Poking around, I located what was almost certainly the pit where they'd made charcoal for their furnace. My heart was pounding as I rode back to the ranch, and I could hardly wait till after supper to share the news with Elena.

We got out the map Luiz had given me and looked at all the markings and signs that were indicated on it. There were lots of small caches shown, and each had a different set of markings. It seemed that there was no standard set of blazes or arrangement of rocks but that in each case there'd been a completely new way of locating the cache.

This certainly didn't look like it would help in finding the big cache. The method of locating the mine itself, as shown on the map, was especially involved and seemed like an awful lot of trouble. However, had it been easy, the mine would have been found before now.

We were getting ready to bed down when I said, "That cache has got to be in that canyon. If I just had some time to look closely, I could find it. From what Luiz told me, there's enough gold in there to make us as rich as old King Solomon. When I read about how much he got every year, it boggles my mind, and to think we may have something like that right here on our ranch."

"It's exciting to think about, and if we build our herd of cattle and keep improving the horses, we'll have something better than gold. We'll have done what God directed you to do. Is anything as good as that?"

"Lord, you gave me the best wife any man's ever had. Thanks for doing that. It's sure nice that she's the prettiest thing you ever made, too, but she keeps me on track like nobody else ever could. I'll never figure out why you decided to give her to me, but sure am glad you did. It'll be really good if you keep making her wise enough to keep me from chasing after things that aren't important. I love you, Lord. Thanks again."

She said, "Lord, you have given us so much we can hardly imagine it. We have this fine home in a place so beautiful it seems like a fairy tale. We have a son who's so perfect we can't quite think it's true. I have the best husband in the world. I'm so happy it almost scares me, and it's all from you, LORD. Please keep giving us your wisdom and direction so we don't forget that it's a gift from you. My cup is running over, LORD. Lead me so I'll be the wife Reuben needs and deserves. I love you, LORD. Thanks."

"Whoo, boy, that's good, isn't it?" I whispered.

"Yes. I can't remember ever feeling this close to Jesus before."

"Makes me understand better what he means when he says we are in him. To be in him together like this really makes it special. Do you have any idea how much I love you, sweetheart?"

Her voice sounded like it came from way down inside her. "Yes, because that's the way I love you, my darling."

After a long, sweet kiss, I said, "As soon as possible, I'll take two days and go look for that cache. We can afford to give it that much time, then we'll set it aside until later, after we do the important things."

"That's wonderful. Now, come here and let me show you how much I love you."

"You'll get no argument about that."

So many things clamored for my attention that it was two weeks before I could get away. I took off at daybreak and headed up the park. On the previous trip I had determined where the canyon opened into the lower country and decided to approach it from below. Upon reaching the mouth of the canyon, I tied my horse so he could feed easily in a small pocket back in the timber. Changing from boots to moccasins, I started up the canyon.

I was barely under way through sparse timber that sort of feathered out into the edge of the park when I located a beacon blaze about a quarter mile away in the edge of thicker timber. Heading for it, I watched carefully for any other markings but found nothing until I was beyond the beacon. It was undoubtedly placed there to guide someone across the region where there were relatively few trees to blaze. Continuing up the hill, the blazes made three switchbacks. A tree at the upper end of the last switchback had the regular two blazes—one on each side to indicate the direction of travel. Another long, slender one was about a third of the way around the trunk on the downhill side, facing away from the trail, and toward a clump of scrub spruce a couple of hundred feet away. Going down there brought a surprise.

In the center of a clump of saplings, completely hidden from view, was a good-sized hole, excavated in the shale. Inspection left no doubt that it had been dug by hand. I'd found one of the small caches. It was over two feet across and full of leaf mold.

Hoping that there would be a pack in the hole, I quickly dug away the leaves and dirt, only to find it empty. However, as had been the case when I looked at the hole from which Luiz had taken his sacks of ore, there were some small fragments in the bottom, and they were just like the ore Luiz had given Elena. I had absolutely no doubts that this was the canyon where we would find the major cache. If it had been necessary to use small hiding spots for the overflow, the cavern might be even more packed with treasure than we had assumed.

I went back to tracing the markings. The trail was easy to follow for several hundred yards then disappeared completely as it got within a hundred yards of the top of a low ridge.

Searching carefully, I crossed the ridge in a straight line and found the blazes again about the same distance from the top on the other side. Those old Spaniards were wise in the ways of the mountains. They didn't want the trail to be discovered by some hunter, trapper, miner, or anyone who happened to be passing that way. They knew most folks tend to follow ridges if they offer reasonably good going, because they offer much better chance for looking over the surrounding country. If the blazes had continued across the top of the ridge, they would have been easy to spot by anyone used to watching where he was. I couldn't believe that there'd ever been much traffic in that remote spot but appreciated their concern.

The trail led to the edge of a deep ravine. As I approached it I saw a blaze on the side of a tall pine across the gully. Wondering about it, I searched the area close to me and finally spotted a similar mark on a pine of about the same size on the side where I was standing. The two blazes faced each other. If you were at the tree across the ravine, the blaze on the side where I stood would be easy to see. Crossing over, I located more blazes a short distance beyond the tall pine and followed the marks easily for the next half-mile. The blazes were generally small and slender but were fairly close together. They followed the slope of the mountain and along a rather smooth bench. There was an occasional blaze that was easy to see and a few unexpected changes in the course, but it seemed fairly ordinary otherwise. Time to time, I knew, appearances can really fool you.

The blazes ended abruptly in a clump of thick timber about a hundred yards from what I recognized as the campsite I'd found on my first visit. On that trip I'd been all over the ground where I now stood and hadn't spotted the trail I'd just followed to get back to the park where those old boys had camped and made their charcoal. There was no evidence of trees having been cut. Luiz had said the miners always used trees that had fallen from natural causes so there would be no sign of the work they'd done, and that the waste rock had been packed to slide areas and scattered there so the location of the mine and cache wouldn't be noticeable.

I could see that the old Spaniards had been experts in the art of hiding things, so I made an all-out search of the area on each side of the line of blazes from the old camp back to the edge of the ravine. Recalling the things Luiz had told me, along with things indicated on the map of the mine, I started looking for a pattern of the three pieces of the puzzle, namely, a complicated pattern of blazes, artificial arrangements of natural objects, and markings on rocks. I was looking for anything out of the ordinary but thought it would probably be easiest to spot a pattern to the tree blazes. Without the information given me by Luiz and that on the map, I would never have figured it out.

Following the trail back to the ravine revealed nothing, so I started back to the north. In less than two hundred yards, I noticed a change in the pattern of blazes that hadn't come to my attention earlier. One tree had a big open mark on it, facing south, which was the direction of approach. That blaze was made real noticeable on purpose to grab your eye. From this tree the line of markings turned sharply to the left, or northwest, for a distance of seventeen paces. Four trees in a straight line in this short distance were marked with small but easily seen blazes. Three of them had a mark on each side opposite the other, but on the fourth tree, the second mark was only a quarter of the way around. It was on the right side of the track facing back toward the regular line, some twenty steps away where another noticeable mark was on a spruce.

Two other trees on this new line were also marked. They stood about four feet apart and directly opposite a balsam ten steps southeast, near what would be the regular line of blazes, if they'd been made in regular order. Among the branches about eight feet up on the trunk of this balsam, a blaze had been cut in the form of a "dumbbell," or Indian club. This had been done with a knife, and the marks of the blade were still easily seen. That unusual mark faced northwest on a line that would be directly between the two blazed trees opposite. Sticking out of the pile of leaf mold at the base of the balsam was the rotted remains of a "lop," or top of a young tree. This was about three feet long, had been cut with an ax, and was placed here to indicate direction. It pointed directly northwest between the two marked trees, the same direction as indicated by the Indian club blaze. So here was the pattern of a right-angled triangle with a direction indicator pointing a line that would cut across the side opposite the right angle of the triangle. This was a pattern I'd never seen in any trail and must have considerable importance in the locating of the cache. But what did it indicate?

There was nothing significant in the immediate area. This was a flat bench with no possibility of an underground cavern here. I could see none of the other makings of the mystery such as natural objects artificially arranged either. The only explanation, or so it seemed to me, was that this was a signal of a direction to something else of importance. Taking my bearings from the dumbbell blaze, I walked as straight northwest as I could. The area wasn't especially rough and wasn't heavily timbered. The regular line of blazes was off to my right and down the slope. As my progress took me farther up the hill, the regular marked trail became farther and farther from my present line of travel, which caused me to wonder.

Several hundred feet up the hill, a heavily timbered ridge that reminded me of a turkey plume extended down toward me. As I approached it, there was a clear view of another strange mark on a tree growing at the crest of the ridge. The sight of it gave me reason to hurry up the steep side of the ridge. There were two peculiar blazes cut into that tree, each showing the marks of a knife plainly in the dry wood enclosed at the edges. The mark facing the direction I had come, or southeast, was about seven inches across and in the shape of a comma with the curlicue pointing down. The other, a quarter of the way around the tree and facing east, was an upside-down comma, with the curlicue pointing upward. The direction it indicated was downhill toward the line of the blazed trail.

Wondering what it all meant, I went as straight away from that mark as it was possible to do and, after several hundred feet, struck the original line at the exact point where that trail made a sharp turn downhill to the right, and a big old tree with a large mark on it stood on the line of blazes. It all made a perfect right angle triangle.

Some of the discoveries were starting to make sense. I paced off the sides of the triangle. It was six hundred feet from the big, blazed tree on one corner to the dumbbell tree on the other. From there to the tree with the commas was a thousand feet, and from there to the big mark was another eight hundred feet. This gave me the natural objects artificially marked. Now I needed to find some natural objects artificially arranged. I followed more false leads than I can remember that day, and I found nothing else of importance before the day ran out and I had to start back to my horse. On the way down, about five hundred feet below the lowest corner of the big triangle, I spotted another large tree standing on the blazed line where it began to make a curve around the end of a rock slide. On this big tree was an especially long mark. Above and to the right of that mark was a spot blaze indicating a southerly direction along a bench that ran parallel to the blazed line. I decided that it would be necessary to wait until my next trip before following out that line and headed on downhill, making it to my horse a few minutes after full dark.

As I rode home, and later as I told it to Elena, many things were strange, but I was hopeful all the same. When I'd told her everything I could recall, she said, "You need to write all of this down. It'll be all but impossible to remember everything if we have to put this aside until next year. Why don't you start a journal and keep a detailed record of what you've done so far. You can add to it every time you go there, and then you won't need to wonder if something's been forgotten. There may be something really important in what you've done so far. If you forget it, you'll need to do a lot of things again."

"Can't it wait until tomorrow? I'm worn out tonight."

"You'll not take time in the morning to do it. If you're going to do it, you need to do it now."

"You're the prettiest slave driver in the whole world," I complained, "but you're pretty enough to get what you want, so I guess there's no use arguing."

Another two weeks passed before I could slip away to the canyon. That time, I rode up the old trail and down to the campsite. Leaving my horse there, I hurried down to the tree I'd spotted on my way out the last time. Taking my bearing from the spot blaze, I started a trip over down timber, big rocks, and thick brambles. After about five hundred feet, I began to wonder if it was worth the trouble, and then there was a single blaze on the east side of a lone tree in a small clearing. Since there were no other marks in the area, it didn't seem like much of a discovery considering all the work it had taken to reach it.

I moseyed out through some fairly thick timber to the edge of a bluff overlooking the narrow valley of the small creek that ran down from the mountain hovering above me. On a finger of the bluff, about a hundred feet beyond the edge of the timber stood a big rock. It was shaped like a pyramid, almost head high, and would weigh at least a ton. On the backside of it was drilled a hole almost an inch across and two inches deep. There was only one way for that rock to have gotten where it was, and that was for someone to have put it there, and the hole had certainly been drilled using steel tools.

I remembered an indication of a similar rock on the map of the mine and that it was the key to locating the portal of the mine. There was an intricate mathematical formula that gave the direction from that rock to the portal, and it appeared that you could actually see the opening from the rock. Based on that, I assumed that the opening to the cache was in sight from where I stood,---if I only knew what to look for.

It was impossible to get down off the bluff at that point, so I backtracked and went to a spot where I could scramble down then returned to the base of the bluff just below the "sentinel" rock. I spent the rest of the day going over that valley, trying to cover every foot of ground that could be seen from the rock. I discovered some strange items but not the entrance to the cache. There was a series of rocks that formed an arc, with another rock that was placed opposite the deepest part of the arc, and in that rock was drilled a series of shallow holes that formed exactly the same pattern. The direction indicated intersected the long side of the big triangle. Taking that line, I ended up within a few feet of the big "sentinel" rock. The rocks in the arc were broken off from others in the area, and each weighed about a hundred and fifty pounds. The one that was opposite the center of the curve of the arc was placed on edge, with a foundation of small stones, and was at the base of a tree that stood at the corner of another imaginary triangle formed by trees with unusual markings.

Close to the arc made of stones was the stump of a tree that had long ago fallen and broken on a big rock. There was no sign of the trunk of that tree, and I was again reminded that the Spaniards had used only trees that had fallen from natural causes, not wanting to leave any cut stumps to indicate activity in the immediate location of the mine or cache. The missing trunk could well be one of the logs used to seal the portal to the cache.

I searched the area until it was dark, then rode wearily home, knowing there was to be no discovery of the treasure that year. I'd used the time we'd allowed and wasn't going to vary from our plan. The ranch was still in its formative stage and couldn't stand for me to be absent any longer.

We were visited by Ignacio and Ouray. They stayed with us two days, and I took the opportunity to renew the arrangement to move our herds down into the high desert south of Ignacio's camp in case the winter storms were severe. It seemed to me that eventually we would face some really deep snow in the parks. The hovering San Juans with several peaks reaching over fourteen thousand feet warned that we could expect some pretty hard weather at times. Ouray was friendly and encouraged Ignacio in his relationship with us.

All of our stock was in good shape when winter struck, and we had a fair supply of hay stacked and cured, but it wouldn't last if the cattle couldn't graze a lot. The hay was to supplement grass that was left uncut and ungrazed on which we depended for the primary winter feed.

CHAPTER SIXTEEN

We made another trail drive in the spring, following the same procedure as before, with four herds gathered and delivered. We were stopped by a group of buyers outside of Trinidad and made a deal to deliver at Pueblo. It was a much easier drive and took less than half as long. Upon arrival, we left the herds in charge of skeleton crews, and the rest of us went to town.

Pueblo was a one-of-kind town. Its main support came from livestock interests, and I especially remember Gann's outfitting store. At night one could find anywhere from ten to thirty cowboys asleep on the counters. The owner turned the keys over to them at closing time, even though he didn't know a tenth of them, while he went to his own home and slept. A man named Gallup owned a saddlery in which the same thing was done. So far as I could learn, neither man ever lost a single piece of goods, and each of them got rich out of the cattle business.

Dealing with cowboys had some funny parts to it. The firm of Wright, Beverly & Co., of Dodge City, ended up with over seven thousand vests during the days of the trail drives. When a cowpoke bought a new suit, he had no use for a vest, and it was left behind to be put back on the shelf.

We had to stay about two weeks helping the new owners get their herds put together for moving to their final ranges. We found Pueblo to be much quieter and the people more interested in meeting the normal needs of cowmen than those in Abilene had been. If there hadn't been so many chores waiting for me at home, I would've stayed and done some buying and selling of the leavings of the herds. There was a lot of money to be made in buying odd lots and filling orders from small buyers. But there were too many important things to do at the ranch for me to seriously consider such an operation.

I'd arranged for Elena and Gard to meet me at Luiz's place in Santa Fe. We took the opportunity to tell him of the things I'd learned about the location of the gold cache and encouraged him to visit us and let us help him locate the treasure we were sure lay in that canyon. His interest was only mild, and we realized that he'd taken an attitude typical of most of the Spanish who had wealth. Having married a lady from a very rich family whose children were all successful, neither of them was interested in roaming the hills in search of something they didn't need.

"Here," he said, "take the map. You can find the cache easily with it."

Elena looked at me, a question in her eyes. I barely shook my head, and she smiled.

"Thanks, but we'll give it another whirl this summer. If we miss again, we'll take the map," I said.

We hurried home, and the ranch was like a beehive since it was branding season. The calves and foals were carefully examined, and only the really great males were left whole and kept for potential breeding animals. We were severe in the culling, not keeping any that didn't come up to the quality we wanted to develop in our herds. The smallest lack was enough to cause an animal to be rejected. We gelded all but fifteen colts and would cull them again the next spring, expecting to keep no more than four for our own use. A few would probably be sold to other ranchers, but not many men were trying to improve their herds.

It was no surprise that the best foal was from Elena's filly, which was technically now a mare. We had hoped for a colt but got a filly. It showed the best of both breeds and was everything we could have wanted. We paired Elena's horse with the same stallion again, hoping for a colt this time. The youngest Thoroughbred had developed into a horse like none of us had ever seen. He stood a full seventeen hands, just four inches shy of six feet, and had the length of his racing heritage. Charlie and I shared the training chores, and he was almost as quick as Elena's filly had been. In fact, he remembered the lessons better than any horse I ever worked with. He seemed to never forget anything, but was ready for something new each session. He didn't have the natural cow sense that she had, but that was no surprise. He learned to work cattle quickly, and by his fourth year was even becoming a good cutting horse. We wouldn't ordinarily use stallions in working cattle, since they tend to get their minds on things other than work, which causes trouble, but we needed to be sure our foundation stock had the ability to do that kind of work.

We were glad for the precise records we kept on each of the young animals, since it enabled us to decide easily whether to use the same mates again. We always duplicated the pairings in the outstanding youngsters and tried new matches when the results were less than excellent. That first year convinced us we were on the right track and would soon see the kind of stock we had set out to breed.

I kept my promise to Miguel and notified him about the foal from Molly's filly. Not only did he come, but so did Señor Martinez, the owner of the ranch.

Miguel took one look at that foal and said, "You've proven your idea. That filly will be better than any animal on this ranch." He turned to his employer and said: "Now you can see why I asked you to sell this one. We are looking at a new breed of horse."

"I can see that. I guess we can take some credit for it. You did well, and I am glad you did it."

They stayed a week, so we were able to show them most of the ranch and explained some of what we planned. Miguel has returned at least once every year and contributed many suggestions that assisted in our ending up with the type of horse we wanted. He's one of our favorite people.

In August Elena said, "Let's leave Gard with his grandma so the two of us can go look for the gold. I want to be there when you find it."

"I'd love that. Set it up, and we'll do it."

We left before dawn ten days later. That would give us close to fourteen hours of light at the canyon. We saw over a hundred elk in one herd, three cinnamon bears, several small herds of deer and a pack of coyotes. Wolves and grizzlies were getting scarce, for which we had no regrets. We never came close to killing all of them, but they'd gotten cautious enough to stay out of sight and generally away from our herds. Grouse, or "fool hens," were plentiful and easy to bag with a hand-thrown rock if you were good at that sort of thing.

We reached the Spaniards' campsite an hour after sunup. The first thing I did was take Elena down the blazed trail and show her the various triangles, rocks, and marks. She noted a few things I had missed, like a small, round spot blaze high up on one of the big trees that formed the big triangle, and opposite that about fifty feet away a small blaze close to the ground, which indicated a dead-end. By noon we'd gone over the area completely and returned to the campsite for a quick lunch and chat.

Elena said, "Would you mind if I try dowsing?"

"I'm ready to try anything. Ever done it?"

"Grandfather taught me, and I've practiced some over the years. He used to hide gold around the house and in the outbuildings, and I was always able to find it. If there's as much here as we've been told, it should be fairly easy."

"That's great. Why didn't you say something before now?"

"I wanted you to find it. If you had known I could dowse, you might have not looked until I could come along. I could not leave Gard last year, and we would not know as much about the location as we do. We at least know the general area to look, with the sentinel rock and all."

"I'm sure enough out of ideas, so it'll be a pleasure to turn it over to you. When I saw Luiz do it up in the high country, it was all a mystery. Now I know a little bit about it, and it'll be fun watching you."

She said, "I think this would be a great time to talk to Jesus. If we ever needed his help, it is now. Will you do that?"

"I'd love to, sweetheart. Jesus, there's no way I can tell you how much you've already blessed me. You've given me the most wonderful wife in the world, and we're together with you here in this beautiful place. If that's all I get today, it'll be more than any other man'll have. Elena's planning to look for the gold her great-great-grandpa put in a hole here in this canyon. Lord, you know, if I don't get anything except to watch her, it'll be better'n a wagon load o' berry pie. We came up here to try to find gold. I ask you to show her where it is. We'll give you all the glory and use it the way you want us to. If there's a way I can help, please show that to me. We believe you for this. If our faith isn't strong enough, will you give us some of yours so we don't fall short? We love you, Lord. You've already blessed us more than we can ask or think. Thanks."

"Lord, being here with Reuben is more than anyone deserves. You have already poured your blessings over us so much we can hardly believe it. We are sure you have led Reuben to this canyon and shown him that this is where the gold is stored. Now we need to find the exact location and want to see it. Please lead me so I'll understand what you are doing and we can find the gold. Just being here and sharing this with Reuben is wonderful. Thank you for giving me the assurance that you are going to make this a perfect day. I love you, Lord."

She rose quickly to her feet, an action that always caused me to wonder at her graceful, easy movements. She still reminded me of a bird soaring in the air. As a horseman I call it an "easy way of going," but as a man watching his wife, I just marveled and enjoyed it. She had regained her willowy figure quickly after

Gard's birth and was as trim as when we first met, just a bit riper. She took off a necklace she had worn inside her blouse. The chain was gold, and a good-sized nugget dangled from it.

"Do you recognize this?" she asked.

"Let me see it. That's the necklace you wore to the Sena's dance!"

"Is it all right to use it for this?"

"I reckon it's all right. Just don't expect to get anything more precious than what I got that night."

"I got you, too, and nothing is better than that."

"Quit stallin', woman! Show me how great you are."

"I'm stalling because I love to hear things like you were saying. Now you're just a slave driver."

"I'll tell you sweet stories all night, sweetheart. We've only got about twelve hours of daylight left, though. Go to work."

"What a mean man! All right, all right! Here I go."

We were both laughing. She started to leave, but I was able to reach her. She left after we'd enjoyed a hug and kiss.

She took the chain between her right thumb and forefinger, swung the nugget in a circle, stopped her hand, then stood very still and watched the nugget. It gradually changed from a circular motion to one like a pendulum, swinging southeast to northwest.

She moved slowly until she faced northeast, directly across the direction of the swing. Keeping her eyes on the nugget all the time, she walked slowly straight ahead. She'd gone about a hundred feet before I had any idea about her purpose. The direction of the nugget's swing slowly changed until it was pointing more to the south, and I could see that she'd effectively determined that the cause of the swing was not to the northwest but in the opposite direction. Had she walked in the direction of the original swing, she wouldn't have known if she were going toward the cache or away from it. Now she knew.

It takes someone with an easy stride to walk so the back and forth swing of something attached to a chain and held in his hand isn't influenced by the movement of the body. It was a joy to watch her move smoothly over the rough terrain of the canyon, and the nugget never varied from its straight back-and-forth movement. There were many trees, rocks, and clumps of brush that caused her to leave the course indicated by the nugget, and when she had to veer away, it always changed to show that she was still approaching the thing that was causing the motion of the chain. Her course went down into the valley then along a steep hillside. The going got pretty rough when she was a quarter mile upstream from the sentinel rock on the bluff, and as I watched the action of the nugget, it changed to a circular motion similar to the movement she had given it when she first started.

She stopped and stood stock-still, raised her eyes, and gazed across the creek for several minutes. The nugget continued to swing in a circle all the time. She looked back down and started slowly across an especially steep bank. She'd gone less than fifty feet when the motion started changing back to a straight swing. She turned slowly and went up the slope, against the direction of the swing, and the nugget continued the same movement. After some fifty feet it gradually changed again, this time swaying more in the direction she was walking. She turned again across the direction of the swing and walked back north until there was another change, at which time she turned back toward the creek bottom.

I guessed that she was virtually on top of what was causing the nugget's actions and was trying to learn the extent of the area as well as determining the exact location of the gold. I crossed the creek and got level with her on the opposite bank, hoping to spot something that would show where the entrance was. Elena continued her test of the area and eventually had paced off a spot more than a hundred feet square. The entire area caused the same circular swing of the nugget. The long part of the rectangle ran up the slope, so the actual length of the cavity would be somewhat shorter than the surface distance. I figured it to be about a hundred feet underground, if her movements were an accurate indication of the size of the cave.

From across the creek, I noticed that the only part of the hillside that had anything but grass on it was at the very bottom of the area Elena was blocking out. Luiz had said that the portals were screened by brush, so I went across to investigate. The brush covered an area thirty feet in diameter. Five feet inside the upper edge was a slight depression. There was a small hole in the upper left corner of the depression, similar to an animal's burrow. There was no dirt around it like there always is when an animal has dug the hole. That would have been a clue, even if we had no other indication.

"I think we've got it, sweetheart," I called. "The portal seems to be right here."

She hurried down, and I showed her the spot. "Let's be careful to disturb it as little as possible," I said. "We'll not be able to take much with us and will need to leave the cache hidden."

"You really think this is it, don't you?"

"Sure, don't you?"

"I hope so. The dowsing left little doubt that something is here."

"That's for sure. You were a sight to behold. Never saw the beat of it. Only you could walk like that and never mess up the action of the nugget. It was a beautiful thing to watch."

All the while I was carefully digging with my hands. It took but a moment to uncover the end of a log lying horizontally across the top of the depression, and I was sure.

"There it is, honey. Luiz said they always laid logs this way, rather than up and down. Boy, I thought I was excited before, but this has my heart going like crazy."

We were on our knees, side by side, and she turned and gave me a hug. "Hurry," she said. "I can hardly wait."

"Gotta be careful. These logs are pretty rotten. If we rush, we'll end up having to find something to replace them with."

"All right, but hurry as much as you can. Did you see how big it seems to be? It must be a hundred and fifty feet long."

"Remember, you were going up the side of the hill. The hole probably goes straight back and won't be near as long. I guess not more'n a hundred feet."

"Even at that, it looked like there was gold all the way. Oh, please hurry."

I had to take myself in hand and make me slow down as I gently scooped away dirt and exposed the entire log. It wasn't the top one after all, and I had to uncover three more before I was sure I had located the one at the upper edge of the opening. The four left a hole big enough for Elena to get through, but I had to take out two more to make room for me. I lowered myself into the hole and saw that it was a small tunnel that went back about five feet and opened into a larger cavern. I had to stoop to get my head inside the tunnel, and it took several seconds for my eyes to adjust to the dark so I could see a little of the bigger hole. Elena was climbing down, so I helped her then lit a candle, and we moved through the entryway.

It took only a couple of steps to reach the interior, and we saw a room bigger than our candle could light. There were open areas ahead and to both the right and left, with a wall some eight feet high that lacked a couple of feet of reaching the top of the cavity. A corner was left open in each of the walls. We went into the area to our right. It appeared to be completely filled with sacks. Upon opening one of the sacks, we found that it was filled with bricks of gold. I opened another and found it filled with ore that seemed to be identical to what we'd seen before. I checked several sacks, and it seemed that about every fourth one contained bricks, and the rest had ore in them. It took nearly an hour to come close to checking the entire cavity. It was almost exactly one hundred feet square, with a path about five feet wide going completely around the outside, and another similar path going down the middle. That left two areas that would each measure about ninety feet by a little over forty feet. Both were filled with sacks of ore and bricks. *It was a king's ransom!*

"What's back there?" Elena asked, and we walked farther into the cavern.

She'd spotted the furnace the Spaniards had used to melt gold from the ore. Along the wall beside it were tools, implements, a complete set of pots and pans, as well as tents and bedding. We inspected the paraphernalia then examined one of the gold bricks. It was about four inches wide, eight long, and two thick. I picked up one that weighed at least forty pounds. It took my breath away, and I just had to sit down to recover some.

Elena knelt beside me and whispered, "What have we found? It's not possible! No one could even dream of all this."

"You reckon ole King Sol had more than this?"

"He must have. He was richer than anybody, according to the Bible."

"He also had more wives than any man could ever want. He sure didn't have anybody like you, or he'd have stopped at one."

"Am I to take that as a compliment?"

"I reckon. No way I could ever want more than you. Just don't make sense to look anywhere else when I've already got the very best in the whole wide world."

"That works both ways, sweetheart. I've got the best man in the world."

"Wonder which of his wives he said this to:

'Behold, thou art fair, my love; behold, thou art fair;
thou hast doves' eyes within thy locks;
thy hair is as a flock of goats,
that appear from Mount Gilead.
Thy teeth are like a flock of sheep that are even shorn,
which came up from the washing;
whereof every one bear twins,
and none is barren among them.

Thy lips are like a thread of scarlet,
and thy speech is comely,
thy temples are like a piece of pomegranate
within thy locks.
Thy neck is like the tower of David builded
for an armory,
whereon there hang a thousand bucklers,
all shields of mighty men.
Thy two breasts are like two young roes that are twins,
which feed among the lilies.
Until the daybreak and the shadows flee away,
I will get me to the mountain of myrrh,
and to the hill of frankincense.
Thou art all fair, my love; there is no spot in thee.
Come with me from Lebanon, my spouse,
with me from Lebanon;
look from the top of Amana, from the top of
Shenir and Hermon,
from the lions' dens, from the mountains of leopards.
Thou hast ravished my heart, my sister, my spouse;
thou hast ravished my heart with one of thine eyes,
with one chain of thy neck.
How fair is thy love, my sister, my spouse!
How much better is thy love than wine!
And the smell of thine ointment than all spices!
Thy lips, o my spouse, drop as the honeycomb;
honey and milk are under thy tongue;
and the smell of thy garments is like
the smell of Lebanon.'"

(Song of Solomon 4:1-11 KJV)

It was, of course, from the Song of Solomon, and we had read it together many times. It was a special favorite of hers, seemed to make her feel romantic. She'd never know how hard I'd worked to get to where I could say it to her.

Then she gave me a surprise—picked it right up where I had stopped.

"Awake, O north wind; and come, thou south;
blow upon my garden,
that the spices may flow out.
Let my beloved come into his garden,
and eat his pleasant fruits."

(Song of Solomon 4:16b KJV)

The candle was some shorter when we took up our conversation again.

"Being here with you is better than the gold, the ranch, and everything else in these hills," I said, my voice husky. "I thought I knew what love was, but this is the very best, sweetheart."

"I wouldn't have missed this for anything," she whispered, her breath caressing me. "Let's keep this place secret so we can slip away and come up here once in a while."

"I'll want to drag you up here every day."

"And I'll want you to, but we'll keep it for really special times." Her voice sounded like it came from deep in her throat.

"You make any time special," I said, and kissed her again.

She snuggled closer and brushed my throat with her lips. Neither of us wanted to break the spell, but at last she sat up, stretched like a cat, pulled me up for another kiss, and said, "Let's look at the gold again."

"Okay, then we best get out of here and close things up."

"What can we take with us?"

"Four of the bars is about all we can handle."

"Is that all?"

I picked up one of the bars and handed it to her. It weighed nigh onto forty pounds.

"Oh," was all she said.

We packed the bars over to the opening. I pushed them up onto the ground and started to climb out.

Habit is a wonderful thing, time to time. It's just natural for me to take a long look around before making a move, and this was once it paid off. With nothing but the top of my head and my eyes out of the ground, I paused and took a long gander. Good I did, because right across the creek, where I'd been earlier, was a man on a horse, bent over looking at the ground.

I jerked back down into that hole and motioned to Elena to keep still.

"That dirty skunk," I whispered. "Won't he ever learn?"

"What is it?"

"The fellow who's been after you since Santa Fe is out there. Probably got his crew with him, too. He's on the other side of the creek, looking at my tracks. Won't be long before they figure out where we are. Dadgum it! How'd they get here?"

"What will we do? If they spot us, they'll have us in a trap."

"We've got to figure a way to get shut of them. And this time, we'll get rid of them for good. I'm plumb tired of having them pestering us. Pa always said, 'Set and think before you go making any moves.' Best do just that."

"How long before it will be dark?"

"Too long. Three, four hours, easy. Can't wait that long. If they spot this hole, we're in for it. Got to get out of here and make a move on them before they have time to get set up."

"There's no cover except right around the entrance. How can you move from here?"

"The brush is thick. I can get in it and see what they do. If one of them comes in alone, I can handle him with no trouble. Use a knife on him. If they come together, I'll just shoot them. Not much danger of them hitting me, shooting into the brush like they'll have to, and it won't bother me much."

"That brush won't stop a bullet," she said. "There has to be a better way. Why not stay in the opening and shoot from there?"

"The brush would bother me as much as them, unless I get close to the edge. But you may have something there if we have to handle them all together. I've got to be outside to take any of them with the knife, though."

"Wait for them to come, and then shoot from the protection of the hole. If you try for one of them and the others show up, they'll have the advantage."

"I'm going back up and see what that bird is doing," I said and peeked out. The rider was going toward the campsite, and I was unable to spot anyone else. I ducked back down and said, "That buzzard's going back toward the horses. Nobody else around that I can see. I'm going out. You keep this rifle handy. Stay inside and shoot anybody who pokes his head in. I'll make certain sure you know it's me if I come back, which I won't till they're all taken care of. If I ain't back by full dark, you scamper out and down that trail I showed you, the one that goes down to the park; then make your way home. Ain't nobody going to follow you down through there horseback, and those birds won't go afoot. Do it quiet, though. Don't you budge till it's as dark outside as it is in here."

"You can't leave me here alone! I'll die of fright. I'm going along if you leave."

"Listen, sweetheart, I'd rather do most anything than go off and leave you here, but there's no other way. I've got to get out where I can see what they're up to. No way to tell anything down here. Those guys are a bunch of fools, as we've seen before, and I'll have an easy time taking care of them once I'm out of here. But cooped up where I can't see or move, they've got all the best of it. Unless I miss my guess, I'll have everything under control in an hour or so, and we can go on home."

"Please don't leave me. I can't stay here, not knowing what's happening to you."

"Have I ever done anything that brought you hurt?"

"No."

"Don't plan to now, neither. You just do like I say, and this'll be over. But it's got to be the way I've said. Just ain't no other way to handle it. Promise you'll stay right here. I can't be wondering what you're doing, along with trying to handle them."

"May I at least peek out once in a while?"

"Reckon that won't hurt none. But watch how I do it. Do it wrong, and you'll give away your position. You know how a prairie dog does? Ease up like one of them, looking around as you do, and never raise up more'n to where your eyes are level with the ground. Don't be moving fast anytime. Stay still and it ain't likely they'll spot you. I figure to stay pretty close by, anyway."

Never in my born days had I done anything harder than climb out of there and leave her in that dark hole. But there really wasn't any other way. I knew the real reason they were here was so he could finally get Elena for himself. When I thought of her in his hands it took me out of that hole with a resolve to see him dead first. If he got her, it would be over my dead body. There was hardly a moment that I wasn't asking the LORD to keep her safe and guide my steps so I could remove all threat to her. I don't think there'll ever be a time when I was more serious in my talk with him. She became more precious than I had known she was until then. God had opened heaven and poured his blessing on me, and I was determined that no outlaw was going to touch her.

CHAPTER SEVENTEEN

The cavern, full of warmth and joy but moments earlier, was now a dark and fearsome place. Reuben was hardly out of the opening before I pushed my head outside, trying desperately to move as he had told me, stopping when my eyes barely cleared the edge.

He was snaking away through the brush, making not a sound. The brush, while it was thick enough to make such soundless movement impossible, appeared to provide meager cover. Still, he disappeared from my searching eyes within a few yards.

When he moved out of sight, I spent long minutes in prayer. Later, I pushed farther out of the opening and searched every shred of cover that could hide an enemy. Reuben wanted me to stay in the cave, but that wouldn't keep me from being involved if there was a way to help. No one would sneak up on him if I could prevent it.

I had hunted with him and tried to remember everything he had taught me. Never moving my head more than an inch at a time and lowering myself when possible, I made a complete inspection of the hillside, valley, and the ridges that rose on two sides above the creek. I was watching across the stream when Reuben dashed into the timber on that side. He was in a crouching run and dived out of sight behind a rock. The next time I saw him, he was fifty feet into the scant cover. It must have taken him ten minutes to move that far, and he stood absolutely still for so long I was sure he had seen something. When he finally moved, it was to take three steps and stop again. He was in sight for a distance of not more than ten feet and spent what seemed like ages to travel that far. What boundless patience he had. But was there enough day left for him to accomplish his task if he continued at that pace? Keeping up my vigil, I tracked his snail-like progress up the hill toward the old campsite. It gave me an abundance of time to reflect on this man of mine.

The glimpses I had of him going through the timber reminded me that our friend Ignacio said that he always walks like he is sneaking up on someone. The fluid movement of his body, unexpected in a man so large, propels him with hardly a sound. Even in the most private moments he is the same.

At last I saw him briefly, close to the campsite, watched as he changed course and made a circuitous trek above, then to the southwest of the camp. Trying to interpret his actions, I looked ever closer at the hillside ahead of him. After what seemed like hours, I spotted a man seated at the base of a spruce, concealed in waist-high brush. Had he been there all the time? The thought struck fear in my heart. I would be of little help if someone could sit in plain sight without my seeing him. How I longed for the field glasses.

Vowing to not let anything else escape detection, I made another complete survey of the landscape before turning back to watch my husband. His actions never varied, or so it seemed to me. He moved a tiny distance then paused for what seemed like ten times as long, moving only his eyes. After every third pause, he would turn completely around, moving so imperceptibly that I could only track his progress by the fact that he was facing a different direction. I'd seen him stalk an elk in a patch of down timber, but he had never been so deliberate as now.

From a quarter mile away, I could see the well-loved hands, scarred and granite-hard.

When he was within fifty feet of his target, I forced my gaze away to look for danger from any other quarter. It was torture to look elsewhere, but I made a complete—and this time, thorough—search. My goal was to move as slowly as Reuben when making my turn. I know he does it better than anyone else ever could, but he was my pattern, and it seemed that I would never complete the turn. I came to a greater appreciation of what it cost him to move so slowly, and it gave me more reason to admire this one I love so dearly.

The other difficult thing was forcing myself to look into every bit of cover and each separate shadow for danger lurking there. After what seemed like an age, I had all but finished the task and almost let my eyes jump over the last bit of screening vegetation in order to get him in view again. It is likely that I would have gone over it too hurriedly, but a movement caught my eye. A man was creeping toward Reuben, not fifty feet from where I had last seen him. It was all I could do to keep from jumping out and shouting a warning, but I could almost hear that dear voice saying, "Set and think before you go off half cocked."

My eyes jerked to the man my husband was stalking. He sat exactly as before. It seemed a long time before I spotted Reuben standing absolutely still fifteen feet behind him. I was surprised but delighted to see that he was even then starting to turn and search behind him. Who else would do that when he had all but reached his goal? It became apparent that, although the man I had spotted was close, Reuben couldn't see him because of a thick clump of spruce between them.

Between the man and the clump of trees was a ten-foot clearing. The man was in the brush several feet from the opening. Would he cross it or take a route around it in order to stay out of sight? I glanced at Reuben again, afraid to let my eyes leave the other one lest he move so I couldn't watch him. Reuben was almost upon his quarry, and I was sure he wouldn't look to the rear again until he'd done whatever he planned. In the meantime, the other one would be moving into position to shoot him.

I pushed the rifle out of the hole, careful to not let the sun shine on it. There was no rest for the gun that would give me a clear shot, and I wouldn't consider taking an offhand shot at that distance, so I climbed slowly out of the cave and crawled toward a boulder fifteen feet away at the edge of the brush. By the time I'd moved those fifteen feet, I had a deeper appreciation of how difficult it is to move slowly enough to avoid detection. I crawled like a snake, pushing the rifle ahead and pulling my body forward with no movement except my hands and elbows. It wasn't possible to look at anything except the brush and grass, and I removed every loose twig so there would be no noise.

After covering half the distance, I could stand it no more and rose up slightly to look up the hill. I could see nothing and dared not rise up any higher. My heart raced as I forced myself to resume that endless crawl.

After an eternity I reached the rock and forced my body to lie still until my breathing was slowed somewhat then removed my hat and ever so slowly pushed it onto the boulder. The rifle was then put atop the hat, cushioned so there would be nothing to cause my shot to go astray. Finally, I took a slow look all around, remembering how my husband had acted. Had he been watching he would have probably said I moved awfully fast, but it seemed to take forever. Finally I allowed myself to creep upward until the rifle was cradled firmly against my shoulder and I was looking down the sights.

Suddenly I remembered the story Reuben had told of shooting his first deer. This situation was similar but with much more depending on the outcome. I could see nothing of the men on the hill. A brushy hillside blocked any view of Reuben and the man he was after, but I should have been able to see the one I was looking for.

He appeared suddenly at the edge of the trees, off to the side of the tiny clearing. I moved so the sights covered his chest then raised them until the point of aim was just above his head. In the corner of my eye, I saw him raise his pistol, pointing it toward Reuben.

SPANISH GOLD

Nothing has ever been more difficult than taking what seemed like forever to squeeze the trigger. Every nerve and muscle wanted to jerk it and get the shot off quickly. When the trigger finally broke, the rifle was as steady as the rock under it, and I saw the man collapse into the brush.

Once again it was as though that voice came to me. "Stay still and likely you can't be seen. Make a move and they'll spot you, shore."

Much as I wanted to leap up and look for him, it would do no good to expose my position. I was in fairly thick brush, partially hidden by the rock. Moving only my eyes, I watched the slope above me. It was but a few minutes before three men came into view, moving toward me in the trees. They probably thought they were moving stealthily, but compared to Reuben or the man I had shot, they were like a herd of cattle. It was easy to follow their movements, and I was suddenly not afraid. Even I could handle these, and I was not alone. I was certain that by now my husband had gotten rid of the man he had stalked and was moving into position to protect me.

The three banditos stopped at the edge of the barren hillside and stood talking and gesturing. Wildness surged through me as I thought of the times they had tried to kill my man, and there wasn't the slightest hesitation as I aimed at the chest of the leader. A perfect calmness came over me, and the sight was steady as the Pyramid when I squeezed the trigger. The shot seemed uncommonly loud in the stillness. I saw him fall then noticed another on the ground and heard another shot. The third man crumpled, and that wonderful voice called to me.

"I'm coming in. You hear, sweetheart? I'm coming, don't shoot."

I wanted to jump up and rush to him, but weakness swept over me. I managed only a welcoming shout to let him know where I was. He fell to his knees beside me and gently lifted me.

"You okay, darling?"

"Oh, yes! Now that you're here, everything is wonderful."

"You saved my hide. That bird had me dead to rights. I'd just slit the other one's throat and turned away when he put his sights on me. Hadn't a chance in the world. Saw his finger tighten just as your shot came. Split his brisket dead center. Some shooting, that. Least a quarter-mile shot."

"I couldn't see you, but I had to take a chance that it wouldn't keep you from getting your man. He was where you couldn't see him. Did he move, or did you?"

"We were where we could see each other. Maybe we both moved."

"Maybe so. I saw him aiming his gun in your direction, so I couldn't wait."

"It was just right. Then we shot at the same time, on the others. We make a team, I reckon."

"I reckon. Who was the fifth man? I recognized all the others."

"Got no idea, but he was some good at getting around with no racket. He'd not been with them before."

"He should have stayed away this time, too. Can we leave now?"

"I'll get the horses."

"Not without me, you won't. Now that I have you back, you are not getting out of my sight again."

"Suits me to a T," he said and pulled me deeper into his arms.

"What about the bodies?"

"Leave them lay. If coyotes can't stomach them, buzzards'll take care of it. We've no time to waste on them. Be dark before we get out of here as 'tis. By the way, we've got five extra horses, so we can take thirty more of those bars."

"How much will each of them weigh?"

"Forty pounds, likely."

"You mean we will have over half a ton of gold?"

"Close to thirteen hundred pounds. Sorta puts a shiver up your spine, don't it?"

"I reckon."

It was almost dark by the time we had the logs back in place to his satisfaction. Sometimes his meticulous nature is aggravating, but I'll never complain. He patted the soil in place and moved some grass from the middle of the hillside, transplanting it over the opening. Satisfied at last, he started to lift me into my saddle. I stopped him for a long hug and kiss, and then we set off. I led the way so he could handle the other horses.

It was over an hour later when we came to the park. I slowed until he was beside me. He reached out to me, and I placed my hand in his.

"Quite a day, darling," he said.

"Quite a day," I echoed.

We rode in silence, immersed in our love. When we were almost home, I said, "Do you have room in your heart for someone else?"

"Who you got in mind?"

"Oh, maybe a little girl."

"You telling me something?"

"I sort of think so."

"When, you think?"

"I think the Lord told me a few minutes ago. If he did, it should be about nine months. I will know more in a couple of weeks."

"You mean—"

He squeezed my hand tighter, peering into my eyes. A grin spread across that craggy face.

"Thank you, Jesus."

"Amen."

Those horses ambled along, setting their own pace and grazing as we went, but it seemed like a matter of minutes before we were home. I hadn't thought of eating but was suddenly hungry. By the time Reuben had cared for the horses and found a good place for the gold, I had a meal ready. We took it to our rooms and ate it in privacy and gratitude. Later, we slipped into Gard's room and watched him sleep. He reminds me so much of his daddy that my heart has to get bigger every time I look at him. I'm almost certain the LORD told me we have his little sister coming, but we'll know soon.

As Reuben said, it's been quite a day.

> Behold, you are beautiful, my love,
> behold, you are beautiful!
> Your eyes are doves
> behind your veil.
> Your hair is like a flock of goats
> leaping down the slopes of Gilead.
> Your teeth are like a flock of shorn ewes
> that have come up from the washing,
> all of which bear twins,
> and not one among them has lost its young.
> Your lips are like a scarlet thread,
> and your mouth is lovely.
> Your cheeks are like halves of a pomegranate
> behind your veil.
> Your neck is like the tower of David,
> built in rows of stone;
> on it hang a thousand shields,
> all of them shields of warriors.
> Your two breasts are like two fawns,
> twins of a gazelle,
> that graze among the lilies.
> Until the day breathes
> and the shadows flee,
> I will go away to the mountain of myrrh
> and the hill of frankincense.
> You are altogether beautiful, my love;
> there is no flaw in you.
> How beautiful is your love, my sister, my bride!
> How much better is your love than wine,
> and the fragrance of your oils than any spice!
> Your lips drip nectar, my bride;
> honey and milk are under your tongue;

the fragrance of your garments is like the
fragrance of Lebanon.
A garden locked is my sister, my bride,
a spring locked, a fountain sealed.
Your shoots are an orchard of pomegranates
with all choicest fruits,
henna with nard,
nard and saffron, calamus and cinnamon,
with all trees of frankincense,
myrrh and aloes,
with all choice spices—
a garden fountain, a well of living water,
and flowing streams from Lebanon.
Awake, O north wind,
and come, O south wind!
Blow upon my garden,
let its spices flow.
Let my beloved come to his garden,
and eat its choicest fruits.

Song of Solomon 4:1-7, 10-16 (ESV)